DOCTOR WHO

THE HOLLOW MEN

KEITH TOPPING AND MARTIN DAY

D1285516

BBC BOOKS

Published by BBC Books
an imprint of BBC Worldwide Publishing
BBC Worldwide Ltd, Woodlands, 80 Wood Lane
London W12 0TT

First published 1998
Copyright © Keith Topping and Martin Day 1998
The moral right of the authors has been asserted

Original series broadcast on the BBC
Format © BBC 1963
Doctor Who and TARDIS are trademarks of the BBC

ISBN 0 563 40582 1
Imaging by Black Sheep, copyright © BBC 1998
Front cover scarecrow illustration by Colin Howard

Printed and bound in Great Britain by Mackays of Chatham
Cover printed by Belmont Press Ltd, Northampton

We would like to thank the following people for their input and encouragement: Ian Abrahams, Alison Bean, Daniel Ben-Zvi, Mark Blunden, Daniel Blythe, Paul Brown, Will Cameron, Nick Cooper, Paul Cornell (for a weekend in Wiltshire that changed our lives), Mark Cullen, Helen Day, Luke Gutzwiller, Jeff Hart, Eva Jacobus, Jim Lancaster, John McLaughlin, Lance Parkin, John Peel (no, the *other* one), John Pettigrew, Eric Pringle, Nathan Rogers, Paul Shields, Trina Short, Paul Simpson, Graeme Topping, Ben Varkentine, Geoff Wessel.

And Ian Atkins and Audra McHugh, without whom this book would have been much poorer.

For Lisa Gaunt
– KT

For Charlotte –
sorry your sister's book has more jokes in it
– MD

'There is no such thing as society.
There are individual men and women,
and there are families.'

– Margaret Thatcher, 1987

FIRST PROLOGUE
THE BLOODY ASSIZES

To some, the moon was the face of an ancient witch, pale against a thunderous sky. To fishermen, grateful to be far from the sea during the howling gale, it was 'the old in the arms of the new', a silver crescent that brought ill luck. Inland, where the storm was at its worst, the moon was visible only when the clouds, like black ink in churning water, parted for a moment. The moon's sad face regarded the storm-lashed land, its cold expression unchanging as it watched a single figure braving the driving rain.

The door burst open and a whirlwind of rain and rusty leaves rushed into the tavern, accompanying a man bent double against the storm. He turned to close the heavy oak door and let out a long sigh of relief as the warmth from a crackling log fire began to draw the chill from his aching bones.

'Is this the foulest night that ever was on God's earth?' he asked, removing his tattered, soaking greatcoat. 'Thy finest ale,' he added quickly, and moved closer to the fire.

''Tis a night when the devil a monk would be, Long John,' agreed the innkeeper as he poured a mug of beer.

The newcomer was tall, with a thin, pockmarked face. The others looked away whenever his cold blue eyes came into contact with their own.

The landlord left the ale just within reach of the man, who removed a dirty copper coin from a small leather purse. 'Old Lucifer 'imself, aye, and no mistake!' said Long John with a guffaw, although the others in the tavern seemed reluctant to share in his laughter.

There was a lull in the storm, and a chilly silence settled over the inn, broken only by the howl of a distant dog and by the clop of approaching horses.

'Two riders. And a coach,' said the landlord, moving to the window.

'Only a wicked man would be out on a night like this,' said one of the taverners, casting an anxious sideways glance at Long John.

Again the door was flung open, to admit two men, swathed in thick black cloaks and broad hats.

'Welcome, sirs,' said the innkeeper as he reached for two mugs.

'Treat me like a stranger, Tom Spence?' said the first man, removing his hat and shaking the rain from it. He was even taller than Long John, and seemed as broad as a barn door. His eyes were a piercing green.

'Joseph Jowett?' asked the innkeeper, nervously. 'Been a long time. Never thought I'd see thee back in these parts.'

'Aye,' said Jowett. 'Nor I, Tom Spence.' He paused and looked around the tavern's dingy interior, moving to the fire to warm his hands. 'My master will stay in thy finest room this night.'

A look of unreasoning terror crossed Spence's face. 'Tell thy master, Joseph Jowett, that 'e ain't welcome in this place,' he stammered.

Jowett looked up with an expression of plain amusement on his face. 'Hear that, Richard?' he asked his companion, who was also chuckling to himself. 'We're to tell the master that Tom Spence o' Hexen Bridge don't want the King's Men in his tavern.'

'Sirs, I never did mean to say –'

'Good,' snapped Jowett. 'Because my master don't take kindly to having his custom refused by the likes of 'ee, Tom Spence.'

'Aye,' said Richard, whose gruff accent indicated the north country. 'He has been known to end a man's livelihood over such an impoliteness. And he must be to his bed afore night is come, or there shall be grave retribution.'

Spence turned, calling into the kitchens. A young serving girl bearing a lantern appeared, and she began to question the innkeeper's whispered instructions. ''Taint no business o' thine,' he snapped angrily. 'The gentleman commands chambers and victuals.'

She hurried off towards the stairs.

'Hold,' said Jowett. He strode across the hushed room, and turned the girl's face towards him. 'What be thy name, girl?'

'Sarah Hatch, sir,' she said, quickly, averting her eyes from Jowett's piercing gaze. There was a slight quiver in her thickly accented voice.

'Ah,' said the man. 'Hear that, Richard?' he asked, to his companion's obvious amusement. 'Sarah Hatch, eh?' He looked her up and down with a lascivious grin, then grasped her slender arm tightly, causing her to wince in pain. 'You're all skin and bone, Sarah Hatch. B'ain't no meat on 'ee, least ways not enough for the King's Bull to go hunting for rabbits, eh? Eh?' He sniggered across the tavern to his friend, then returned his attention to the girl. 'Be kind to old Joseph, and ye shall have a shilling.' He paused. 'Be thy mother's name Mary?'

The girl nodded, mute with fear.

'Aye. The resemblance is plain. She was a fine, strapping woman, your ma. Tell 'er Joseph Jowett o' Hodcombe was asking after 'er.'

'That I will, sir,' said Sarah, pulling free of Jowett and hurrying up the stairs, the candle sputtering and dying as her movement extinguished it.

'Buxom girl, that Mary Hatch,' Jowett said to no one in particular. 'Knew 'er since she was no bigger'n a sparrow.'

'She's old and sick now, Joseph,' said Spence. 'These years ain't been kind to her.'

'They ain't been kind to any of us,' added Jowett sadly. ''Cept for the master.' He looked over to Richard and nodded towards the door. 'Bring 'im to this place.'

'Who be this master he speaks of?' Long John asked the innkeeper in a whisper.

'The most evil man on God's earth,' replied Tom Spence. 'The infamous Jeffreys.'

* * *

3

He was not at all how other men imagined him. The tales of Baron George Jeffreys of Wem had made him a legend in his own lifetime. To those of London, terrified by Monmouth's West Country rebellion, he was a figure of charm and grace, a godly man who carried out the wishes of his King, ridding the nation of sedition and treason. To those in the south-west he was a vile, murderous dog; the killer of Titus Oates and Richard Baxter; the man who had hanged, whipped, fined and transported hundreds of their number – miners and farmers mostly – in a vengeful parody of justice.

'God save the King,' said Jeffreys as he entered the tavern with Richard and four others of his retinue. He was a slight man, in his late thirties, wearing a dark coat, jerkin and long-sleeved blouse, and leather breeches. There was a trace of rural Welsh in his accent.

'Aye,' said Tom Spence. 'God save 'im.'

Everyone else in the tavern stood, respectfully, as the judge entered. He looked around him with a sour expression on his face. He was, clearly, a man used to more lavish surroundings than these.

'Be this the best thou canst do, Master Jowett?'

'Aye, Thy Lordship, 'tis but a poor ale house, known to me from my younger days.'

'Indeed,' said Jeffreys dismissively. 'Curious that temperance did not follow thy misspent youth.'

Someone sniggered briefly and Jeffreys snapped his head around to find the culprit. His gaze fell upon Long John and he moved towards the man, slowly. His eyes were as cold and unblinking as a snake's.

'What is thy name, sir?'

'John Ballam,' he said. 'A blacksmith of these parts.' He looked down at the much smaller Jeffreys and the merest hint of a smile played at the corner of his mouth. 'I am known to all as Long John,' he continued, 'on account of my considerable size!'

Jowett moved, menacingly, behind Long John, and placed a hand on his shoulder, forcing the blacksmith to stoop until his face was level with that of the judge.

'And art thou a righteous man, John Ballam?' asked Jeffreys.

John grimaced. 'No one has ever said to my face that I am not.'

'Knowest thou of Monmouth, John Ballam?' continued the judge.

'Aye, sir. A man of considerable standing with some in these parts.'

'Shall I tell thee of Monmouth?' asked Jeffreys with a savage grin. 'Shall I tell thee, John Ballam, of how that rotting bastard-spawn of the King's father was caught in a ditch at Ringwood and dragged to the Tower, caked in his own filth? How he wept and begged before His Majesty for his life? Him that was proclaimed King by cowards and traitors at Taunton this July, now dead – shall I tell thee of him?' He paused and looked closely into Long John's eyes. 'Or dost thou know? Wast thou at Sedgemoor?'

'No, never,' said Long John. 'I am a loyal Englishman, true to my King.'

'Then thou hast nothing to fear from me, or from His Majesty, nor from God,' said Jeffreys. He turned away from the terrified man, to Spence. 'Master innkeeper?' he asked cheerfully.

'Aye, sir,' he said, bowing.

'Be there a room where a servant of the King can rest his weary head this night?'

Jeffreys was high above the Earth, arms crossed over his chest, as if he had ascended directly from a coffin to the very heavens. He looked ever upward, and towards the face of the Almighty. But there was war in the heavenly realm, and angels were being cast out in droves. They fell like flaming arrows through the chill of space, merging into one great fiery dart that burnt white-hot. Down, down to the planet cursed by God and man, through skies and clouds and air, until the angels fell like rain upon Hexen

Bridge. The village green ruptured as if under cannon fire, and closed over the demons, who immediately set about creating their own hell. Jeffreys looked, and saw filth and abomination everywhere. In this cavern, this microcosm of the world, figures in robes indulged in unspeakable acts. The ground was a writhing carpet of snakes, their tongues flicking up at Jeffreys, heavy with poison. He turned to run, but slipped, and, crying out to God, fell under the shuddering mass of snakes. Hell was cold, and they sought entrance into his warmth, pushing into nose and mouth.

Jeffreys awoke screaming.

Baron Jeffreys of Wem was often troubled by bad dreams. The voices of those whom he had sent to their maker seemed to return, still seeking their vengeance upon him. But the dreams he had in the tavern in the village of Hexen Bridge on the Somerset–Dorset border were the worst. As he tossed restlessly in his bed, the dreams seemed to continue even when the judge lay awake and trembling. This was a bad place. Satan's own.

As Jeffreys exhaled slowly, resting back on the sodden sheets, the answer came to him. With a grim smile he drifted into the untroubled sleep of the just.

Jowett entered Jeffreys's chamber to find the man stooped by the open hearth, jabbing at the few remaining logs with a small iron poker. The judge was not yet fully dressed, his wig hanging from a hook by the door. The shutters were still closed over the windows, and in the sputtering flames of the fire Jeffreys seemed like a little bald-headed imp, tending the ovens of hell.

Jeffreys turned the moment he heard Jowett's footfall.

'The wench said thou hadst orders,' explained Jowett hurriedly.

'Indeed,' said Jeffreys. He seemed to Jowett unusually sanguine – perhaps he had rested well. 'There is much to do, Master Jowett. We find ourselves in the very heart of the villainy. Monmouth's rebels are all around us.'

'This village harboured rebels?'

'Aye, and produced them, I am inclined to think. Thou art a good man, Jowett. The traitors must be known to thee.'

'I knew not of rebellion, sir,' stammered Jowett.

Jeffreys shrugged. ''Tis clear to me.' He turned to look at Jowett for the first time, and the unnatural calmness in his eyes was more terrifying than his usual anger. 'The villagers are to dig a pit. The green afore this inn.'

'For what reason?'

'Thou shalt see.'

It was a bright, crisp day as the men gathered, the storm having long died out. The villagers were nervous – the mere mention of Judge Jeffreys's name was enough to send an icy shiver down the spine – but, while they waited for instruction, they joked together, feeling a certain strength in numbers. Whatever Jeffreys had planned, it would soon pass, and their lives would continue as normal.

Jowett emerged from the inn, and a hush fell. He walked slowly towards them. 'Dig a hole in this green,' he ordered. 'Ten cubits broad.' Uncomprehending, the men hefted shovels, and began to work.

When, after a day, the men had excavated down twenty feet and found nothing, and twilight was fast approaching, the full horror of Jeffreys's plan became evident. The men were still in the pit when the first of the militia appeared at the outer edge of the diggings.

Jeffreys emerged from the tavern. His eyes glittered like the stars. 'God spoke to me in a vision,' he announced. 'In his name I condemn you all for treason against the King, and damn you to hell.' He turned away as the first musket shots sounded.

The gunfire brought Tom Spence running from the inn. Some of the women of the village dared to emerge from their cottages, their eyes wide with terrified disbelief.

'What you do here is wrong!' exclaimed Spence, grabbing the

judge by the shoulder.

'How dare thee, sir?' replied Jeffreys, shaking himself free. 'I speak with the authority of the King. I do *no* wrong.' He turned to Richard, standing behind him. 'Cast this wretch into the pit with all of the other traitors.' As Spence was dragged away, screaming, Jeffreys sighed. 'I had hoped to let one man live,' he observed.

The women, clutching their children to them as their husbands were murdered, began weeping.

'And disperse this gaggle of screeching harridans,' snapped Jeffreys.

'Aye, sir,' said Richard, signalling to two soldiers to remove the women.

Jeffreys watched as one of the villagers tried to pull himself from the pit, but he was spotted by a rifleman, and kicked in the face. He flew backward, on to the writhing, moaning mass. The soil was already soaked red.

Jeffreys turned, Richard still at his side. 'Order the soldiers to begin filling in the pit.'

'But, sir, we cannot be certain that all the traitors have perished.'

'It matters not. Bury them alive. I wish to leave this godforsaken place within the hour.' He shook the dirt from his boots as he strode back into the deserted tavern. In time the vile village would surely disappear without trace.

When the killing was done, Jowett and Richard stood alone in the gathering gloom, cleaning the mud and blood from their boots by the village duck pond. The thunderous clouds were gathering overhead once more. It would be another hellish night.

'Savage occurrences, and no mistake, Richard,' said Jowett, his voice heavy.

His companion gave a short, harsh laugh and swept his fingers back through his blond hair, winking broadly at Jowett. 'Thou old rascal, Joseph, thy stomach for such deeds is not usually so weak.'

'There is something down there, Richard,' said Jowett suddenly. 'I felt it this day when the men were dying. Something in the ground. Something... hungry.'

'What?' There was both astonishment and curiosity in the Yorkshireman's voice.

Jowett cast a last, horrified look at the scene of the massacre. 'There is something in the green,' he said.

SECOND PROLOGUE
STICKS AND STONES

The boy was dreaming. Bad, bad dreams.

He was running through a cornfield, the stalks snapping and falling to the floor like tiny hollow corpses. The sun was setting, etching the golden corn with splashes of blood. And the ensuing darkness would mean something terrible.

He pulled himself through another untidy mass of plants, whipped together by the wind into a thicket of yellow. The leaves snagged on his blazer like rose thorns; when he glanced down, his clothing was covered with crushed ears of corn.

Ears? They weren't ears. They were tiny eyes, staring at him. Unblinking, pupils wide and accusing. They knew where he was.

'No!' he shouted, trying to brush off the corn as he ran. If only he could make his uniform clean again, they wouldn't be able to track him, and he'd be able to push on to the edge of the field – if it had an edge.

Oh God, what if the field went on for ever?

Something crashed through the tall plants behind him, causing his next cry to die in his throat. With a sudden surge of strength, he pulled himself free, and ran on, all the while glancing over his shoulder.

The thing that tramped through the corn after him was at one with the plants and the grinning, empty sky. It moved as quietly as a summer breeze over carved chalk hills, or rats' feet on a cellar floor. Terrified, he stumbled on, his breath coming in short, harsh rasps. No… way… out.

He tripped and fell just as the grotesque uniformity of the rows of corn was threatening to give way to the safety of the scrub grass of the field's edge, and the trees beyond. His world spun, sun-bleached gold, dappled sky-blue, then the solid, enveloping musty brown of the earth.

He forced himself to look around, trying all the while to pull himself to his feet. His chest throbbed with the impact. He pushed with his legs, but they refused to work. The boy dug his fingers deep into the ground, seeking roots and old branches on which to pull, striving to drag himself forward.

It was no use. He felt fingers of bone and twig grip him tightly, then flip his body over as easily as if he were a rag doll.

Another sickening surge of colour, finally settling to show the face of his pursuer, the one who taunted him every night. A blank expanse of cloth, with stitched slits for eyes and mouth. Ears of corn rained down from the squashed head like spilled blood.

And a straw-stuffed hand pulled back the mask.

He awoke to the distant sound of Elgar's *Enigma Variations*. It was just on the periphery of his hearing, as unreal and intangible as the dream he had emerged from.

He rolled over on to his side, then sat bolt upright, his cheeks flushed red. He swore under his breath, ashamed and cross and guilty. The bed was soaking wet. Again.

If word got out, tomorrow would see another round of taunting and abuse, another stylised beating. And he could rely on the teachers being less than sympathetic, too. He glanced at the alarm clock on his bedside cabinet. Tomorrow? Make that today. It was just after five in the morning.

He pulled himself from his bed, rummaged around for his slippers and, as quickly as he dared, another pair of pyjamas, and then padded silently down the length of the long, tall chamber and towards the bathroom further down the corridor.

The school was eerily quiet, but for the sounds of Elgar. Ironic that he was taunted by his peers as a stupid, Scouse spasmo, and yet none of them would be able to tell Elgar from Debussy, or Schumann from Schubert. Ignorant bloody straw-sucking peasants, the lot of them.

The boy changed swiftly in the bathroom, and then pulled his dressing gown around him, tugging the cord tight. There was an Everton logo on the lapel, a rebellious link to his former life, the life that most of the children despised. Some of the stitching had been loosened in a recent attack, when his head had been shoved into a dirty toilet bowl; he really ought to get around to fixing it, but the thought of being caught with needle and thread was deterrent enough.

He walked slowly down the corridor, towards the library and the source of the music. He strained his ears to hear. The ninth and most famous variation, 'Nimrod', was just beginning. The strings ebbed and flowed, like the song of an angel, or those rare dreams of light and life that he wished he could dream again.

He pushed open the door, and stepped into the library. At the bottom, on a low table covered with the previous day's newspapers, stood an enormous ghetto blaster, garishly painted and like none that the boy had ever seen before. In front of it, his back to the boy, sat a small, dark-haired man in some kind of pale suit. An array of charts and photocopied sheets surrounded him, propped against the beatbox and strewn all over the floor. He seemed to be taking notes, but had stopped, his head aloft as if he'd heard the boy enter. Just for a moment the head dipped, as if bowed down by some vast pressure, and then rose again as the music swelled.

'I'm sorry if I woke you,' said the man, without looking round.

The boy paused. He didn't know the man, but he obviously wasn't an intruder. Presumably he could be trusted. Certainly his voice, somehow warm and dark at the same time and with a Scottish burr rolling the consonants, seemed… reliable. Despite his size, he was clearly a man of great authority.

'Elgar,' said the boy at last, walking towards the man. 'One of my favourites.' He paused, thinking of the reaction of his friends and enemies. 'I mean, don't get me wrong, I like rock and roll, too. New

Order, the Fall. Me ma used to call it "hooligan music". She's –'

'You don't have to justify anything to me,' said the man.

The boy sat down, surprised by what he'd already said. He hadn't mentioned his mother in weeks; indeed, he had tried actively to banish her from his every waking thought. But the man's very presence seemed to enforce honesty.

'Pretence saddens me. So does fear. And hurt,' continued the man. His words were strong and confident, but there was an underlying melancholy, so palpable the boy felt he could reach out and touch the man's own anguish. What was all the more surprising was that the man's face was wet with tears, but he was talking perfectly calmly, as if nothing was the matter. 'Life is complicated enough without adding to its problems,' he concluded with a half-hearted grin.

The music from the ghetto blaster swelled again, reaching its conclusion.

The man pointed, as if the rising strings and brass, the rolling drums, the very essence of the music, was something tangible. 'Here. Listen. Just as you expect an overblown conclusion… It fades away with only the string section. It's like a butterfly you can't quite grasp. Elusive. It's so beautiful.'

The boy listened intently. It was like hearing music for the first time.

The man introduced himself as the Doctor. 'I'm a sort of governor here. I often come to the library to clear my head. It's so quiet you can even hear the past, the heritage of this lovely old building.'

The boy wasn't quite sure what he meant, but he nodded anyway.

'And you are?' the Doctor asked politely, smiling.

'Shanks, sir,' replied the boy without thinking. He was about to add his Christian name, too, but the Doctor seized on this revelation as if that was all he needed to know everything about him.

'Shanks,' said the Doctor, turning the word over a few more times. 'Shanks. Ah, yes.' Doubtless he was familiar with the names of the students, and was ticking off some kind of mental register. 'Shall we go for a walk? I find sleep… troublesome.'

Shanks hadn't even mentioned his nightmares, but it seemed that the Doctor knew most things without their having to be spelled out. The boy nodded dumbly, and, some time later, found himself walking around the school grounds, pouring out his heart to a complete stranger. The first hint of the sun was lightening the horizon.

'So, you've been here a few weeks?' inquired the Doctor, his face serious despite the umbrella that twirled around his hand like something from a slapstick comedy.

'A month, I think. Time passes so slowly.'

'It's difficult being exiled,' agreed the Doctor. 'Those around you claim to understand, but they never can. Not fully.'

Shanks nodded. He was *exiled* from his home town. He'd never thought of it in those terms before.

'Although in your case,' continued the Doctor, 'I doubt your peers are very sympathetic.'

Shanks nodded. 'Yeah. But a couple of 'em are brave enough to be my friends. Don't you worry about me,' he said with a certainty that seemed to stop the Doctor in his tracks, 'I'll sort it out here. You'll see. They all will.'

The Doctor paused. 'I'm sure you will. But don't let the people of Hexen taint you. Not *everyone* is as cruel as that.'

Shanks scratched his head for a moment. He'd seen some pretty bad things up on the council estates of Liverpool, and the children here didn't seem any worse than the crackheads and pushers that loitered in the shadows of Toxteth and Garston. 'They're just the same as other people,' said Shanks, although he could barely believe that he was defending his tormentors.

'No,' said the Doctor firmly. 'Don't think that for a moment.' He changed the subject abruptly, pointing towards the field that ran

15

alongside the school rugby pitch. 'Have you ever noticed how many scarecrows there are around here?' he asked.

Shanks shivered. He could just make out the stickman half slumped in the middle of the field. 'Yeah. They give me the creeps.'

'Unusual for an area only partly dedicated to arable farming,' continued the Doctor. 'I mean, that fellow over there makes sense. But you must have noticed those that skirt the periphery of the village.'

'Can't say I have,' admitted Shanks, following the Doctor towards the scarecrow. 'Are you interested in them?' the boy queried, remembering the Doctor's maps and documents.

'Oh, I'm interested in lots of things,' said the Doctor. 'I'm especially interested in you.'

Shanks laughed. 'What makes me so special, then?'

'You're an outsider, like me. In this village, that makes you as unique as a man with two hearts.'

The boy snorted. 'I'm nothing special.'

'Oh yes you are,' affirmed the small man gently. He turned again towards the scarecrow, where a rook had alighted on the sackcloth face. It began picking intently, like a vulture at a corpse. 'You're very important,' the Doctor concluded with a sigh. 'And that's the most frightening thing in the world.'

PART ONE
JACK OF ALL TRADES

CHAPTER 1
LITTLE ENGLAND

'Pastoral. Wicked!'

There was something perfectly natural about seeing an anachronistic 1960s London police box standing in the middle of an English field in the early years of the twenty-first century. The solid blue oblong was as bright as an eye against the interlocking fields of green and gold, the little frosted windows glinting like diamonds in the early-morning sun. It looked as if it had always been there, but the crushed grass underneath spoke of a recent arrival. What summer breeze there was pulled the last murmurings of the box's advent high over the downs and into the cloudless infinity of the sky.

The couple that emerged from the box surveyed the land intently. The man was small, somewhat shabbily dressed, and inconsequential but for his eyes, as dark and unfathomable as the deepest well. His companion, a girl in her late teens, wore a short pleated skirt over dark tights, a narrow-striped T-shirt, and a badge-festooned jacket, the word ACE! prominent on her back. Her long hair was pulled into a ponytail behind her head. Just as she slipped a pair of mirror shades over her eyes she sneezed.

'Aw. Hay fever,' she exclaimed. 'I *hate* the countryside. Always have done.'

'Really?' asked the man with a rich roll of the tongue as he closed the police box's door behind them, ignoring his young friend's abrupt change of mood. 'This is one of my favourite places on Earth.' He stooped and retrieved something from the ground, then straightened himself up, beaming. 'Look, Ace!' Between his fingers he held a four-leaved clover. 'Now that's got to be a sign of something, surely?'

'I don't believe in all that. And neither should you, Professor.' She paused, and looked around the lush green vista. In the distance, on the faraway rolling downlands, she could just make out a chalk horse carved into the hillside. 'The West Country, right?' she asked.

The man nodded. 'Wessex,' he announced grandly. 'Over there is Thomas Hardy country,' he said, pointing with a ruler-straight arm. He turned. 'The Isle of Avalon is somewhere over there.' He gestured again. 'And that is the way to Camelot.'

The girl smiled as if at a recent memory. 'Great. And I'll bet it's three miles from the nearest pub, but when we get there they'll all be out playing cricket, or something.'

'More like two hundred yards,' said the man. 'But we're not going there yet.' He paused, gnomically. 'A military campaign is only as good as the intelligence reports it is based upon.'

For the first time, the girl looked worried.

Russ Sloper placed the last milk bottle on the doorstep and shivered despite the rising sun. This was normally Daniel Cottle's round and, frankly, he was welcome to it. Sloper wasn't one to trust innuendo and rumour over logic – for that reason alone he preferred broadsheet newspapers to the tacky tabloids of his colleagues – but the village of Hexen Bridge was different. No small area could produce so many stories and legends if there wasn't at least a grain of truth in them.

Sloper walked back towards the float, the empty milk bottles chinking against the plastic carrier. Behind the cottages and terraces of orange-yellow stone the faintest sounds of early-morning movement could be heard: water running in bathrooms, radios being switched on in kitchens. Somewhere a car engine was being coaxed into life.

Best get out before he actually saw any of them.

The village was a maze of tiny lanes, surrounding an ancient green and a duck pond. To the north and east rose great chalk hills variously patrolled by sheep and cows; to the south, trailing gently out of sight, was a ring of woods and a crazy paving of small fields. The main road out of Hexen ran to the west, just wide enough to accommodate two lanes of traffic. Not that the roads bristled with many cars, even during the holiday season. Somehow, people knew.

Everyone knew about Hexen Bridge.

Sloper manoeuvred the float towards the west road, feeling the tension fall from his shoulders as each second took him further from the damned village. He began to hum under his breath, a tuneless conglomeration of sound to help block out the whine of the milk float's electric engine. Even after all these years, he'd never entirely got used to the noise. Still less the gentle ribbing he received when he arrived anywhere in his car. 'Left your float behind, have you, Russ?' went the cry. It hadn't been funny the first time. It was almost enough to –

He slammed on the brakes as a couple appeared around a bend in the thickly hedged lane. 'Watch out!' he shouted, just missing them.

The float came to a halt, and Sloper jumped down. 'You OK?' he asked the short man.

'I am, thank you,' said the man with just a little dignity.

'Never walk with your back to the traffic,' Sloper scolded, though realising that at this time in the morning his float had probably been the first vehicle they would have encountered.

'Ah,' said the man solemnly. 'I take your point.'

'Fancy a lift?' Sloper asked, in a calmer voice.

'That's very kind of you,' said the man, jumping into the front of the float next to Sloper. 'I've only been on one of these once before, and that was many years ago.' The girl positioned herself on the edge of the seat more gingerly.

Sloper regarded the couple for a moment. The man didn't look attractive or daring enough to be eloping with this young thing, but she seemed to be close to school age. Still, there was only a week or so of term to go, and Sloper remembered bunking off lessons when the fine weather arrived. She was pretty, this girl, although she studiously avoided eye contact.

Perhaps they were on holiday. Whatever. That was their business. They were walking away from Hexen Bridge, and that was good enough for Russ Sloper.

'You not from round here?' he asked, hoping to strike up a conversation to while away the journey back to the dairy.

'No,' said the man. 'We've only just arrived. We want to visit a library.'

'Tourist brochures, a bit of local history, that sort of thing,' said the girl, piping up brightly. 'Isn't that right, Professor?'

'Professor, eh?' inquired Sloper. 'Writing a book or something?'

'Perhaps,' said the little man. 'I'm usually known as the Doctor. "Professor" is just an irritating affectation my companion has picked up.'

'Then you're not a professor?'

'Yes and no,' said the man, as if that was answer enough.

'I'm Ace,' said the girl.

'I bet you are,' said Sloper with a chuckle.

Ace glared at him. Her eyes spoke of things that Sloper could never imagine. Sloper shivered. It was his turn to avert his eyes.

Sloper suddenly remembered an Asian kid he'd got to know at school. The boy had turned up one term, exotic and alien, and calm, despite the bullying. With his faraway look he made Sloper feel mundane and trivial. So did this girl.

'Are you all right?' asked the Doctor.

'Fine,' said Sloper. 'Just glad to be away from Hexen Bridge.'

'Ah,' said the Doctor. 'Why am I not surprised to hear you say that?'

Ace glanced at a passing road sign. 'That village seems very isolated,' she announced. 'Miles from anywhere.'

'I've often wondered about that,' said the Doctor.

'Don't wonder too hard,' said Sloper. 'I'll happily drop you off at the library in town but, if you want my advice, you'll have a much nicer holiday if you stay there. Hexen's good for nothing.'

And with that, and despite the sun rising into the azure sky, Sloper lapsed into brooding silence.

A magazine can tell the observant many things about the person who is reading it. This particular magazine was a music-and-fashion monthly, one of hundreds that cluttered the newsstands and kiosks of Britain. Its garish, brightly coloured cover was in stark contrast to the drab, grey formalism of the *Daily Telegraph* that lay on the plastic-topped table. Nails painted bright red grasped the pages of the magazine tightly.

The summer sun nervously pulled itself above the brow of a solitary hill, blinding the train passengers with its unexpected brilliance. The girl cursed under her breath, swayed slightly as the carriages clattered through a series of tightly positioned points, and lifted a pair of vampish plastic sunglasses from her handbag. She had put the bag on the aisle seat next to her to discourage anyone from sitting there. Personal space is very important to the average train user, and it was particularly, obsessively, important to Nicola Denman.

She glanced back at the magazine, but she had lost the thread of the article on the Star Jumpers' comeback tour. She picked up the bottle of mineral water, but the taste was bland and insipid. Then the sun lost itself in the clouds again, and Nicola removed her glasses, and shivered.

Anyone in the train compartment with an active imagination, and too much time on their hands, might have paused to wonder at the way in which the girl and her bearded companion seldom made eye contact. They talked to each other in snatched bursts of clumsy embarrassment.

'I still don't know why you made me come,' said Nicola, stopping abruptly as if the danger of initiating a proper conversation was too horrible to contemplate. Her voice was soft and singsong, cut through on occasions with a strong, nasal Scouse inflection.

'You're not staying in the 'Pool on your own,' said the man flatly. 'If I've told you once I've told you a million times…' He paused, aware that he was raising his voice. Again.

'But, Dad…'

Her voice faded away as the train entered a tunnel and the compartment was, momentarily, plunged into darkness. By the time the train emerged a silence had settled between them, Nicola's father turned his attention to the *Telegraph*'s article on the new Home Secretary's latest crackdown on youth crime.

'I'm twenty, for goodness' sake,' exclaimed Nicola suddenly. 'I can look after myself.'

'Then act your age and stop sulking.'

Nicola Denman recoiled as if struck. Her father glanced up and saw that her eyes were swollen and red, as if on the verge of tears.

'I'm sorry,' he said.

'It's OK,' replied Nicola. 'I just hate travelling.'

'Remember that holiday on the Isle of Man?' asked Denman. 'You must have been about eight.' He stared at the countryside that passed, a blur through the carriage window. 'You were so bored. Your mother and I were at our wits' end…'

Denman gave Nicola's hand a pat of reassurance, but she withdrew it quickly. 'You made me behave by threatening me with Jack i' the Green.' She paused for a moment, but the giddying momentum of her words carried her on. 'You said that Jack took all the bad little girls to Hexen Bridge to do terrible things to them.'

Denman's face was like thunder. 'You mark me well, Nicola Denman,' he said. 'The last thing I need right now is mockery.'

'I was just saying –' she replied, but was cut short.

'Well, *don't*,' he snapped. 'This reunion is important.' He stared out of the window again. 'We've been trapped by the past for too long.'

The library was a modern slab of a building, coloured concrete offset by large windows and an overfussy entrance. It stood, awkwardly, halfway between its former location in the centre of the town and the new estate that was eating into the green land to the east. As a consequence, only the truly dedicated sought it out, a line of miserable-looking old people passing through to read the newspapers.

'Why are we here, Professor?' asked Ace.

'Well, I like books, and…' The Doctor affected bafflement at Ace's question.

'You know what I mean.'

'Why,' the Doctor shrugged, 'does there have to be a reason for everything?'

'Where you're concerned there is,' said Ace. She ran a few paces in front of the Doctor, and turned to face him, both hands out in front of her. 'Whoa,' she said, stopping him in his tracks. 'C'mon. Spill the beans.'

'Here…' The Doctor held out his hand. In it was a crumpled, yellowing piece of card. The writing on it had almost faded , but the top line was still visible:

      HEXEN BRIDGE SCHOOL REUNION – 14TH JUNE.

'You went to school here?' asked Ace, incredulous.

'Not exactly.'

'Then…'

'It's a long story.'

'I'm listening.'

'Let's go inside, and I'll tell you.'

Some stories have no ending, but they all have a beginning. And in this case, the beginning came when the Doctor, then in his third incarnation, was exploring the area around the Wiltshire village of Devil's End, after his defeat of the Dæmon, Azal. The Doctor never quite knew what it was that made him take Bessie up the unmarked side road, the same road that, four regenerations later, he and Ace walked along before the intervention of the local milkman. But the Doctor had, and what he found made him curious.

'Perhaps it was the lack of birdsong,' he explained to Ace, reaching to right a toddler who had just collapsed, face down, in front of him. The child's mother emerged from the romantic fiction section and withdrew the boy without a word of thanks. An expression of fear had tightened the woman's soft, pleasant face, and Ace couldn't tell if she was afraid of them or of their conversation.

'There's certainly a strange, oppressive atmosphere over that village,' continued the Doctor at length. 'You'll see what I mean when we get there.'

'So that's where we're going?' quizzed Ace.

'That's where the battle will be fought,' continued the Doctor, using the same image as earlier. 'I always meant to return to Hexen Bridge and investigate further, but time never seemed to allow. In fact, it wasn't until my exile on this planet had come to an end that the place came to mind again. I was in the area once more. Another spot of bother, just a few miles down the road.'

'What happened?'

The Doctor paused. 'I've always thought I'd make a good teacher. The responsibility of disseminating information to young, inquiring minds...'

Ace was used to these tricks. 'Professor, you're changing the subject.'

'Am I?' said the Doctor absent-mindedly. 'That probably explains why Ian and Barbara and I got on so well, doesn't it? Anyway, to cut a long story short, I managed to get a place on the board of governors at the Hexen Bridge school. I've kept an eye on the place ever since.'

'And this?' asked Ace, gently tapping the invitation card.

'Oh yes, I've had that for decades. Of course, in Earth terms I would have picked it up two weeks ago from a dead-letter office in London. I'd almost forgotten about it. I mean, when I got it I had a different face. You know how it is.'

'And when is *now*, incidentally?'

'The early years of the next millennium.'

'It's not changed much from my time,' said Ace.

'No,' smiled the Doctor. 'And that's why I like it.' He got to his feet, and made his way towards the stairs that led up into the reference department. 'To business.' He glanced back over his shoulder at Ace, grinning apologetically. 'It's not very exciting, but it will help to oil the wheels later on.'

'Really?'

'Oh yes.'

The Doctor spent the next couple of hours photocopying dozens of maps, photographs and pages from books of local history.

Ace found a recent newspaper and turned to the sports section. 'Aw,' she wailed. 'Look where Charlton are now. GM Vauxhall Conference...'

'It could be worse,' replied the Doctor. 'Have a look at Arsenal.'

The Doctor and Ace struck up a conversation with Mark, a young librarian who had been keen to show the eminent visiting professor of history as much as he could. While Ace busied herself looking through a huge bundle of papers and feeding two-pound coins into the photocopier, the Doctor – having glanced around nervously in case of being overheard – asked Mark about Hexen Bridge.

'If you'd asked my old dad about Hexen you'd have got a right mouthful in return,' the young man replied.

'Is that so?'

'Yeah. All the old 'uns reckon it's a *bad place*. You know what West Country traditions are like? They're stories to frighten the children, aren't they?'

'You don't believe in them, then?' asked the Doctor.

'Oh, no. Well...' Mark paused. 'I'll tell you something for nothing:

very few people ever go anywhere near the place after dark. It's stupid, but for a long time there were stories of people going missing and the like. I suppose most folk think it's better to be safe than sorry.' He paused as he found another reference for the Doctor, which he slid across the desk towards him. 'There's a lot of local rivalry with the Hexen lads, mind you. We always called them "thick Hexies", and told the same sort of jokes about them as other people do with the Irish.'

The Doctor picked up a map of the area and circled Hexen Bridge with his finger.

'Nothing within ten miles?'

'Never has been.'

'Never?'

'No,' said Mark, seeming to realise for the first time how strange this was. 'Well, they like to keep themselves to themselves, if you know what I mean.'

The Doctor nodded. 'And you're sure there's no aerial photographs?'

'Positive. Just maps.'

Ace overheard this last comment. 'Significant?' she asked the Doctor.

'Possibly,' he replied, before turning back to Mark. 'Thank you very much for your help. Ace, come on.' He scurried towards the door. 'Places to go, people to see, things to do.'

'Terrific,' said Ace sullenly. 'No chance of anything to eat, I suppose?'

'As soon as we get to Hexen Bridge,' he said.

An old man, walking into the library, stopped and called after the Doctor and Ace. 'I heard that,' he said. 'You don't want to be going there, boy.'

'I beg your pardon?' said the Doctor. He wasn't easily surprised by anything, but he hadn't been called a boy for almost a thousand years.

'Hexen Bridge,' said the old man, his weather-beaten face

cracking into a scowl. 'Terrible place. Terrible. They do things, you know.'

'Really?'

'Yes. Terrible things. And they're all scum, them Hexies. Be better if they dropped a bomb on the lot of them.'

The Doctor seemed distracted by something in the distance, like a dog when it hears a high-pitched whistle. 'The children I've met in Hexen Bridge seem very bright, academically speaking,' he said, dragging his attention back to the old man.

'Ah, that's what they *want* you to think,' the man said. And with that, he turned into the library, leaving the Doctor and Ace staring after him.

They had just enough change left to pay for a taxi into Hexen Bridge. The driver said he would drop them off outside the village. In fact, when they turned the first corner, expecting to see the cluster of cottages, they saw only the lane twisting into the distance.

It meant another walk in the broiling sunshine. If Ace had been surly when they left the town, she was positively fuming by the time they passed the field where the TARDIS had landed.

'Two hundred yards, you said,' she moaned.

'Indeed,' said the Doctor. 'As the crow flies.'

'I'm not a crow.'

'No,' said the Doctor. At length they rounded a corner, and Hexen Bridge lay before them.

The village seemed less sinister than Ace had expected. There was a certain picture-postcard quality about the place, little thatched cottages jockeying for position around the green. The people who sat at wooden tables outside the pub looked normal enough. Ace had expected extra limbs and Elephant Man deformities, at the very least.

'You sure this is the right place?' she queried.

The Doctor nodded. 'Relax, just for a moment. What do you feel?'

Ace paused. 'I feel hungry and sunburnt,' she exploded. 'Isn't there anywhere to eat in this hole?'

'As I promised,' said the Doctor.

He turned Ace around, and there, on the left-hand side of the lane, was a Chinese restaurant. A large sign proclaimed it to be A TASTE OF THE ORIENT. Its façade resembled that of a Buddhist temple and, in the context of the village, it was almost an eyesore. Ace rather liked it.

'Wicked!' she exclaimed. Two massive carved lions the colour of green jade stood on either side of the door, and Ace couldn't resist patting one on the head. Its eyes were coloured glass, cut to resemble precious gems. 'Purpose?' she asked with a hint of mocking humour in her voice, parodying the Doctor's usual inquisitorial style. She had been in many Chinese restaurants, but had never seen anything like these giant statues before.

'Other than the purely decorative?' replied the Doctor with a wry grin. 'I'd say they were to ward off evil spirits.'

'Guess what?' said Ace. 'I just *knew* you were going to say that!'

They stepped into the restaurant. Fans in the ceiling and shutters over most the windows kept the interior cool and dark, a welcome relief after the sun. Golden dragon murals trailed along walls; brightly coloured paper lanterns hung from the ceiling. It was an absolutely unremarkable Chinese restaurant. What Ace couldn't work out was what it was doing in a place like Hexen Bridge, and how it managed to stay open.

She gestured towards the few diners seated at the tables. 'It's not exactly seething, is it?' she queried.

'It *is* one thirty,' responded the Doctor. 'And, before you ask, you'll find the people of Hexen a strangely cosmopolitan bunch. They're quite happy for this place to stay here – on their terms.'

'You come here often?'

'I've met Mr Chen and his family on several occasions.'

As if on cue, a middle-aged Chinese man emerged from the shadows, bowing politely. 'Good afternoon,' he said. 'How pleasant it is to meet one of the family of Dr Smiths again.'

'I've not broached the subject of regenerations with him,' whispered the Doctor. 'Hello, my friend,' he continued, more loudly. 'Sorry to turn up unannounced, but –'

Chen looked puzzled. 'You rang last Monday, Dr Smith,' he said.

'Of course I did,' bluffed the Doctor. He quickly withdrew a notepad from a pocket, and used a piece of pencil lead under his thumbnail to scribble a note. Ace saw that the page was headed 'To Do List' and, under items 25 ('Leave settee in Perivale') and 26 ('Return to Planet 14 to check up on provisional government'), the Doctor added a note to remind him to book the table.

'You are a little late,' said Chen diplomatically. 'But as you can see, we are not busy at the moment. Let me show you to your table.' And he walked across the room towards the window that afforded the best view of the village.

Ace sat down before Chen could hold her chair for her, and grabbed a menu, leaving the Doctor to do the small talk.

'How are things?' asked the Doctor vaguely.

'Some matters have worsened since your last visit, Doctor,' said Chen stoically. 'My family have lived in this village for twenty years, but we shall always remain outsiders,' he continued, presumably for Ace's benefit.

The Doctor sighed. 'In a village where everyone else can trace their ancestry back to the seventeenth century, that's hardly surprising.'

Chen nodded. 'But… other factors are worrying.'

'You mean the racist graffiti?' asked the Doctor. Ace looked up from her menu.

'You saw it?' asked Chen.

' "Chinks Out", "Yellow Pigs", the usual mindless drivel. Yes, I saw it. I also saw how hard you'd scrubbed the walls in an attempt to remove the writing.'

'That's terrible,' said Ace, angry and shocked. 'Why don't the police do anything about it?'

'This town has one police officer, miss,' said Chen passively. 'Like most other people in this village, he is related to almost everyone.'

'They all marry each other, Ace,' explained the Doctor. 'Everybody is everyone else's cousin.'

'Isn't that illegal?'

'No,' said the Doctor, 'but it's not healthy.'

'The policeman is a good man,' said Chen, 'but he is also loyal to family ties, yes? In my culture the family is more important than anything else, so I can understand his reluctance to do anything. And people do not want to involve him in family disputes.' Chen clapped his hands together eagerly. 'But this is no time for such morbid talk. You are here to sample our cuisine. My hope, as always, is that it will take you somewhere better.'

'I am sure it will, Chen,' noted the Doctor.

'Excellent.' Chen motioned to a young man in a white shirt and bow tie across the room. 'Most of our children have gone now,' said Chen, 'but my youngest son, Steven, will be glad to take your order.'

'Well, you can start with a lager,' said Ace cheerfully. 'And two portions of prawn crackers.'

It was a 1980s-style wine bar, hopelessly out of time. Everything spoke of a bygone era, from the songs on the jukebox and the pictures on the wall, to the plastic decor and the overpriced cocktails.

'Trevor!' A female voice cut through the murmur of conversation and the chiming guitars of a Stone Roses song. The man in his late thirties snapped his head up from his vodka and orange, and their eyes met. Instantly he was sixteen again. And she was fifteen, and the most beautiful girl in the world.

'I...' He stammered briefly, like a nervous schoolboy. He shook his head, feeling stupid. Get a grip. 'Hi, Rebecca.'

'Am I late?'

'Yes, as usual,' he smiled. She moved gracefully through the bar, her black dress clinging to her hips. She swept a fringe of auburn hair out of her eyes and widened her arms as he stood to greet her. They kissed, at first clanging teeth with the clumsiness of unfamiliarity, then with the passion that time cannot dull.

Trevor released his grip and stood back. He tried to think of something witty or urbane to say, but that would have cheapened the moment. They had never been scared of silence.

'You look *fabulous*,' he said eventually. And he meant it.

'You don't look too bad yourself,' she said with a silly smile that left him wondering whether she had meant it, too.

They moved to a corner table with two seats and ignored the faintly patronising looks from the other people in the bar.

'We have something they'll never have,' she said, reading his mind in that annoying way of hers. Just as she had in the days when they used to sit by the riverbank in Hexen Bridge and recite Keats, Shelley, Wilde and Morrissey to each other.

'You needn't have come,' he said simply. 'We could have met later. At the reunion.'

'I wanted a few hours of you to myself, Trevor Winstone,' she said. Her eyes were wide, and sparkled in the dull light of the bar. Trevor realised, as he had done three months ago when they had met for the first time in ten years, that she was no longer the most beautiful girl in the world, and *his*. She was the most beautiful *woman* in the world, but she didn't belong to him any more. Or to anyone. He had learnt that hard, cruel lesson outside a grubby Iranian bed-and-breakfast in Victoria, and it hurt him badly. 'I love you,' he had told her. 'Grow up,' she had replied, and he'd spent the last few weeks trying.

Rebecca's voice, rich with laughter, brought him back to the present. 'This reunion, Trev. Is it business or pleasure?'

'Both,' he smiled. 'You know, the usual. Deals to be done…'

'Keep greasing those wheels,' advised Rebecca.

'Matt Hatch told me he's keen to get away from that wife of his,' said Trevor. 'I've heard she's desperate for kids, but Matt's not. I reckon he's got a bit on the side.'

Rebecca started making pointless small talk about who was married to whom, or divorced from whom, or shagging whom, in Hexen Bridge. You mistake me for someone who's interested, thought Trevor as he cleared his throat, waiting for her litany of 'hatched, matched and dispatched' to end. 'Rebecca, we really need to talk.'

He had been looking at the table when he said this, and when he raised his eyes to meet hers he found that she was staring out of the window at the street outside. A boy and a girl, no older than sixteen, were holding hands and skipping across the road, high on love. It was a magical sight. After a moment she looked back at him, smiling.

'I'm sorry, I wasn't listening.'

Trevor shook his head. 'It doesn't matter. Small talk.'

Just then 'There is a Light that Never Goes Out' came on the CD jukebox, and they grinned at each other.

'Remember when this was *our* song?' she asked, as if he could ever forget. They waited until the song finished, without saying anything, just looking at each other and mouthing the words. When it ended, Rebecca stood up and straightened her dress.

'Come on,' she said, simply. 'Let's go home.'

'London's my home,' said Trevor with a wicked grin.

'Hexen Bridge'll always be thy home, boy,' she replied, mocking the local accent. 'Till Jack i' the Green lets 'ee go.'

Ace scooped the last of the Beef Szechwan into her mouth and belched contentedly. 'You're right, Professor, this is serious nosh.'

The Doctor smiled warmly. 'You make it sound like I'm in the habit of not telling you the truth.'

'You have your moments,' said Ace. 'And this is one of the better ones. Even if you *didn't* let me have that lager.'

'You should treasure your youth, Ace, not fight against it all the time.'

'That's easy for you to say.'

The Doctor poked at his food. By his own standards, he had eaten heartily, but Ace couldn't help but notice that most of his food remained untouched. It probably hadn't helped that he seemed to have chosen his food by the quality of the name alone: Seven Stars Around the Moon, Wandering Dragon, Happy Family...

'Shall I help you with some of yours, Professor?' Ace asked.

'By all means,' said the Doctor, sliding his bowl away from him.

Steven Chen returned to their table. 'Everything is OK?'

'It's fine, Steven,' said the Doctor.

'More than fine,' agreed Ace.

'My father has told you what we have to put up with?' Steven asked while clearing away the empty bowls.

'Indeed. I'm very sorry,' said the Doctor.

'The attacks have become more frequent.' Steven stopped and checked that no one else in the restaurant was looking at them. He leaned forward, conspiratorially, and dropped a piece of paper on to the table. 'My father considers you a friend, Doctor. May I ask a favour of you?'

'Certainly.'

'You will be staying at the Green Man, I take it?'

'The Green Man?'

Steven smiled. 'The pub on the green. It changed its name recently.'

'I have stayed there in the past,' confirmed the Doctor.

'Then could I ask you to deliver this note to Mrs Joanna Matson, the publican's wife?' He again glanced around like a frightened animal. 'I would take the message myself but Mr Matson and I... do not get along.'

'I'll deliver it,' said Ace, snatching up the note and giving Steven a wink of encouragement.

'I am very grateful, miss,' said Steven Chen, before turning away for the kitchens.

The Doctor gave Ace a curious sideways glance. 'He was asking me. Why involve yourself?'

'I felt for him. He's obviously having a bad time with the fascists. And I hate fascists as much as I hate clowns.'

'That much?' asked the Doctor, amused.

'You bet!'

'Come on, Ace,' said the Doctor, getting to his feet. 'We'd better be going. I have a reunion to prepare for.'

CHAPTER 2
THE BUTTERFLY COLLECTOR

Billy Tyley was smashed out of his skull, as usual.

He took another long swig from the two-litre bottle of cider. The drink was horribly warm and flat, but it had a hint of apple about it, and was perfect in the summer sun. Billy pulled the sleeve of his T-shirt up to his lips to wipe them dry, swinging his legs against the wall. Then he stopped, deciding that it probably made him look like a kid.

Billy Tyley certainly wasn't a child any more. And he'd smash the nose of any scumbag that said he was. Soon school would be over for ever and an adult life of doing nothing all day and getting paid for it would be waiting for him. The teachers knew about his bunking off, but they let him get on with it because he was a disruptive influence on everyone else. Outside the school gates he was, essentially, someone else's problem, so it was a pretty cool arrangement all round.

Billy glanced at his digital watch and smiled. He should be in an exam, but he didn't give a monkey's. Better just to sit here and enjoy the sun.

'Oi, Billy!'

Billy Tyley turned, and saw a gaggle of younger children approaching him from the direction of school. He recognised most of them – dirty, freckled kids much like himself. 'Yeah? What do you want?'

'Thought we'd hang out with you,' said one lad through teeth clogged with metal braces. 'We're skiving off PE. We thought, sod that for a lark.'

Billy grunted and jumped down from the wall and screwed the cap back on to the bottle.

'Aw, Billy, can't we have some?' whined one of the others.

Billy shook his head. 'No, it's mine.' His eyes – slowly – lit up with an idea. 'We could nick some. That'd be a laugh.' He trudged towards the post office with the chuckling youngsters in his wake.

Decades ago, the living room of one of the terraced cottages had been transformed into a shop with the addition of bigger windows and a counter. In the 1950s it became a post office, and a decade later Mrs Cluett took over the day-to-day running of the shop. Now, some forty years later, she was still in charge, and her shop was packed to the rafters with ice creams, toilet rolls and bunion ointments.

As soon as Mrs Cluett saw Billy Tyley's bulky frame in the jangling doorway, she knew there'd be trouble. Trouble followed that boy like a bad shadow. A troop of little Tyley clones came into the shop after him.

'Afternoon, Mrs Cluett,' said Billy. 'I'd like a quarter of midget gems, please.'

Mrs Cluett kept an enormous array of sweets in old-fashioned glass jars on shelves at the back of the shop. She had decided on this, as a way of preventing petty theft, and had doggedly stuck to imperial measures, in contravention of European law. No one in Hexen Bridge saw fit to report her to the proper authorities. The children often chose the bottled sweets over the pre-wrapped chocolates that edged the cash till as it meant that old Mrs Cluett would have to rummage around behind the counter for the pair of wooden stepladders – which gave them all the time in the world to steal from elsewhere in the shop.

Today, however, Mrs Cluett was having none of it, and she ignored Billy's request. 'Can't you read?' she said. 'Only two children at a time.'

Billy glanced back towards the door, as if he'd never seen the handwritten notice before. 'Ah well,' said Billy, with an attempt at a charming smile that only succeeded in drawing attention to his broken nose and close-set eyes. 'You see, Mrs Cluett, I barely count as a child, seeing as I'm about to leave school. And Bingo 'ere… Well, I'm not sure Bingo even counts as a human being, do you, Bingo?'

The boy in question was already scrabbling around on the cobwebbed floor like a dog, woofing animatedly.

'Get up!' screamed the old postmistress. 'Get off the floor, you little hooligan.'

Bingo found a bag of dog food and began yelping.

'Look,' said one of the other children. 'The poor kid's got BSE. Too many school dinners.'

Bingo's *pièce de résistance* was to pretend to cock his leg against the bag.

Mrs Cluett flipped open the counter, and marched towards the lad. 'Get up, you tearaway, and get out of my shop!'

With that, Billy Tyley clicked his fingers, just out of sight of the woman, and two of the boys ducked into the aisle that contained the alcohol. 'Now, Mrs Cluett,' said Billy, using what he assumed to be his most adult-sounding voice. 'He don't mean any harm. He's just mucking about.'

Bingo got to his feet, partly because the diversion had worked, and partly because his left ear lobe was caught in Mrs Cluett's pincer-like grip. 'You little so-and-so,' she said, ignoring Billy. 'If my husband were alive he'd give you a damn good hidin'.'

'If you don't let go of my ear,' said Bingo suddenly, 'I'll get my dad on to you.'

'Will you, indeed?' queried the woman. 'Now, that might work with your teachers, Mark Luston, but I know your father well. I think he'd be quite keen to hear my side of the story.'

There was a sudden clanging crash as two boys pushed their way out of the shop, laughing hysterically. Mrs Cluett recognised the bulges under their blazers.

'Oi!' she screamed, letting go of Bingo's ear. 'You come back here with that!' She went to open the door, but Billy's friends blocked her way.

'Mrs Cluett,' said the ringleader in a quiet voice. 'I only came in for some sweets…'

The boys started laughing, but Mrs Cluett recognised the darker tone to Billy's voice. 'All right, lads,' she said. 'Just be on your way, and no more will be said.' At least, until PC Stuart Minton came in for his evening paper.

Billy Tyley advanced on her, his face hard and fixed. The room was silent and even more claustrophobic than usual. 'Who's to say that we've finished. Eh?' He took another step forward, a sick, leering grin on his face. 'Maybe we want to *borrow* some more things from your shop.' Now he was only inches away from the old woman, who recoiled at the smell of the drink on his breath. 'Maybe we should just take what we like.'

'No, lads, don't.' Mrs Cluett's appeal was to the whole group. Some of them glanced away nervously, but no one responded to her.

'Don't?' Billy shouted in the woman's face, making her flinch again.

'Don't be wicked,' continued the woman in a low voice, her eyes half closed, 'or the hollow men'll come for you.'

With a scream of rage, Billy Tyley shoved the old woman in the chest. She sprawled backward, pulling a shelf of sugar and flour down with her. The back of her skull clipped the hard metal edge of the ice-cream freezer, and her body thumped into the floor like a dead weight.

A little pool of blood emerged from her silver curls, like a halo.

'Jesus,' whispered one of the boys, his eyes as wide as saucers. 'You've gone and done it this time, Billy.'

Billy Tyley snorted, and pushed a path through his now frightened disciples. 'Come on,' he said. 'We've got what we came for.'

* * *

Rebecca drove the red sports car down the twisting country lanes towards Hexen Bridge. The roof was down and the wind caught her hair, billowing it behind her like the plume of a comet. Trevor was whistling something tunelessly beside her.

'What was that?' she asked through the roar of the engine.

'Nothing,' he said, then he turned to her. 'I've got tickets for the Star Jumpers at Wembley in August. Interested?'

She shrugged.

'Johnny Astronaut are supporting!' Trevor continued.

'Oh, well, in that case...!'

'Their last song was about a vicar's daughter. I thought you'd approve!'

She began to laugh, a throaty snigger that died away as they approached Hexen Bridge. 'You're still the funniest man I know, Trevor,' she said.

'I wish you weren't seeing so much of Matthew,' announced Trevor suddenly.

For the briefest of moments it seemed that the ice-cool exterior of Rebecca Baber melted under Trevor's piercing gaze, and she almost lost control of the car. By the time the car steadied itself, her composure was re-established.

'Needs make for strange bedfellows,' she said.

'If your reasons are what I think they are,' began Trevor, with a look of clear concern on his face, 'then he'll gobble you whole, chew you up, and spit out the bones.' He shook his head. 'Just watch yourself,' he said.

Rebecca leaned across the car and kissed him on the cheek. 'I will, my love,' she said, revving the engine.

'I think I could get to like this place,' said Ace as she and the Doctor arrived at the Green Man, the village pub. '*Not*,' she added, as much for the Doctor's benefit as for her own.

The Doctor seemed momentarily distracted. He was staring at the wooden sign above the door and shaking his head.

'Problem?' asked Ace, snapping him out of his solitary musings.

'Hmm? Oh, it's odd. As Steven said, they've changed the name. Recently, too.'

'Under new ownership?'

The Doctor shrugged. 'Maybe. It used to be the Jack Something-or-other. Unusual name. You were saying?'

'I was being sarcastic, Professor. A village straight out of *Dracula Has Risen from the Grave*, locals with a Hitler-fetish, and I'll *bet* I don't get served in here!'

The Doctor chuckled. 'Patterns, Ace. Connections. There is a theory that everything in the universe is connected, and that nothing can change without affecting everything else. Haven't you ever read *Hsi Yu Chi*?'

'I must have bunked off the day we did that in English,' said Ace, laconically. 'I'll tell you what, though: if the guy behind the bar says, "Don't get many strangers round these parts", I'm off!'

The interior of the Green Man provided a welcome relief from the sticky heat of the village. With a number of curtains drawn across the windows, the only illumination was provided by the golden bars of light that slipped through gaps in the fabric and by a television above the bar. Copper pots on hooks hung from the exposed beams of the ceiling, and corn dollies and horseshoes nestled in shadowy alcoves. Ace scanned the patrons for signs of trouble, but they all seemed content enough, supping cider and waiting for the cricket coverage to resume. A vague hush had fallen over the place, but that didn't bother Ace. Something similar had happened when she had walked into a pub in Willesden with Manisha to find she was the only white person there.

Ace turned to the Doctor, and was irritated to note that he was staring with innocent fascination at the TV screen.

'Oi, Professor, snap out of it!'

'Look, Ace!' said the Doctor with a smile.

'What is *that*?' asked a horrified Ace.

'These little creatures are very loving,' said the Doctor. 'They have a wonderful quality of life.'

'Come off it, Professor,' said Ace, disgusted that the Doctor was going all soppy on her again. 'It looks like *Play School*, with a bigger budget.'

The Doctor nodded, sadly. 'Ah, but if only we could repel alien invaders with the offer of a big hug and some tubbytoast…'

'You're still just an old hippie!'

The Doctor finally tore himself away from the television, and turned his attention to the rather stern-faced man behind the bar. He was, ostensibly, taking no interest in his new arrivals, having been casually reading a copy of the *Daily Star*, but Ace knew that he had been watching every move.

'Good day,' said the Doctor, tipping his hat. 'I believe we have two rooms booked under the name of Smith.'

'That would be Mr and Mrs Smith, would it?' asked the man, his eyes barely leaving the newspaper.

'Doctor and Ms Smith,' corrected the Doctor with a charming smile.

Reluctantly, the publican left his stool at the bar and walked the short distance to a small reception area. After opening a leather-bound journal he seemed to take an eternity reading a yellow Post-it note. Ace fidgeted nervously.

'You're late,' he announced at last.

'My apologies,' said the Doctor conciliatorily.

'I can't do you any food now. Kitchen's closed.'

'That's quite all right. We've already eaten. At the local Chinese restaurant. You know it, I assume?'

Ace noticed the man stiffen. He had an imposing stature and Ace didn't like the look in his eyes at all. As the man returned his attention to the hotel register Ace whispered to the Doctor. 'Candidate number one for the nasty paint job?'

'Eh?' said the landlord, his head swinging upward.

'My niece was just admiring your magnificent collection of butterflies,' said the Doctor, walking towards the nearest of several cases containing specimens. A row of glass-topped cabinets ran along one wall of the pub, up to the bar. 'This must represent a lifetime's work,' he continued.

'It must,' snarled the landlord bluntly.

'I used to be a bit of a lepidopterist myself,' noted the Doctor. 'May I?'

'Help yourself.'

The Doctor turned the key and opened the case. His fingers brushed against the closest creatures. He snatched his hand back sharply with a brief exclamation of surprise.

He turned and smiled beguilingly at the publican. 'Mr Matson, isn't it? Yes, if you'd like to show us to our rooms, please.'

Matson grunted and moved towards the stairs, without any indication that the Doctor and Ace should follow.

'What's up?' asked Ace, again in a whisper.

The Doctor glanced at her quickly. 'They were freezing cold,' he replied.

'Arrgh!' Ace leapt out of the shower, dripping wet, and swore violently under her breath. Typical of a place like this: just when you're enjoying yourself, the hot water runs out. Ace shivered as her bare shoulders were caught by a blast of cold air from the extractor fan, and she hurriedly wrapped a towel around herself. Time to ask a few more pertinent questions, she thought, and she marched unceremoniously through the connecting door to the Doctor's room. She found him lying on the bed, his hat over his eyes, apparently sleeping.

'This is a right dump,' she said moodily.

No response.

'I said –'

'I heard you,' came the muffled reply. The Doctor sat up suddenly, and stretched. 'I think it's time I set the wheels of time in motion.'

'Meaning?'

'The reunion waits for no man.'

'You want me to do anything?' Ace asked eagerly.

'Yes,' said the Doctor absent-mindedly. 'Put on some clothes, and wait for me here. And try to stay out of trouble, Ace. I don't want to come back and find a crater where the village used to be.'

'You take all of the fun out of life, you know that?'

The Doctor stood to leave. 'Ace,' he said simply. 'This could be very dangerous.'

'But you know what you're doing, right?'

The Doctor shook his head. 'I'm stumbling around in the dark, acting on hunches and hoping for the gift of vision.' He paused, as though surprised by his own expressed lack of confidence.

'You could still tell me about your hunches, Professor,' reasoned Ace, used to these debates.

'I could,' said the Doctor with a straight face. 'But then I'd have to kill you.' The Doctor gave Ace one of his rare and genuine smiles. 'Just in case I don't come back immediately, continue the research for me. Stay in the village, though.'

'You will come back eventually?' asked Ace, almost afraid.

'Of course,' said the Doctor, after a long pause. 'Time will look after us, Ace. It always does.'

'Be careful, Professor,' said Ace as the Doctor left the room.

From the outside, Hexen Bridge village school looked as though it had been torn from the pages of some Wellsian scientific romance. Every block in the great sandstone three-storey building spoke of history and learning, of children running down corridors and of terrifying teachers bearing canes.

Which is ironic, thought the Doctor, walking up the gravel drive, because there are times when you can count the number of pupils on one hand.

It had taken the Doctor some time during his previous visits to work out the demographics of Hexen Bridge precisely, but the inspiration came suddenly one lazy summer day in 1986, while he was reading a first-edition Byron in the west wing.

They're all related.

The population of Hexen Bridge was numerically static: the odd person left through ambition or a need for change, and very occasionally a new family, like the Chens, would turn up. But, by and large, the numbers within the village remained constant, and over a period of time the number of deaths would match the number of births. Every twenty years or so, there would be something of a baby boom and the school would be full for the next decade. The children would grow, and would then begin the next cycle of procreation to populate Hexen Bridge. And each couple of decades there would be a period when the numbers of local children in the school would reduce to a trickle, and the school would survive only by taking in boarders from elsewhere.

As a chilling experiment in eugenics, it would have been dismissed as a freak show. But there it was, seemingly accidental, but as regulated as a colony of rats in a lab.

The school's façade was somewhat reminiscent of a Gothic castle: all mock turrets and leering gargoyles. The entrance hall stood beyond a pair of doors that could have kept the Hounds of Hell at bay. Within, a smattering of children stood waiting to usher the arriving guests up to the great hall on the second floor. The Doctor removed his hat and paisley scarf, giving them to the nearest child. 'And you are…?' the Doctor asked.

'Fuller, J., sir.'

'Ah yes. I knew your father. And your mother. Class of '93, unless I'm very much mistaken.'

The boy looked uninterested. ''Spect so,' he said, and, with a hint on insolence, he turned and dumped the Doctor's hat and scarf on a chair behind him. 'You know the way to the great hall?' he continued.

'Indeed. Thank you, Fuller,' said the Doctor.

'The pleasure was all mine, sir,' said the boy in a voice dripping with sarcasm.

The Doctor merely smiled and headed for the grand staircase, his nostrils filled with the must of chalk dust and old books. Earth schools often made him think of the Academy. They, too, held secrets, and terrors, and lies.

On the stairs, the Doctor passed the massive 'Pupil of the Year' board. The names of the head boy and girl from each year had been etched into the wood in gold letters. Star pupils, destined for great things in life outside academia – if, indeed, any of them could escape the clutches of the village. The names stretched back to the late eighteenth century, and contained future politicians and statesmen, those who went on to industrial or sporting greatness, and… some notorious names.

'It's an impressive list, wouldn't you say?' came a voice from behind the Doctor.

'Quite,' said the Doctor, turning to find himself facing a studious-looking man in his late thirties with short, dark hair, and thick-rimmed spectacles. 'I'm sorry, I don't believe we've been introduced?'

'Vessal,' said the man quickly. 'Michael. Class of '87.'

'But of course,' said the Doctor, briefly casting a glance backward to find Vessal's name sandwiched between those of 'Hatch, M.' and 'Brown, D.'. 'Illustrious company,' he noted.

Vessal smiled. 'Indeed. A Cabinet minister on one side and, erm… Well, poor David. I knew him very well. He opened the bowling for the house even though he was a year younger.'

The Doctor nodded and found himself thinking of the evening in 1995 when he had been resting in a Cornish fishing village pub with Romana watching a Globelink News report from Bosnia. It had been interrupted by a newsflash that told a shocked nation that the beloved captain of the English cricket team, David Brown, had been found dead in his Mayfair apartment, seemingly the victim of suicide. And apparently this happened shortly after he had murdered the naked woman (who was not his wife) found beside to him. The next day the Doctor had tried to gain access to the flat but, not surprisingly, was refused permission.

Another link. Another wasted life.

The Doctor shook his head. 'I've followed your career with interest,' he said, forcing the memories to the back of his mind.

'Really?' asked Vessal, with a trace of surprise in his voice.

'Yes, it's always nice to see the old boys doing well. Chairman of four multinationals now, or is it five? I get so lost with figures.'

'Seven,' said Vessal bluntly. 'I'm desperately sorry, but...'

'Smith,' said the Doctor, abruptly. 'I'm on the board.'

'My apologies, Mr –'

'Doctor,' corrected the Doctor.

A glint of recognition crossed the man's face. 'Ah, the Doctor. Forgive me, but you have changed.'

'Yes,' said the Doctor. 'Most things do, given time.'

Ace stared at her cola sourly. As she had suspected, Matson – 'Call me Bob' – had refused to serve her a lager. 'It's the law, miss.'

'You don't even know how old I am,' Ace had replied.

Bob Matson had grinned lasciviously. 'I wouldn't dare to speculate.'

And so Ace sat and tore a beer mat into tiny pieces, avoiding the odd looks she was getting from the other patrons. When a hand rested on her shoulder she turned quickly, ready to deck someone.

'Hello,' said a young woman, flinching at the anger in Ace's face. Ace relaxed, and the woman smiled. 'It's not just an age thing. I'm sure he thinks women in general shouldn't drink.'

'Strange attitude for a publican,' said Ace. 'And you are?'

The woman extended her hand. 'I'm Rebecca Baber. I teach in the local school.'

'I don't like teachers,' said Ace sullenly.

'You should try working with them.' She shrugged disarmingly.

'When I was at school I didn't like teachers either.'

'What went wrong?'

'I decided I wanted long holidays. I wish I'd known then how busy I'd be.'

'My heart bleeds for you,' said Ace.

'Don't be cynical, or I'll start confusing you with the locals. Your name's Ace, right?'

'Word travels fast.'

'It does in a place like this. It can come back to you before you think you've finished.' She shrugged. 'Can I buy you a drink?'

'That man won't serve me what I want.' Ace stared at her glass as if she'd been offered hemlock.

'We'll sort something out,' said Rebecca. She strode to the bar, ordered a Coke and a lager, assured Matson that the latter wasn't for the girl, and then motioned to Ace to find a table outside.

Once seated, and safe from Bob Matson's prying eyes, she swapped the drinks around. 'There you go. You look old enough to enjoy this.'

Ace sipped the lager eagerly.

'Anyway, its biblical,' continued Rebecca.

'What is?'

'A little wine for your stomach. St Paul's advice to Timothy, I think. And this is the modern equivalent.'

Ace looked at the schoolteacher suspiciously. 'You're not a Christian, are you? You didn't buy me this as a way of showing that Jesus loves me?' Ace could think of few things worse than a Christian teacher – except possibly one who wore sandals.

'Good gracious, no,' said Rebecca. 'My dad's a vicar, though. It's amazing what you pick up.'

'As the actress said to the archbishop.'

'Indeed.' Rebecca looked around her, at the shadows lengthening across the green and groups of people sitting at the pub's tables. 'What brings you here?'

'Research.'

'Really? That'll go down like a brick in Hexen Bridge.'

'Yeah, I can imagine.'

Rebecca paused. 'Do you fancy coming over for lunch or something tomorrow?'

'Suppose so.'

'You could do with some time away from the Green Man, and I could do with some company. I'm swamped by homework at the moment – I'm not in Hexen Bridge most weekends.'

'I didn't think anyone left Hexen Bridge.'

'Well,' said Rebecca, 'it's the only way *I* can stay sane.'

Ace nodded. 'This is such a weird place.'

'Ten times as weird if you were born here,' said Rebecca.

'Is that why everyone hates the Chens?' asked Ace.

'Not everyone hates the Chens.'

'I'm surprised that Steven Chen hasn't left, though.'

Rebecca leaned forward conspiratorially. 'I'm told he's bonking Bob Matson's wife.'

'Blimey,' said Ace. 'So Matson *is* painting that filth on the restaurant.'

'You don't have to be Sherlock Holmes to work that one out,' said Rebecca.

'I've got a message from Steven,' said Ace. 'He wanted me to pass it to Matson's wife.'

'Well, you'd better be careful. Poor Joanna is long-suffering personified, but I doubt if their marriage could take another major confrontation.'

'It's under pressure, then?' said Ace.

'An understatement. Bob Matson plays away from home more often than the local football team. I'm amazed she's stayed with that slob for as long as she has.' Rebecca nodded to her right. 'Don't look now, but she's over there, picking up empties.'

Ace glanced up, and saw a comfortably attractive woman in a dishwater-grey-coloured sweater and tight blue jeans wiping down one of the tables. 'I'll give it to her when she comes over here.'

'Just be careful, that's all.' Rebecca got to her feet, swapping the empty pint glass round with the slim tumbler of Coke. 'I've got to go now. The reunion.'

Ace nodded. 'The Doctor's already there.'

Rebecca smiled. 'I remember him from way back. A very tall gentleman, as I recall.'

Ace cleared her throat. 'Well, it's funny how your memory can play tricks on you sometimes, isn't it?'

'I'll see you tomorrow?'

Ace nodded.

'Any time in the morning,' continued Rebecca. 'The vicarage. You can't miss it.'

'See you,' said Ace, watching the schoolteacher head off for the distant outline of the school. When she turned back to the pub, she saw Bob Matson framed in the Tudor window, impassive and solid, and she wondered how long he'd been watching them.

Before reaching the great hall, the Doctor found the visitors' book and briefly scanned the pages, before signing it himself. All of the names he had followed through the years were present: Hatch, Burridge, Winstone, Luston, Shanks, Bingham and Price. Only Baber was missing and, as a teacher, she would surely make an appearance before the evening was done.

The Doctor entered the great hall. It was an imposing room, full of the extravagant trappings of history and wealth. The walls were adorned with numerous paintings, but he was especially pleased to see the epic Turner cricketing landscape *Hambledon versus All England (1796)* still hanging above the door. The Doctor had presented it to the school upon his acceptance to the board of governors, and it had been there ever since. Dear Joseph, he'd had a dreadful cold when he painted it. 'As the run-stealers flicker to and fro,' said the Doctor brightly, remembering an afternoon at Lord's with Francis Thompson long, long ago.

He absent-mindedly took a glass of chilled white wine from a passing waiter, his eyes still fixed on the groups of people who circled the room. He recognised many of them. Some he had observed for years, following their lives with the intensity of a stalker; others were window-dressing to the main event.

'We're all Thatcher's children now,' said a man at the Doctor's side.

'Pardon?'

The man pointed to a series of prime-ministerial portraits that dominated one wall. 'I'm Timothy Carlton. I teach history.'

'Pleased to meet you,' said the Doctor.

'You see, I think we're reaping what the 1980s sowed,' continued the man. 'All the current staff feel it. Self, self, self. No time for others, individuality is God.'

The Doctor nodded, but found himself only half listening. His attention was elsewhere, diverted by the recent arrival of someone he recognised. An immaculately dressed man in his late thirties had just entered and was walking towards a small knot of men in the middle of the room. As he strode through the crowd, it seemed to part for him. There was something almost mythical about the entrance, and the Doctor watched the man with catlike curiosity. The newcomer nodded his recognition to several in the room but didn't stop until he had reached the three similarly dressed men, whereupon he shook hands with each, and manfully slapped the back of one. They shared a brief joke, and then took their glasses to a quieter corner of the room.

Carlton followed the Doctor's gaze and sniffed, haughtily. 'Matthew Hatch,' he said. 'Our guest of honour.'

'The Minister of State for Defence in His Majesty's Government,' noted the Doctor.

'Is that what he is this week?'

'Do I detect a hint of malice towards our honoured Old Boy?' asked the Doctor, amused.

Carlton paused, aware that he may well be speaking to one of Hatch's oldest friends, but he ploughed on anyway. 'I don't trust the man,' he said bravely. 'I dislike anyone who crosses the floor for political expediency rather than conscience.' The Doctor nodded, encouraging the man to continue. 'His extremist past is well enough documented.'

'We all do stupid things when we're young,' noted the Doctor. 'I expect he would argue that people can change.'

'Maybe,' continued Carlton. 'But every time I see that man on television, I get the feeling that one day he's going to be in a position of ultimate power, and then, God help us all.'

Ace glanced down at the note Steven Chen had given her. She wondered what it said, but resisted the temptation to open it.

She looked up guiltily as Joanna Matson collected the empty glasses from her table. Ace glanced back towards the pub, but couldn't see Bob Matson.

'Don't say anything,' whispered Ace, sliding the piece of paper towards Joanna. 'Just pick it up.'

Joanna looked confused, but did as she was instructed, pushing the note into the pocket of her jeans. She moved away without a word, but kept looking back at Ace, her eyes cold and suspicious.

Rebecca wasn't enjoying the reunion. Her fellow teachers were a dull, niggardly bunch: they just about tolerated each other in a professional environment, but strip that away and all that remained was a clumsy, patronising embarrassment. Worse still were the former pupils, many of whom seemed to have had one drink too many and were now intent on telling her how much they'd fancied her when she was teaching *Romeo and Juliet*.

She scanned the room for a saviour, and found him in the unlikely form of the large bearded man towards the edge of the room who wore his casual suit as neatly as he would his uniform. He was clearly even more lost in this ocean of inconsequential niceties than she was.

'It's Sergeant Denman, isn't it?' she said, tapping the man on the shoulder. In fact, Rebecca knew only too well what the man's real rank was. It wasn't just the people of Hexen Bridge who kept an eye on Denman.

'Chief Constable,' said Denman automatically. He'd been watching a small group of men on the edge of the hall, and he switched his attention to her with apparent irritation. 'No one's called me that for more years than I care to remember, young lady,' he said at last, looking her up and down.

'Well, you *were* a sergeant when I knew you,' said Rebecca, returning the smile. 'It was the week before you left for Liverpool. You caught me and Trevor Winstone in the Hatch orchard scrumping for apples. You said eight was old enough to know right from wrong and took me back to the vicarage where, I'd like you to know, I got the hiding of my life!'

'Rebecca?' asked an astonished Denman. 'My stars, but you've grown.'

'But of course,' said Rebecca with a grin. 'Twenty years is a long time in anybody's book'.

'The last time your father wrote to me, you were about to go to university. Then your ma died. I was sorry about that.'

Rebecca took a sip from her Malibu and orange and patted the policeman's arm. 'It's OK.'

'Is your father well?' asked Denman.

Rebecca hedged her bets. 'Much the same as ever.'

'I must call in and see him before I return,' said Denman.

'I'm sure he'd like that. Have you been back long?'

'We arrived today.'

'We? Is Nicola here?'

'No,' said Denman forcefully.

'That's a shame,' said Rebecca.

'She never went to school here,' explained Denman.

'I didn't know the invitation was as strict as that,' said Rebecca. 'I'm sure you could have –'

'She's staying with a friend in Bristol,' interrupted Denman.

'They've not seen each other in a while. I'm picking her up on my way back tomorrow.' The disappointment in Rebecca's face must have been obvious. 'I'm surprised you even remember Nicola. She was only two when we left.'

'I used to play with her in your front garden, don't you remember?'

'Well, yes,' said Denman, 'but there's quite a difference in age between you…'

'It would have been nice to have seen her, that's all,' said Rebecca. 'Anyway, the bonds of Hexen Bridge are hard to break. You of all people should know that. I mean, here you are.'

'Seemed rude not to come,' said Denman bluntly. He quickly glanced over to the other side of the room, and Rebecca followed his gaze. 'Your boyfriend seems to be moving in exalted circles these days,' he continued.

'Oh, Trevor's not my boyfriend any more,' said Rebecca hurriedly. 'Not since he went off to Oxford when I was seventeen. We lost touch for a long time. And, a lot of things can happen to two people in "a long time", can't they?'

Denman nodded, and Rebecca found herself staring across the room at Trevor. He'd seemed so like his old self when they'd met earlier, but she knew that, paradoxically, he was a quite different man now. There was a deeper melancholy that she couldn't quite fathom. Of course, those summer days down by the river had been laced with their own teenage sadnesses, but nothing like this.

She remembered the little wicker basket that her mother dutifully packed for them, full of cheese sandwiches, fairy cakes, and strawberry lemonade. With a shiver she recalled Trevor letting her hair down and clumsily unbuttoning her blouse. Then there was the time Trevor had tried to climb the old wooden bridge and ended up falling into the river, and he'd had to wear her sweater to cover his dignity while the soaked clothes dried on the riverbank. They had been two poets, inspired by the beauty all around them. And now… Now, he was a man who worked with dangerous people, and she… She was talking to a policeman.

Rebecca glanced at Denman, but his eyes hadn't moved from the group. His expression had darkened, like a black thundercloud on a summer's day.

'You must excuse me,' Denman said. 'I think it's time I…'

One of the men glanced around, and appeared to notice Denman for the first time. He seemed amused, made a brief apology to Trevor and the swaggering Hatch, and strolled towards Rebecca and Denman.

'What brings you down to these parts, Sergeant?' asked the man in a thick Liverpudlian accent. He looked about forty and was beginning to lose some of his blond hair. He was thin, almost gaunt in appearance, wearing a collarless white shirt and a waistcoat from which clanked a chain containing his car keys. The impression was that of extreme wealth but a complete lack of social grace. A rich vulgarian.

Denman didn't even attempt to correct him, clearly used to the insult. ' "Down" is about right,' he snapped.

'I didn't think you'd be caught dead in Hexen Bridge again.'

'But here I am.'

The man from Liverpool nodded, and looked at Rebecca. 'Aye, it's the vicar's daughter, innit? Trevor's bird?'

Rebecca returned her attention to her drink. Her mother had always said that if you ignore people like that then they might just go away.

'I see your taste in friends hasn't changed,' said Denman, nodding towards the group.

'Matty Hatch and Phil Burridge were the only friends I had when I was in this crap-hole,' said the man angrily. 'And you spent all your time trying to stop us breathing.'

'Just doing my job,' replied Denman.

'And loving it, too.' The man smiled. 'Though I didn't expect

56

you to follow me back down here.'

'I'd follow you to hell, Shanks.'

Without further comment the man turned and stalked back to his friends. Denman shook his head, sadly. 'Kenny Shanks,' he explained. 'A thug from the first day I set eyes on him. I've spent most of my life trying to put that piece of scum away from society. Here and in the 'Pool.'

Rebecca finished off her glass of wine. 'I don't like him.'

'Nobody in their right mind would like Shanks,' said Denman.

'And then there was that terrible business with Michael Forster,' said the former headmaster. The man, mumbling his words through a mouthful of champagne and oysters, seemed to have recognised the Doctor. The Doctor was sure they'd never met before, but thought it impolite to pursue the point.

'Yes,' nodded the Doctor sadly. 'I remember...'

And he did. He remembered the noise of the Glastonbury crowd as Comanche Bloodbath, resplendent against a painted backdrop of *Apocalypse Now* helicopters and Native American faces, finished their opening song in a squeal of feedback. And he remembered Michael Forster coming to the microphone and saying, 'I am the Resurrection, and I am the Life!', and then pulling a combat knife from his jeans pocket, telling the one hundred thousand people in the audience that life was cheap and worthless and that the only answer was death, and plunging the blade into his chest.

Oh, yes. The Doctor remembered.

He was beginning to think that the entire reunion had been a waste of time, and that he should be getting back to Ace, and the TARDIS, when the mention of the proposed village memorial to Michael Forster brought him up short. It was as if he'd forgotten for a moment what the point of it all was, and the mere mention of Forster's name had been enough to remind him.

The Doctor glanced around the room, and for an instant he saw the faces of the shocked band members, spotted with drops of sweat and blood. He shook his head, and the hideous image faded. And the Doctor noticed that Hatch and his friends were no longer in the room.

He apologised to the old headmaster, and made his way towards the door. He spotted a tall, well-built individual with a full beard looking similarly bewildered by the men's sudden disappearance. 'Denman,' the Doctor muttered to himself. 'Another complication.'

The Doctor walked down the grand staircase and out into the grounds, slipping past a burly man in a dark suit who was trying to light a cigarette.

It was dusk now. The sun, a huge orange fireball deep in the west, was almost gone and in its place came a clear midsummer night. The smell of freshly mown grass and the buzz of small insects almost overpowered the Doctor's senses. As he walked out towards the rugby fields, he felt a prickly sensation along his spine. Perhaps he should have heeded the premonition, but the Doctor's strength of purpose was absolute. The answers that he had sought for three hundred years and four of his lives were here somewhere. Voices. Somewhere nearby. And a flashlight.

'...and that journalist woman...?'

'Floating at the bottom of the Mersey, Matt. The lads tied her feet to a block of concrete and dumped her near the cast-iron shore. She'll never be found.'

'Good. That's what I like, an absence of loose ends.'

The Doctor strained his eyes in the gloom. It was the four men from the reunion: Matthew Hatch, Trevor Winstone, Kenneth Shanks, and Philip Burridge. They were standing around a four-by-four, and two of the men were busy pulling back a sheet of tarpaulin. The revealed metal glinted under a flashlight.

The Doctor crept as silently as he could towards the big Jeep. Suddenly one of the figures swivelled on the spot, and the Doctor was blinded by the torchlight.

'Stop where you are!'

The Doctor obeyed without question. Although he couldn't see it, he sensed that there was a gun pointing at him.

'Who's this?' asked Hatch.

'Dunno, matey,' said Shanks. He advanced, cautiously, and a glimmer of recognition crossed his features. A moment later, it was gone, and Shanks was pressing the gun into the Doctor's chest. 'A spy?'

'Get him in the car,' said Hatch angrily. 'If he moves, shoot him.'

Ian Denman left the reunion as soon as he realised that his quarry was no longer in sight. He had allowed himself to be distracted by an eighty-year-old woman governor extolling the virtues of his public stand on school discipline.

He moved out into the twilight, pushing impatiently past one of Shanks's goons who stood at the door. Denman scanned the school grounds for any sign of movement. The noise from the party above drifted down to him.

Nothing. Except, yes, there in the distance on the playing field. Movement in the gloom. Denman jogged a few paces, crouching as he did so to try to get a look at what was going on. There was a flurry of movement as those he sought got into a sleek black saloon car. He counted five figures, but from this distance he couldn't tell who their friend was. After a moment one of the men got out of the car and moved off some distance just as the vehicle burst into life. Headlights flashed across the ground in front of Denman and he hurriedly stepped back into the shadows. When he emerged again, the car had crawled on to the gravel driveway and was heading slowly for the gates. In the distance, Denman heard another vehicle heading in the opposite direction. 'Damn,' he muttered angrily to himself.

'Where do you want me to drive to?' asked Trevor Winstone as he swung Hatch's car through the school gates and off towards the open countryside beyond.

'Anywhere,' said Matthew Hatch, red-faced. 'Just put your foot down.'

In the back of the car, the Doctor sat quietly, very aware of the gun Kenny Shanks was aiming at a point equidistant between his hearts. 'Could you be very careful,' the Doctor eventually exclaimed. 'Country roads tend to be rather bumpy…'

'Oh great,' said Shanks. 'We've got a comedian here. Go on then, crack us a joke.' Shanks lifted the gun to the Doctor's face and poked it at his nose. 'I'm waiting.'

'Shut up, Ken,' said Hatch, who was half turned in the front seat. He seemed to be considering his options. In the dull light of the car, the unflappability for which the politician was famous had been replaced by a high-octane nervous energy that crackled like static electricity. Hatch looked closely at the Doctor.

'I'd advise you to be frank with us,' he said with a voice that had lost every trace of the West Country. 'Because we certainly intend to be frank with you. We'll start with your name.'

'The Doctor.'

Shanks's pocketed the gun. 'Turn on the light, Trev,' he said, looking at the Doctor closely. 'Now I remember you,' he continued. 'You've aged well.'

'So who is he, then?' asked Hatch.

'One of the governors. We met years ago.' Shanks gripped the Doctor's collar as though any reminder of those painful days was unwelcome. 'You picked a bad night to take a stroll, Doctor.'

'I'm so sorry,' said the Doctor. 'If you want to drop me off here, I can assure you that your schemes for world domination will remain our little secret.'

There followed a lengthy silence until Hatch let out a bellow of laughter, slapping his thigh theatrically.

'What are we going to do?' asked Trevor as he slowed the car into a lay-by.

'Looks like a nice spot for a quiet execution,' said the Doctor ruefully. His own stupidity had led him to a shallow grave in a field in Wiltshire. The only consolation would be the surprise on the faces of the three men when a man with a completely different face would sit up after the shooting, asking where he was, what was going on, and could they possibly direct him to his TARDIS?

'May I ask you one question?' said the Doctor.

'Certainly,' agreed Hatch.

'Why?' asked the Doctor.

'Why what?'

'The gunrunning?' The Doctor paused. 'You're all intelligent men, surely you could find something better to do with your time than peddle weapons of destruction?'

'You have an alternative?' asked Hatch, amused.

'Many people on Earth are starving,' said the Doctor.

'Food makes you fat,' said Hatch cynically. 'Weapons make you strong.'

'Goering said something similar.'

'One of my heroes,' noted Hatch before turning to Shanks. 'Aren't you going to add anything into this conversation? He's your friend, after all.'

'Nope,' said Shanks.

'Well,' said Trevor Winstone. 'Guns mean jobs in this country, which means food on the table and less men on the dole. If we don't supply arms, some other country will.' The words flowed out like a well-rehearsed mantra. 'Things aren't as black and white as you think.'

'Few things in life are,' said the Doctor, sadly. 'Except Laurel and Hardy films.'

'A philosopher, too?' asked Hatch.

'Don't start any of that pyschobabble with me, pal,' Shanks said, turning on the Doctor angrily. 'A whole city cacks itself every time I get mad.'

'Remarkable,' said the Doctor. 'When I first met you, you couldn't even control your own bladder.'

Anger flared across Shanks's face. 'Can you sew?' he snarled.

'A little,' said the Doctor, surprised by the question.

'Well, stitch this, then,' said Shanks, head-butting him just above the nose.

CHAPTER 3
THE VILLAGE GREEN PRESERVATION SOCIETY

The door exploded inward, and the masked men rushed into the house. 'Bring him out!' they shouted. 'He belongs to us now!'

A light came on somewhere, and a prematurely aged couple appeared at the top of the stairs, nervously pulling on thick dressing gowns despite the thunderously oppressive midnight air. 'What the hell is going on?' shouted the man. But there was a quaver in his voice, as if a terrifying realisation were washing over him.

'You know why we're here,' said the leader of the group. His voice was muffled through the rough sackcloth mask that had been pulled over his face, his thin lips just visible behind a ragged slit. Like his companions, he wore a long, dark cloak over black jeans. He held a scythe in his hands, the blade orange with rust.

'You have no right,' said the man, coming down the stairs. His wife seemed rooted to the spot.

'Don't be a fool,' snapped the leader. Then, in a calmer voice: 'We all know how we live, Don. And the punishments that await us if we stray.' A weather-beaten hand gestured towards those grouped behind him, and a number of them ran up the stairs two at a time, pushing past the man, who steadied himself uncertainly, his bony hands pale against the mahogany banister. He made his way to the bottom, a tiny figure before the might of the masked intruders.

'Please,' said the man. 'It'll kill 'er.'

'This is the way of things,' replied the leader, his dark clothing incongruous against the wallpaper of irises. 'Your son has been chosen.' He angled his face back towards the stairs.

All the doors on the landing had been thrown open, and a boy, still weak with sleep, was dragged out of one room. The elastic in his pyjamas had gone, a safety pin holding them around his skinny hips. His feet barely touched the ground.

The old woman fell to the floor, her lips moving soundlessly. One of the dark figures bent down to help her to her feet, but was pushed away by the others.

'William Tyley,' said the leader in a strong, clear voice. 'You have been chosen.'

Billy Tyley tried to say something, but he was pushed forcefully down the stairs. He stumbled over his feet towards the bottom and landed in a heap on the floor. He was grabbed by the group of black-clad men, who carried him swiftly through the still-open door, and out towards the village green. They lifted him high above their heads, Billy screaming at the stars above him.

The remaining men swept out of the house. Soon only the leader and the old couple remained. It was impossible to tell what thoughts crossed the mind of the cloaked man, but he did not move for some time, seeming to listen intently to the woman's sobs.

Then he turned, and ducked out through the doorway.

Out on the green, torches were being lit.

Ace woke to the sound of screaming. She was on her feet before she knew where she was, and was standing at the window by the time she remembered the dull evening spent cadging pints in the village pub. 'What…' Her words trailed away as she gripped the curtain. She knew the difference between drunken larking about and absolute terror. She shivered, ice-cold needles in her arms and legs.

'Don't do it, miss,' came a voice from the door. Despite the screams it was like a gunshot in the graveside stillness of the room.

Ace spun round.

Bob Matson was standing in the doorway, framed by the landing light, a bunch of keys in one hand.

'What the –'

'Don't open the curtains,' Matson repeated, more insistently than before. Despite her shock, Ace could perceive something different in his voice. Surely it couldn't be fear?

'Get out, toerag!' shouted Ace, her words still leapfrogging over each other in surprise.

'Shh, keep your voice down.' As Matson walked into the room Ace noticed for the first time that he'd barely looked at her. The sole object of his attention was the curtains that separated Ace from whatever was going on outside.

'I could have you arrested,' said Ace. Matson's distracted manner was both irritating and frightening.

'No you couldn't. Not in Hexen Bridge,' said Matson, finally positioning himself between Ace and the bay window. This done, he seemed to relax for the first time. 'You'd not thank me if I let you look out on the green.'

'What's going on down there?' Ace could see flickering lights through the curtain fabric. The screams – it sounded like a girl – were beginning to fade.

'Nothing that you could interest the constable in. He's my cousin, you know.'

'Oh yeah?'

Matson pointed at the window. 'Drunken young farmers.'

'Don't talk crap.'

'They have some sort of initiation ceremony.'

'I don't believe you.'

'It doesn't matter,' said Matson, placing his hands on his hips. 'You ain't looking out of that window.'

Ace thought briefly about running at the man, but he was too big. His biceps looked like most men's thighs.

'I don't want you to get hurt,' said Matson by way of explanation. 'I like you.'

'What does your wife think about that?'

Matson said nothing.

Ace suddenly remembered that she was standing in front of a man, old enough to be her father, in just T-shirt and knickers. She fought to keep the embarrassment from flushing her features. 'Thanks for the concern,' she said. 'But I can look after myself. If you don't get out of my room in two seconds flat, I'll throw myself on the floor and start screaming. You got that?'

Matson was unmoved.

'I'm serious,' Ace continued.

'I know you are.' Matson turned away from the window, and Ace realised that the village was quiet again. The silence that enfolded Hexen Bridge was so hushed and complete that it seemed to mock her memories of the screams. Matson smiled. 'I've always known when I'm out of my league, Miss Smith.'

If that was a backhanded compliment, Ace wasn't impressed. 'That sort of thing might work with the schoolgirls, but –'

'You're too mature for such flattery?' Matson stared evenly at her james T-shirt. 'Maybe. But when you grow up, you'll see things differently.'

'Really?'

'Yeah. You'll certainly learn not to get involved in other people's marriages.'

Ace was incredulous. 'What are you on about?'

'I saw the note you passed to my wife.'

'What note?'

Bob Matson stabbed a blunt finger in her direction. 'You pass any more messages from that slant-eyed yellow bastard to my wife,' he spat, 'and I might decide you are in my league after all.'

Ace aimed a kick at the man's groin, but he was swift for his size, and moved aside quickly.

'Don't be an idiot,' said Matson, walking towards the door. 'I've said what I came to say.'

'I've not started,' said Ace. 'You're a sad, pathetic, evil –'

Matson turned, affecting hurt. 'Such nasty names.' He nodded towards the window. 'And I've just done you a favour, an' all.'

And with that he was gone. Ace heard him pad down the landing. Back to his wife, tucked up in bed. Poor cow.

She ran to the window and pulled back the curtains, but in the darkness the green was as black as the midnight sea. Nothing moved, and barely a light could be seen in the cottages beyond.

Whatever had happened had happened quickly, and seemed to have left behind little or no evidence. She considered investigating further, but the thought of running into Bob Matson again sent a chill down her spine.

Best wait until morning when the Doctor would doubtless have formulated a plan of attack. She glanced at her watch. It really was very late. Where was he?

Ace locked the door and climbed back into bed, pulling the sheets around her, despite the humidity. She fell into troubled sleep, and dreamed she could still hear the screams.

Billy Tyley was being reborn. Like a plant seed, he was sending out roots and leaves, searching for light and moisture. Or... Was the vegetation rooting into him, clearing out the deadwood? Twigs pushed their way into his arms – what used to be his arms – and sent tendrils into the corpse that was no longer his. He was becoming one with something he recognised, something that had always lived within him. Shooting. Branching. Searching for a new purity, a new way of living.

He was Jack's, and Jack was his.

The crunch of gravel underfoot sounded like a thousand marching soldiers. Matthew Hatch reached the door of his parents' home and fumbled in the pocket of his suit for the key. They would be enjoying their regular summer trip to Rimini now and the house would be deserted. Perhaps Mrs Barnwell, the cook, would have left a light supper for him in the kitchen, just as she had in the past. Hatch remembered arriving back from university at obscure hours of the morning and finding a little note to 'Master Matthew' folded neatly under a large plate of ham-and-cheese sandwiches.

Music was coming from the drawing room. Hatch moved cautiously to the door, one hand gripping the frame, the other searching his jacket pocket for the handgun Trevor Winstone had given him six months ago at a clandestine meeting in a smoky room in South Kensington.

As Hatch shifted his weight the floorboard beneath him squeaked in protest.

'Come in.' The husky female voice cut through the industrial sounds of the band Stillborn on his parents' CD player. The record clearly did not belong to them.

'Nice tune,' he said, strolling into the room, 'but haven't you brought along any Jesus and Mary Chain? You know I can't stand anything post-1990.'

Rebecca Baber lay on a blue velvet couch, naked but for a bright plastic watch and a pair of spectacles. She peered over the tiny round lenses at Hatch, dropping the thin paperback she was reading to the floor.

'I've been here for *ages*,' she said coyly. 'I thought you were never going to come.'

'I had business to attend to,' replied Hatch, moving over to the CD player and turning it off. 'I'm a busy man,' he announced, with just a hint of self-mockery.

'And a grumpy one,' said Rebecca, strolling over to his side and running a hand down Hatch's cheek. 'What's the matter?'

'Nothing that can't be dealt with,' he said. 'I know how to deal with things. Dealing with things is my job.'

Rebecca closed her eyes as Hatch pulled her closer.

'I think we'd better adjourn the meeting in favour of some informal interaction behind closed doors,' he whispered, his lips just brushing her ear. 'What do you think?'

'Anything you say, Minister,' said Rebecca, walking nonchalantly past him and towards the stairs. 'Will sir be requiring minutes to be taken?'

'Get up those stairs!' said Hatch with an animal grin.

* * *

Ace was woken by blinding sunshine, church bells and birdsong. So much for the peace and tranquillity of the countryside.

'Shut up,' she said.

She waited for her mind to sort fogged images and memories into order. Rebecca had left the pub... A teacher, she had said, but you couldn't hold that against her... Then the note had been passed to Joanna, and some lad had tried to chat her up, and she'd said, 'If you don't get your hand off my leg, Worzel, I'll shove your brand-new combine harvester so far up your arse you'll have to use the windscreen wipers to brush your teeth.' Then a drunken collapse into bed, and... Sleep. And screams.

Ace sat bolt upright. The Doctor still hadn't returned, and the screams had been real.

She ran to the window, and pulled back the curtains. She remembered having gone to the window in the night, although the recollection was blurred by sleep.

The green extended from the front of the pub to the edge of the lane that most of the cottages were clustered around. It was lush, despite the dry weather, and billiard-table-flat.

Ace peered more closely. Right at its centre, like some childish stick drawing, lay a humanoid shape. It was made of threads of brown and yellow, clumsily clothed in what appeared to be striped pyjamas. The face was a grotesque parody of human features, all skewed by rough branches and knotted stalks of corn.

Ropes held the scarecrow's arms and legs on to the green, running to hastily banged-in stakes. A single torch had been dropped some feet away.

Ace scratched her head as she began to get dressed. That was some initiation ceremony.

Hatch rolled over in bed expecting to feel the warmth of Rebecca. Instead, he found a cold, empty space. He opened his eyes, and saw Rebecca standing in one of his mother's dressing gowns, looking out of the window, across the village.

'Morning,' said Hatch sleepily, flopping back on to the pillow.

'You hurt me last night,' said Rebecca, still looking out of the window.

'You didn't complain at the time,' noted Hatch, closing his eyes again.

Rebecca turned, her eyes puffy and red. 'You treat everybody like something you scrape off your shoe, Matthew.'

'Most people are,' said Hatch.

A momentary silence settled between them before Rebecca came back to the bed and sat on the corner, putting a hand on Hatch's bare arm. 'Matthew,' she asked in a hushed whisper, 'did you hear the screaming last night?'

'Yes.' Hatch smiled, though his eyes were still shut. 'That was you, wasn't it?'

She ignored his remark. 'It was the Chosen.'

'Rubbish,' said Hatch with a dismissive grunt, turning away from her.

'No, it isn't,' said Rebecca, returning to the window. 'I heard the Chosen screaming in the night when I was five. She screamed until I thought the devil himself would come and take us away. I've hated the night ever since.'

She turned back to Hatch again, but he was asleep, snoring soundly into his pillow.

Ace's trips to her local cemetery in Perivale had normally been at the dead of night, on a dare to do something outrageous like spray 'Satan Lives!' on a gravestone. She'd got out of that phase by the time she was thirteen, although Midge and Jay had carried on doing it for a while. Prats.

They were cool places, though, in every sense of the word. And she stood beside one now, wondering what to do next.

She had got dressed as quickly as she could, but there had been no sign of the scarecrow by the time she came out of the Green Man. There were half-formed boot prints in the scuffed-up earth towards the centre of the green, but nothing more. She had returned to her room again, just in case the Doctor had magicked himself into existence with a puff of sulphur, but his room was as he had left it. So, he wasn't coming back in a hurry, and the only course of action was to do what he had wanted her to, and carry on looking... for something. But since she didn't have the faintest idea of what that something was, Rebecca Baber – clearly the only civilised and vaguely intelligent person in Hicksville – seemed a good place to start.

Ace stood, distracted by a large stone cross just outside the churchyard. It was a memorial for the thirteen men of the village killed while serving in Prince Albert's (Somerset Light Infantry) Regiment during the First World War.

Pte Daniel Burridge: Killed defending the
lines, Ypres, 31st October 1914
Sgt Thomas Baber: Gassed, 24th April 1915
Major Nicholas Hatch: Died of shrapnel
wounds, the Somme, 8th July 1916
Pte Walter Smith: Killed, saving his officer's life,
Passchendaele, 20th September 1917
L/Cpl Edward Luston: Shot, Marne, 19th
March 1918

Ace felt a terrible prickling sensation behind her eyes and cursed openly. It was *stupid*. Why was she upset by the fate of men who'd been dead for over fifty years by the time she was born? She *hated* that side of her nature, and had spent months on Iceworld trying to pummel her sentimentality out of her. There were times when she so wanted to be hardened to the cruelties of the universe, to just let the sickness wash over her.

She reached out and touched the memorial, and said something under her breath. Then, like a rabbit caught in the lights of oncoming traffic, she stepped back, bewildered and lost.

'Bye, lads,' she said, glancing around in case anyone was watching. Then she turned her back on the plain stone memorial and the ghosts of the past.

A black metal fence ran along the graveyard boundary, pointing the way to the vicarage. It was a lovely old thatched cottage that backed on to the church. It reminded Ace of picture postcards from the 1950s.

Ace found the back door open and saw a harsh-looking man in his early fifties sitting at the kitchen table. His brow was creased in concentration as he wrote in a scuffed leather-bound journal with a fountain pen. Presumably this was Rebecca's father, the vicar. Ace thought she could smell fire and brimstone from where she stood.

Most churchmen in Ace's experience – even the doddery old simpletons – had an agenda more sinister than the Cybermen. Despite this, she decided to be pleasant, and see how far it got her. After all, the man's daughter did seem to be a fully fledged member of the human race.

Ace coughed and tapped lightly on the door, smiling as the man's head slowly raised from his book.

Instantly, Ace knew what sort of person the Reverend Baber was, and that her initial suspicions had been correct. It was in the eyes. She really *was* in a Hammer film, and this was the local Peter Cushing.

'Yes?' he asked in a haughty tone that put Ace's back up straight away.

'Morning,' she said. 'I'm here to see Rebecca.'

'Are you indeed?' The vicar stood, and moved his glasses to the edge of his nose, peering at Ace the way she would have scrutinised a slug. She thought him tall, for a vicar, with a thin, pinched face. 'May I ask why a young girl like yourself isn't on her way to church?' His tone was brusque, but with a hidden menace. Ace was really annoyed now.

'First off, right...' she began, about to give him her considered opinion that she wasn't a 'girl', and how she spent her time was her own business, and why didn't he go off and perform an exorcism or something? Fortunately, she was interrupted by Rebecca bursting into the kitchen behind her father.

'I thought I heard voices,' she said in a bubbly voice. She wore a pretty floral summer dress that made her look much more countrified and less sophisticated than the previous day. Rebecca gave Ace a wink and said, 'Hi, come in.' She turned to her father. 'I trust you've been making our guest at home?'

Baber said nothing, but Ace could see the aggression draining from his features, replaced with something akin to embarrassment.

'Thanks very much for your help,' said Ace as she walked past the man, following Rebecca up the stairs and into her bedroom. It was a large, pleasant room that faced south, and a huge bay window allowed the sunlight to flood in. It afforded a magnificent view of the village and the scattered fields beyond. The rest of the room was spacious and uncluttered, nothing like her own bedroom either in the TARDIS or back in Perivale. There was a desk with a touchscreen computer on it, and hundreds of books dotted across every possible surface and shelf.

Rebecca flopped on to the bed, and giggled as if at some private joke.

'What's so funny?'

'Oh.' Rebecca sat up. 'Daddy. He's always like that with new people. Very stuck in his ways.'

'Why isn't *he* at church, then?'

'He's finishing his sermon, I think. He'll be gone soon.'

'Good.' Ace glanced out of the window again. 'Great view you've got here.'

'Awesome, isn't it?' asked Rebecca. 'In the summer, when I was a kid, I used to sit out on the ledge, and dangle my legs over. It was *so* thrilling. It's only twenty feet to the ground but when you're ten, that's like being on top of the world. All the boys used to come by on their way to play football and I'd flirt with them. It was great.'

Ace was surprised. The old man didn't look the sort to allow his daughter to get away with flashing her pants at the first, second and third eleven. 'Didn't your dad have something to say about that?' she asked.

'Oh yes, but Daddy's always been tolerant of my excesses. He says we are what we are.'

This didn't sound at all like the Reverend Baber that Ace had just met. She sat down on the swivel chair next to the computer, picking up one of a stack of orangy-red school exercise books in a pile on the table.

'Just marking my year-eleven general studies class,' Rebecca explained. Essays on the social effects of the Great Drought of '02.'

Ace had loathed history at school. She picked up an exercise book, glancing at the beautifully looped handwriting. 'What're they like, your kids?' she asked.

'Oh, they're little horrors. The girls are the worst actually, really bitchy and obsessed with sex. Just like I was!'

Ace smiled.

'The lads are more difficult to teach because their minds are always on other things,' continued Rebecca. 'Usually football. But they're bright enough. Which one have you got there?'

'Gail Burridge.'

Rebecca made a pained face. 'One of the great trials of my life. Really clever girl, her potential is enormous, but she wastes it by acting the fool. Her family environment probably doesn't help. Her father, Phil, is the local thug. Always seems to have loads of money, though nobody's ever seen him do an honest day's work in his life, unless you count brown-nosing around Matt Hatch. And he's always down the Jack... er, sorry, the Green Man. And he gets violent when he's drunk.'

'To his family?' asked Ace.

'To *everybody*,' replied Rebecca. 'But yes, his wife's been seen around the village with a few black eyes in her time. I'm pretty certain he gives Gail a slap every now and then, too.'

'Why doesn't anybody *do* anything about it?' asked Ace, plaintively.

'Why?' Rebecca paused. 'Because he's our cousin,' she said, as if that answered everything. 'Who's next?'

Ace picked up the next book. 'Zoë Luston,' said Ace.

'Zoë's a little tease,' said Rebecca with a smile. 'But a bright lass.'

But Ace wasn't listening, she was looking at the handwriting. She glanced back at the book belonging to Gail. It was the same. She picked up another, this time one of the boys'. Again, the familiar effortlessly beautiful handwriting. She remembered her own at their age, which Miss Birkett in computer studies had once compared to 'a spider on drugs trying to get home from the disco'. The next exercise book was the same.

'Have you seen this?' she asked Rebecca. 'The handwriting.'

'Shocking, isn't it?'

'No, it's all the same.' She passed the books over to Rebecca, who glanced at them dismissively.

'Yes, I suppose they are a bit similar. Never really noticed it before. From an early age they're taught to write in a certain way, that's all. I don't think they've been cheating, if that's what you mean.'

Ace wasn't sure exactly what she did mean, but when she opened the next book something caught her eye. At the bottom of a previous essay was a small note in red, again in an almost identical hand to that of the student to whom the book belonged: 'Paul, this is an excellent piece of work, a *huge* improvement. Congratulations.' Ace looked up at Rebecca, who moved away from the bed to pull down a reference book. As she did so a cloud passed across the sun, cutting the stream of light through the bay window.

CHAPTER 4
I BETRAY MY FRIENDS

Matthew Hatch walked towards his old school with a spring in his step. The bright sun made his back prickle, reminding him of Rebecca Baber's fingernails as they clawed at his shoulders. However, there were conflicting emotions to consider and control. A return to Hexen Bridge should be a source of triumph for its most famous son, but, more than most, Hatch was aware of the suffocating pressure of heritage.

It had been that way since his youth, when, day by day, the Hexen culture had been drummed into him. His fierce intelligence, which even his critics now conceded, had been recognised by his parents, who had indulged his precocious eccentricities, turning a blind eye to the succession of loud, *common* friends. Others might have been upset by the thought of their son mixing with the likes of Kenneth Shanks and Philip Burridge, but the Hatch family had a long history of using those from the lower classes to do their dirty work.

At university, freed from the ominous expectations of everyone in Hexen Bridge, Matthew was *magnificent*. It was inevitable that he would go into politics – with his ruthless intellect and ability to manipulate even the largest crowds, he was a natural.

It was then, however, that Matthew Hatch made the first big mistake of his life. He picked the wrong side. The losing side. It took Hatch five years of grovelling and the dedicated support of the back benches, but at the previous election he had been given what he had always craved: a safe government constituency, and a job in the Cabinet.

'Pleased to see you, Matthew,' the Prime Minister had said, standing as Hatch entered his office with a handsome smile.

'Prime Minister,' said Hatch respectfully as they shook hands.

They sat, and talked about the election, and the implementation of manifesto commitments.

'There is a feeling in the party, is there not, that you can't entirely be trusted?' the Prime Minister had said suddenly. 'That there is something of the night about you.'

'I think that's a little harsh,' countered Hatch. He'd had this discussion many times on doorsteps and in television studios. 'I felt strongly I had to follow my convictions when it would, perhaps, have been easier to have remained silent.'

'Of course,' the Prime Minister had noted. 'A new beginning. I share your hopes, Matthew. That is why I fought to have you in the parliamentary party when others would have cast you to the wolves. But I admired your stand. We believe in similar things. Education. Opportunity. Community Spirit. Choice. We're two of a kind…'

'Indeed.' And, in that moment, Matthew Hatch knew that he had achieved *everything*.

'How do you feel about defence?' the Prime Minister had asked.

Hatch had smiled, nodding slowly. 'I have always been interested in defence…'

Hatch shook the memories from his head as he made his way into the school's plush reception area.

Hatch had rather enjoyed his time here. He was King of the World inside these walls, a modern-day Flashman. He didn't bully people – he got others, chiefly Phil Burridge, to do that – and the teachers were in awe of him. Some were plain terrified.

'Morning, cousin Matthew,' came a woman's voice, and Hatch turned to find himself looking at a girl in her early twenties in a bright summer dress.

'Which one are you?' he asked with a handsome-devil smile, and she tittered coyly behind her hand.

'Belinda.'

'Ah, Josie and Michael's girl.' Hatch nodded. Like most of this village, she was distantly related to him. It took a bewildering form of mental dexterity to keep tabs on the entire family tree, but it did make business easier. Trevor Winstone, for instance, wasn't just his business partner, but was also his second (or was it third?) cousin. And, in Hexen Bridge, business and family most certainly mixed.

Matthew engaged in pointless small talk with Belinda for a few moments, then made his excuses and headed for the library in the west wing. The coolness of the room was in sharp contrast to the atmosphere outside. Hatch found himself alone in the echoing circular chamber. He headed towards the section devoted to nineteenth-century history, and removed the copy of *The Peninsular War and Its Causes* from the top shelf, depressing a hidden button set into the case.

The tunnel behind the bookcase was narrow, and Hatch had to stoop to prevent his head banging on the wooden ceiling. After twenty yards the floor beneath him gave way to four stone steps cut into rock the colour of bleached bones, the tunnel widening as it continued downward. Despite the gloom, Hatch could see the rough footprints beneath his feet. Ever since he had first come to this place, as a fourteen-year-old, he had been aware of following his ancestors.

Then came the still incongruous sight of an ornate, seventeenth-century, gold-trimmed mirror set in the rough rock. Hatch stood before it. He remembered the terror he had felt when he had faced his own reflection in this place as a boy.

''Tis I,' he said, his voice no longer Oxford-and-London English, but rich and filled with West Country inflection.'Where art thou?'

In the mirror, Hatch's reflection had gone, replaced by swirling mist, from out of which stepped a tall figure in the rough clothing of long-dead centuries. His eyes were the colour of blood, his cheeks as ruddy as a funeral-parlour corpse. He looked at Hatch with an animal intensity.

'What be thy business?'

Hatch had met this avatar before.

'Inform thy master, John Ballam, that research into the cure goes well. I'm expecting to have the latest results within the next four days.'

'The master grows impatient,' cut in Ballam with a snarl.

'Jack i' the Green has waited nigh on three hundred years for his coming,' said Hatch contemptuously. 'He can wait another week.' And with that he turned and walked back up the tunnel.

In the mirror, John Ballam faded into the mist. But a gaggle of voices followed Hatch up the tunnel.

'The work must be influenced to serve the master better.'

'The time is almost upon us.'

'Delay frustrates us, but soon we shall be free.'

The Reverend Thomas Baber knelt down as the parishioners began trudging through the final verse of 'Oh for a Closer Walk with God'. Was it him, or was the organ even more out of tune than normal? That really would need attention again, when funds permitted.

Baber shook his head to clear the babbling, interminable clutter from his mind. Concentrate. He rested his head against the pulpit of oak, knowing that it shielded him from the rest of the church, affording brief sanctuary. He sighed, trying desperately to find God within his heart... And found something else, as dark and gnarled as the wood that surrounded him like a dry and dusty womb.

> So shall my walk be close with God,
> Calm and serene my frame:
> So purer light shall mark the road
> That leads me to the Lamb.

Baber sighed. Fine sentiments, but they were alien words, with no relevance to Baber's inner life. This was the lull before the storm.

He rose to his feet, a snivelling, fidgeting hush coming over the congregation. He surveyed them slowly, heads all turned up towards him, faces bright with expectation and fear. Baber closed his eyes. 'May the words of my mouth and the meditation of our hearts be pleasing in your sight, O Lord, my Rock and my Redeemer. Amen.'

The murmur of assent from the villagers echoed down the main aisle, bounced off the high Gothic arches, before finally dissipating on the stained-glass window of Jesus raising Lazarus from the dead. Very precisely, Thomas Baber opened his leather-bound volume of notes. But he barely glanced at them.

'Saint Paul, I think, put it well in his epistle to the church in Rome. "I am unspiritual," he wrote. "Sold as a slave to sin. I do not understand what I do. I know that nothing good lives in me, for I have the desire to do what is good, but I cannot carry it out. Instead, I keep on doing the evil things I do not want to do." ' Baber paused, as if the words were too painful, too intimate to relate. ' "What a wretched man I am!" ' he exclaimed, his knuckles white as he gripped the edge of the pulpit. ' "Who will rescue me from this body of death?" '

Baber paused, leaving the heartfelt plea hanging in the air like an accusation. 'Good men and bad have pondered this ever since. Who will rescue us from the turmoil – the war, as Paul puts it – that we feel within?' He scanned the faces arranged below him. 'As I walk the village, I notice many things. I see delinquent, drunken children, completely out of control.' He glared at Mr and Mrs Tyley. Only the man returned his gaze. The woman's cheeks were still wet with tears. 'I see abominable practices and brutality that defies description.' There were nervous coughs from pews towards the back of the church. 'I see infidelity, unfaithfulness and sexual immorality.' He glanced at the Matsons, sitting in the side aisle. They stared forward, unblinking, like children at assembly, their hands limp in their laps. The space between them was the chasm of their lives. 'Racism, fornication, contempt for the Lord and his day. I see all these things, and am appalled.'

Baber's voice was rising in volume and pitch now. He wasn't quite shouting, but the anger in his voice was like a flaming brand. Dust motes sparkled and danced in the air, lit by a beam of sunlight through one of the side windows. 'As Saint Paul said in the letter to the Galatians, "The acts of the sinful nature are obvious: impurity and debauchery, idolatry and witchcraft, hatred, discord, jealousy, selfish ambition. I warn you, as I did before," concludes Paul, "that those who live like this will not inherit the kingdom of God." '

Baber licked suddenly dry lips. 'I warn you, the kingdom of God is at hand. It is close by! Even in Hexen Bridge!' The affirmation was so strong, so surprising, it almost shocked Baber. He could feel the sharp intake of breath in the congregation. 'And if we do not follow that narrow road that leads to the Lord, we shall instead find ourselves on the wide and easy road that leads to hell and destruction.' There was a snigger from somewhere, some blasé, contemptuous child. 'Hell is no laughing matter,' Baber continued, louder still. 'The valley of Hinnom, to the south of Jerusalem, is the Old Testament picture of hell. A place of slaughter, where children were cut open and sacrificed to Molech, a rubbish dump that burnt continuously and shifted like quicksand. In the New Testament, we hear of a lake of burning sulphur, a place of torment, an underworld, a bottomless pit. Our Lord himself spoke of a fiery furnace, the outer darkness, where there is weeping, and gnashing of teeth.'

The boy who had dared to laugh was staring at his shoes, his face pale. 'You think the filth of Hexen Bridge, the filth in your own black hearts, is terrifying beyond description? If you stay on the wide road, that will be as nothing to what awaits you when reunited with your true master. The author of the turmoil and conflict in your hearts.'

Thomas Baber closed the journal as firmly as one would close the book of life on the unrepentant. ' "Who will rescue me from this body of death?" ' The answer was clear to Baber, but he knew that he could never say it, not in this place. 'Who indeed?' he concluded, turning sadly away from the villagers.

Hatch emerged back into the library to find Trevor Winstone sitting in one of the leather-covered reading chairs, his feet propped up on a stool, smoking a cigar. Hatch's younger partner looked decadent, and the initial inclination was to hit him hard. Hatch found himself having these urges more and more, especially in the House. The desire to take three steps across the chamber and slap the opposition spokeswoman on defence across the face was enormous.

'You shouldn't be smoking in here,' he said, closing the secret entrance. 'It's very bad for the books.'

'You're right, of course,' said Trevor, easing himself out of the chair and turning to face Hatch. He stubbed out the cigar in the fireplace. 'Mind you, I don't imagine the novelists, poets and historians who wrote these magnificent works would approve of them being attacked by grubby little hands, either,' he continued.

'You were young yourself once,' said Hatch. 'I can remember what a snot-nosed brat you were. You and Becky Baber. The Romeo and Juliet of Hexen Bridge.'

'All right,' said Trevor defensively. 'That was a long time ago.' He looked at the politician more closely. 'You look knackered,' he observed.

'I should be,' noted Hatch with a wicked smirk. 'I've been up half the night giving your ex-girlfriend one.'

Trevor winced but said nothing.

'Well, you'll know yourself, she can be pretty energetic,' continued Hatch.

'Like I said, that was a long time ago.'

'The consignment is safe?' Hatch asked, changing the subject abruptly.

Trevor nodded. 'Phil's got it, not far from here.'

'Good.' Hatch grinned.

'And our little visitor?' queried Trevor, not sharing Matthew Hatch's boyish enthusiasm.

'Oh, he'll be dealt with up in Giroland soon enough.'

'Fine,' said Trevor, heading for the door. 'I don't want to know the details.'

'Squeamish?' asked Hatch.

'No,' said Trevor flatly. 'Just not interested.'

An hour later Trevor sat in his car three miles from the village, listening to the bleak thrash of Strawberry Horse. Longman's copse was a secluded enough place for a secret meeting, the arch of trees on either side of the road creating a dark cathedral, into which it was virtually impossible for prying eyes to see.

Another vehicle pulled up behind him, the engine just audible above the music. Trevor was out of the car in seconds, his fingers tight on the trigger of the sub-machine-gun which he held out in front of him.

And there stood Rebecca, her hands on her hips, a scowl of suppressed amusement on her face. 'Is that thing an extension of your penis, Trev?'

'Jesus, Becky…' He tossed the gun on to the front seat of the car and came towards her, kissing her savagely on the mouth.

'Ah, ah, ah,' she tutted, pushing him away with a look of disapproval. 'Business before pleasure, matey. I had to make more excuses than the captain of the *Titanic* to get here.'

'Trouble?'

'Not really. That girl who came with the Doctor is snooping around. She's harmless enough, though. Apparently the Doctor's missing. You wouldn't know anything about that, would you?'

Trevor shook his head mutely.

'I've had to leave her at the vicarage,' continued Rebecca. 'I made up some cock-and-bull story about needing to see a sick friend.'

'Charming,' said Trevor ironically.

'Come on,' said Rebecca impatiently. 'I've got to get back. You said you could show me some merchandise.'

'Well,' said Trevor, 'As I told you in London, it depends on the amount of collateral damage you hope to cause.'

'I want to blow the whole world ten feet off the ground,' said Rebecca with an anger that Trevor had seldom seen before.

'I've got plastic explosives that'll shift it off its axis if that's what you want.' There was a dour sadness in his voice. 'Untraceable, too. If you're careful.'

'Aren't I always?' she asked angrily. 'Just show me what you've got.' Trevor tugged at the tarpaulin in the back of the car to reveal rows of crates and boxes, stuffed with bubble wrap and terrifying weaponry. Rocket launchers, machine-guns, mines, timers and a bewildering array of explosives. Many of them still carried small white tags, as if giving the prices of Action Man's latest accessories.

'I like your showroom, Trev,' smiled Rebecca.

'I don't,' he said sourly, glancing around him nervously. 'OK, what are you interested in?'

Ace had let the rest of the day slip through her fingers like sand on a beach, and she felt a familiar frustration that the Doctor hadn't been more explicit with his instructions. Actually, if truth be told, she had assumed that he would turn up, as ever, and was more irritated than concerned when he hadn't.

She'd hung around the village, watching people come and go, but they seemed wary of her. She had the feeling that important things were happening, but it was always just out of sight, and whenever she approached people they would stop talking and let her pass, continuing their business only when she was out of earshot.

She glanced out of the window. Black clouds had come in from the west, and night had fallen quickly. There was rain in the air, but none fell. Ace could sense the nervous energy of those that braved the seats just outside the Green Man, and she wondered if Hexen Bridge was like this all the time. No wonder everyone here was a loony.

From her room, high up in the inn, she could watch the entire village. In her position the Doctor would probably stand, brooding, hatching plans and schemes, alert for anything that went on beneath him. Ace found herself being distracted by the sound of a lovers' tiff, and the constantly changing, endlessly rolling grey-black clouds that reached down to brush the church spire and the Gothic pinnacles of the school.

The school. That was the place to start. After all, the Doctor had been there the previous evening, and as far as she could tell no one had seen him since. The obvious answer was that he had found out something he shouldn't, and was trussed up like a pig about to be spit-roasted.

She walked down the rickety back stairs and into the bar. Bob Matson was noticeable by his absence, which suited Ace down to the ground.

Out on the green the lovers had come to some sort of sobbing truce, while their mates laughed and joked and pretended they hadn't heard the argument. A lingering embarrassment hung in the air like the claustrophobic storm. Thunder rumbled distantly.

Ace had noted that a lane ran from a point just shy of the Chinese restaurant towards the back of the old school. Good. She didn't really want to go marching up to the front entrance, demanding the release of all prisoners.

A Taste of the Orient glimmered in the distance, the stone lions looking even more powerful than usual. It was as if they sensed the atmosphere, and had puffed up their chests in confident expectation. The car park was empty, but the restaurant seemed full, dark shapes visible through the windows.

As she came closer she noticed a figure moving towards the restaurant. While Ace was walking confidently, so that if challenged she could play the innocent with ease, this person stuck to the shadows like a child playing at war. He moved with the artless clumsiness of a large man, and seemed to be looking away from Ace and towards the restaurant. Ace took her chance, and ducked behind a tree. When the man looked back towards the village, he saw nothing and, emboldened, he stepped through a small lit area and towards the side door.

It was Bob Matson, looking as guilty as sin. He carried a plastic bag with him.

A Taste of the Orient's side door was simple and wooden, brightly painted and lacking all the mock opulence of the restaurant's main entrance. There was a door buzzer to one side, and a brass letter box in the centre. Gingerly, Matson opened up the letter box – even from where Ace was watching she could tell it was one of those finger-crushing ones that postmen hate – and he began forcing the contents of the bag into the house. Matson had his nose buried into one expansive shoulder.

Ace could hardly believe it. The man was posting excrement through the letter box.

When she was growing up, she had thought that racism was maybe something that affected just her street or her school. As her consciousness expanded, the limits were continually pushed back. Birmingham, Martin Luther King, South Africa, the Second World War. Her travels with the Doctor had expanded her viewpoint still further, the dizzying scope of their explorations almost trivialising the problems of Earth.

But this was a shocking reminder of the mundane hatred that goes hand in hand with everyday life. If she'd resented Matson before, she loathed him now. She had half a mind to cross the road and confront the man, sod the consequences and Hexen Bridge's inability to deal with the appalling behaviour of its own people.

But the Doctor's voice came clearly through her mind. 'The bigger picture, Ace. Always remember the bigger picture. Sometimes, you'll find that if you concentrate on that, the smaller details will fall into place, too.'

Hell, she hoped so. And, if not, she'd deal with Bob Matson before they left. She didn't know how, yet, but she'd happily devote the next couple of days to considering her options.

But, as Matson moved away quickly, she remembered the Doctor, and the school, and she waited for her emotions to calm. They did, moments after Bob Matson disappeared from view.

Ace emerged from the shelter of the tree, and turned into the lane that led to the school. It sat some distance away, a large building darker than the hedgerows it seemed to sprout from, studded with one or two resolute lights.

The wind picked up just as the rain started to fall, and Ace swore under her breath. The leisurely stroll became a dash for shelter as she ran towards the school, past what seemed to be a staff car park and a bedraggled, tacked-on row of workshops and science labs. She crashed into the back door, thankful for the overhanging roof, and pressed the doorbell, no longer interested in subtlety.

At length the door opened, and a ratlike man stood in the doorway. 'Yes?' he asked, suspiciously.

Ace tried peering around him, as if the Doctor would be somewhere within sight, but saw only a wall of lockers and the doors to some toilets. 'I got caught in the rain.'

'Yes.'

The man seemed unconcerned, but Ace ploughed on regardless. 'So, can I come in? Out of the rain, I mean.'

'No.'

Ace opened her mouth to protest, but the man cut her short.

'Rules,' he said, 'are there to be obeyed by one and all.'

'Yeah, but surely I can –'

'And your friend is no longer here.'

If Ace was surprised by the man's sudden burst of intuition, she didn't show it. 'But he was?'

The man nodded. 'Of course. Last night. The reunion. He departed some time before midnight.'

'But I haven't seen him since.'

'Not my problem.' The man peered out into the darkness, as cold as the grey rain that was falling in sheets. 'Now, leave the school premises, or I'll set the dogs on you.'

In a different context, the threat would have been laughable, but Ace had spent long enough in Hexen Bridge to recognise that the man was deadly serious. She turned away, trying to think of something witty and abusive to say, but managed only a brusque 'Well, up yours, then.' The door closed with a muffled thump.

She walked down the little driveway back towards the lane, feeling one or more pairs of eyes watching her as she went. Only when she turned the corner and the school slumped out of sight did she relax. As if on cue, the rain slowed to a pathetic drizzle.

What next? She supposed it was just about feasible that the Doctor had headed back to the TARDIS, and either been injured on his way, or had collapsed inside. 'Professor, I hate this!' she exclaimed out loud.

She recognised the bushy copse close to the field where the TARDIS had landed, and walked in that direction, clambering over a rust-red gate and cutting through the ascending pastures.

She slapped her forehead. Perhaps the Doctor had left a note there, and Ace had frittered away her day chatting with Rebecca Baber, waiting for something to happen. Tomorrow, Ace resolved, she would seize the initiative and... do something.

She found a break in the hedge surrounding the field, and strode swiftly towards the area where the TARDIS nestled. A dark shape emerged from the deeper shadows, and Ace let out a sigh of relief. She hadn't realised how frightened she'd been of not finding it at all.

But something was wrong: the shape was all amorphous and rounded, not angular and square. Ace ducked back under the overhanging trees that skirted the edge of the field, approaching more cautiously.

The night-time clouds receded. As Ace walked closer she could see that an unmoving *something* had surrounded the TARDIS on all sides. Actually, make that several somethings.

A group of figures appeared to have encircled the TARDIS, their arms touching in an attempt to make a human cordon. They were motionless, only the wind tugging at them causing an approximation of movement. They were scarecrows, straw-filled faces staring blandly out into the fields and down into the village.

Breathing heavily in relief, Ace strode over towards the TARDIS. Probably some straw-sucker's idea of a joke, she thought. Just shift these out of the way and open the door and –

The faces were terrifying, and Ace stopped dead in her tracks, suddenly remembering the manikin she had spied on the green earlier that morning. Twigs and roots ran over skin-coloured cloth faces in a parody of veins and arteries; bunches of corn ears and brown leaves formed muscles and features. The eyes and mouths were savage slits in the cloth.

Steeling herself, she approached the first scarecrow. It wore a thick checked shirt and scuffed chinos, and when she gripped its shoulder she could feel the strong, straight branches underneath that supported the straw stuffing.

She pulled, expecting the thing to topple over, but it was locked solid. She pulled again, harder, and some dried grass came away in her hands, but the impassive figure hadn't budged an inch. She glanced down at the broken boots and stick legs of the scarecrow, but there were no obvious means of keeping it in place. It was as if the entire thing had been cast in bronze, and rooted deep into the ground.

She walked around the sinister group. All were motionless and immovable, resting against the solid walls of the TARDIS as if seeking warmth. There was no gap, no way through.

Ace swallowed down her rising panic, and turned back for the village. As she glanced over her shoulder, the wind tugged at the scarecrows. It was as if they were turning their faces to watch her.

PART TWO
JACK IN THE BOX

CHAPTER 5
PROMISED LAND

The Doctor sat on a mountain top. Below him, a thousand miles away, friends, family and companions were calling to him. He could hear the voices clearly as they echoed up through the clouds and the thin air towards him. He tried to answer, but his tongue was tied. Above him there was nothing but the vast rich blue of the universe. A scattering of stars, as bright as a hundred suns, cascaded their light upon him… And there was Pogar, his guiding star. The light that always brought him home from the furthest reaches of time and space.

He was dreaming, of course. He had known that for some time. The Yeti who had asked him, in halting Old High Gallifreyan, if he had any cigarettes probably gave the game away.

Get up.

Consciousness overwhelmed the Doctor's mind, and for a moment he lost all sense of where he was. When he finally opened his eyes – focusing on a beautiful woman sitting on a cream leather sofa – he was none the wiser. She was blonde, with high cheekbones. She wore a strapless full-length dress that, the Doctor supposed, probably curved in all the right places. In her hand was a half-smoked cigarette. She glanced at the Doctor and noticed that he was awake. She got to her feet without a word.

'Those are very bad for you,' observed the Doctor, but the woman had already gone.

He looked around the room keenly. He seemed to be in some sort of luxurious apartment, and he noticed for the first time that he was slumped in an armchair that would, in other circumstances, have been hugely comfortable. His wrists and ankles were bound, and he couldn't feel his feet at all. When he tried to push himself into a more upright position, the cramp in his legs caused him to cry out in pain.

'Are you *compos mentis* yet, or what?' asked a familiar voice.

'You always were good at Latin, as I remember,' said the Doctor, still wincing against the terrible ache in his legs. 'Nice place you've got here.'

'Ta,' said Shanks, looking almost embarrassed, although there was no one else in the room to hear the Doctor's remark. He knelt beside the Doctor, beginning to loosen his bonds. 'The drug will take a while to wear off, so don't do anything too energetic just yet.'

'I know,' said the Doctor, feeling as though his head was stuffed with cotton wool. He had a vague memory of Shanks injecting him with something during the long journey from Hexen Bridge. 'I am a pharmacologist. Amongst other things.'

'You poor bloody divvy,' said Shanks with a seemingly genuine sadness. 'You ain't gonna like what I've got planned for you.'

On her second morning in Hexen Bridge, Ace awoke to the sound of smashing crockery. The Matsons were clearly having a big argument in the kitchen. Ace didn't like listening in on private conversations, but the volume employed made it impossible not to.

'I saw you at the stinking yellow restaurant!' It was Bob Matson in full flood. 'Try and deny it.'

'I was talking *business*.' Joanna's voice was calmer, but the anger in it, too, was unmistakable.

'Oh, don't give me that. You're screwing that chink kid.'

'That's rich coming from you. At least *he's* over sixteen.'

'What the hell are you on about, woman?'

'That bit of jailbait you've been knocking up. Our "guest". There are laws in this country.'

Ace couldn't help but shiver; the entire idea was too gruesome for words.

'You're round the bloody twist! Anyway, she's over sixteen.'

'Oh, you know, do you?' shrieked Joanna, the first touch of

hysteria audible in her voice.

Ace had heard enough. This had gone way beyond soap-opera funny. These were real people self-destructing beneath her feet, and it was time to get out. She pulled on her clothes as quickly as she could, and bolted out of the back door.

She let out a long sigh as the door closed behind her. The only thing you could say in the Matsons' defence was that they probably deserved each other. Anyway, she had work to do.

What she needed was an outsider's point of view, someone who had been in the village long enough but hadn't been swept away by the festering insanity. Someone she could trust. Rebecca was the obvious choice, but she'd been born and raised here, and the thing with the handwriting still spooked Ace. The Chens seemed the next-best bet.

Ace strolled down the lane towards A Taste of the Orient, wondering whether to mention what she'd seen Bob Matson doing the previous night. When Steven Chen pulled open the door, his smile was so full of bitterness and fear that Ace decided to leave the subject well alone. The Chens must have known who was behind the racist attacks, and it seemed foolish to raise the matter so abruptly. Perhaps they had their own way of dealing with it. Maybe some strange Chinese rite could breathe life into the stone lions, who would devour Bob Matson next time he came calling.

'Hello,' said Steven. 'What can I do for you?'

'I delivered your note,' replied Ace brightly.

Steven immediately put a finger to his lips. 'Come inside,' he whispered, holding the door open for her.

Steven Chen led Ace into the kitchens, which were deserted. He seemed to be in the middle of washing the floor, the metal work-surfaces already looking clean enough to eat off. Which, decided Ace, was probably just as well, given the number of tacky takeaway joints in Perivale that had been closed by Environmental Health.

'My parents do not approve of my friendship with Joanna,' said Steven.

'I suppose you can see their point of view,' said Ace cautiously. 'I mean, she is married to –'

'Of course,' said Steven Chen hurriedly. 'I sometimes think what we're doing is stupid.' He sighed. 'Anyway, it doesn't really matter. I hope Bob Matson hasn't made life... difficult for you.'

'No more so than usual,' smiled Ace. 'I came to ask you about the school. The Doctor disappeared during the reunion the night before last.'

'Really?' Steven looked genuinely surprised. Whatever village grapevine there was, it obviously bypassed the Chens completely. 'What's happened to him?'

'No idea,' said Ace. 'From what Rebecca's told me, the school's an odd sort of place.'

' "Odd" is one way of putting it,' said Steven. 'I've spent the last five years trying to forget about it.'

'Was it that bad?'

'If you're an outsider, they make your life an absolute hell. I know a lot of kids have to put up with bullying, but this was systematic torture.'

'But you've lived here so long...'

'But I wasn't *born* here,' said Steven. 'Thank God. None of my family were. You're either one of Jack's children, or you're not.'

'Jack?' queried Ace, surprised.

'Just one way they put it. I don't know what it means,' he added, hurriedly.

'I noticed that the pupils' handwriting all seemed very similar.'

Steven laughed. 'In most other places, interbreeding causes extra limbs or close-set eyes. Here...' He paused, looking around as if someone were listening. 'You wouldn't believe what it gives rise to here.'

Tara Hatch was a formidable woman. A stunning Aryan beauty

and an hourglass figure masked a tempestuous nature and a voice that could strip paint. She'd been a model when she first met Matthew, then a rising star in the last days of a hated, radical government. If there was one thing Matthew Hatch had a weakness for it was the blonde models who frequented the society parties of Knightsbridge and Kensington. A whirlwind romance followed, during which time they holidayed on the Riviera on her father's yacht. They made love for the first time at dusk, as dolphins leapt around them. Then they got married, and things were never quite that awesome again.

Tara stood facing Matthew. 'Ah, the master has returned from carrot-cruncher land,' she announced.

'Shut it,' snapped Hatch. 'I'm just not in the mood.'

'You never are,' agreed Tara.

'Then you'll just have put up with it.'

'Oh, I've put up with a lot for you, Matthew. I've put up with Daddy's disapproval. I've endured your mood swings and your blasted depressions. I'm not even bothered when our former friends call us traitors any more.'

'Yeah,' said Hatch, with something approaching a genuine smile. 'Crossing the floor was about the one good idea you've ever had.'

'I've kissed babies for you. I've stood by you, like a politician's wife should.' Her voice took on the slow, measured tones she used for her innumerable interviews. 'Of course I stand by Matthew. His decision is courageous, but I think he will be vindicated in time.'

'You're the only person I've met who can beat me for bullshit.'

Tara ignored his remark. 'I've even turned a blind eye to your screwing your PA.' Her fingers tightened around the glass of vodka in her hand.

'One affair, darling. Not bad for an MP.'

'Don't lie to me!' she shouted.

Hatch sighed. 'Look, if this is the best you can come up with after a weekend away then I'll get the doctor to increase the strength of your happy pills.' He turned to the correspondence that awaited him, muttering 'Frigid bitch' under his breath.

'Oh, that's good!' exclaimed Tara angrily, flinging the glass at Hatch.

He was used to her aim now, and ducked out of the missile's path easily.

'Down, and a smidgen to the left,' he said, offering her his own glass for a second attempt.

Tara moved menacingly towards him. 'Maybe I should find myself a real man,' she said in a low voice. 'Somebody who doesn't shoot blanks the whole time.'

Matthew Hatch raised a fist as if to strike her; Tara's eyes invited him to do so, mockingly. A tap on the door silenced them both. For people who fought so regularly, and so often, they could be surprisingly discreet.

Matthew casually picked up the stem of the broken glass and dumped it on the table while Tara straightened her hair and made for the door.

'Come,' said Matthew casually.

'We'll continue this another time,' said Tara, as the door opened. She left, casting an ominous glance at the new arrival.

Melanie Jenkinson was Hatch's personal political adviser. She was a matronly woman in her early thirties who wore her dark hair pulled tight into a bun. A pair of very unflattering black-rimmed spectacles dominated a severe face that any ex-public schoolboy would have been terrified of. Despite appearances, she was one of Matthew Hatch's closest friends, a warm and generous woman who had stuck by her mentor during his difficult years in the political wilderness. Her patience, and skilful reading of the climate of the country, had steered him through one crisis after another until now, finally, she had dragged him towards real power. They had also enjoyed a brief and torrid affair three years ago, which began during an official visit to Eastern Europe, and ended in a night of terrifying thunder and lightning at his parents' home in Hexen Bridge.

Melanie closed the door and gave Matthew a quizzical look. 'Tension?'

'The usual.' He stared out of the window, a faraway look in his eyes. 'One day,' he said softly, 'she'll go too far.'

'Matthew,' said Melanie urgently, 'I have some grave news.'

Hatch turned briskly. 'Well?'

'The Proteus Research building near Birmingham has been bombed. Ten dead, including Jeffrey Squire. Nobody's claimed responsibility yet, but...'

'Bloody animal-rights activists,' said Hatch, sitting down, the colour draining from his cheeks. 'Terrible.'

'It gets worse. The warning included a reference to the CJD research they're carrying out. Nobody's supposed to know about that, Matthew. There's been a leak somewhere, and the PM thinks it must be at this end. He's going ballistic, and the other EC countries have already lodged an official protest.'

'Damn them all,' said Hatch gruffly. 'Research is research.'

'Not in this area. Too sensitive. Too many skeletons in closets.'

'It'll blow over,' said Hatch, reaching for the telephone on the edge of the desk. 'I ought to phone Jeff's widow. What must she be feeling? Her husband sacrificed to save some blasted monkeys.'

'Your own position is being questioned,' continued Melanie, doggedly.

'What?'

'Some journalist has already looked up Proteus's board of directors, found your name and Squire's...' Hatch swore under his breath. 'I'm already investigating the circulation of memos and confidential reports at this office, Matthew. I have one or two ideas where the leak might have originated.'

'No need,' said Hatch, deep in thought. 'Leave it with me.'

Melanie nodded curtly, and stepped out of the room. Hatch sat quietly, drumming his fingers against the desk. Given that he trusted his own team, and that there was no way that Squire or any of his people would have compromised themselves, only one person remained.

Rebecca Baber.

That slippery, calculating little bitch had wormed her way into his bed and taken more than a good time away with her. He should have realised sooner, of course, but when you've known somebody since they were three years old, it's hard to see into their dark corners.

Hatch picked up the phone and dialled a number. As he waited for an answer he cursed again. Taken in by a vicar's daughter. Unreal.

'Phil?' he said urgently when the other phone was picked up. 'Listen, mate, I've got a job for you.'

Chief Constable Denman swept into the room, and a million trifling conversations ebbed away. His uniform was immaculate, the buttons gleaming like diamonds. The assembled officers sat upright in their seats, straightening ties and tucking in shirts and blouses.

'I want to keep this short,' said Denman. He stood at the head of the table, hands held behind his back. 'I have a radio interview in forty minutes, and then a meeting with the Home Secretary. Now, Shanks. Chief Inspector Ross has kept me informed. You know how important Shanks is to me, so I thought I'd drop in and have a word. I don't think the cocky little bugger is on to us, but time is clearly of the essence. James, what's the latest on Green?'

DI McMahon was a good-looking young man who'd accelerated through the ranks under Denman's tutelage, just before Denman himself had been promoted 'upstairs'. He looked up from the folder in front of him. 'Still unwilling to testify, sir. I think Shanks's boys have been putting the choke on him, but it's difficult to prove. I've hinted we'll be lenient with the burglary charge if he squeals, but –'

'Do more than hint,' said Denman. 'Give him a copper-bottomed guarantee if you want. Just get that man in court.'

'Sir.'

'Brian, I've heard you've made progress on the stolen electrical goods.'

DC Kennedy, seeming to enjoy the opportunity to wear jeans and T-shirt in the station, looked up with a wide grin. 'Yes, sir. We were told about a lorry-load of VCRs and DVDs destined for Shanks's chain of ex-rental shops. We trailed the vehicle to a lock-up on one of his estates, and then the goods themselves right into one of his warehouses. Photographic and video evidence, the lot. Jeremy Beadle wants to use some of the material on his next show.'

There was laughter, but it was not shared by Denman. 'I had hoped to get him on something more serious than receiving stolen goods, but it'll still carry a prison sentence. That's good. And the CPS are convinced?'

'Yes, sir. We'll start proceedings any day now.'

'Excellent. Paul, what's the latest on the internecine drug conflicts?'

'The Yardies are still fuming, sir,' replied DI Paul Hill, whose expensively tailored suit looked as much a uniform as Denman's formal attire. 'They and Shanks have carved up the city between them, but now Shanks's tribe is moving into Yardie territory. I've got a few good contacts there, and hope to be able to get a result pretty soon.'

'Including actual interception of consignment?'

'I hope so, sir. There's a shedload of Colombian on its way, plus enough crack to keep his pushers supplied for the next decade. And we've just had word that he makes synthetics on site. Supposedly he's got a chemist drop-out from the university producing stuff to order somewhere in Everton, but nobody's talking.'

'More than enough in that summary to nail him for good,' commented Denman.

'Let's hope so, sir,' replied Hill.

'Well done,' said Denman, scanning the room for further

contributions, although none were offered. 'I want you all working on these lines of inquiry as hard and as fast as you can. If previous experience has taught me anything, it's that you can't skewer Shanks just the once. We need to hit him hard, with multiple charges. And then finally the streets will be safe again.' And with a final nod, Denman was gone.

The remaining officers began to file out of the conference room in their teams. DC Fielder paused in the doorway, turning back to Hill, who remained seated, deep in thought.

'Coming, guv?'

'I'll be along in just a minute, Mick.'

Fielder smiled and left, leaving Hill alone in the room. Hill pulled a mobile phone from his pocket, and stared at it momentarily as if he'd never seen it before, his brow creased with concentration. Then, with feigned casualness, he strolled towards the window. With his back to the door, he tapped in a number, holding the mobile to his ear.

'Tell Shanks,' he snapped when someone answered at the other end, 'if he's going to have a pop at Denman, he'd better do it now.'

Ace passed the war memorial with a curious sideways glance. 'Back for more, boys,' she said with a grin, patting the stones tenderly. 'I wish you lot were here. I might get some straight answers then.'

She found the Reverend Thomas Baber tending to his begonias in the front garden. He was a picture of childlike contentment, entirely absorbed in his flowers. Ace decided to try the 'little Dorothy' act once again, hopeful that it would get her further than the day before.

'Hello,' she said brightly. 'Lovely day, isn't it?'

Baber snapped up to his full height, seemingly taken aback. 'Err… Yes, yes it is,' he said, wiping the dirt from his hands. 'I'm afraid Rebecca is in school today, so…'

'Actually, it was you I came to see,' said Ace with a dazzling smile.

'Oh,' said Baber.

'I wonder if it would be possible for me to have a look at the church records. Parish registers, that kind of thing.'

'They're church property,' said Baber quickly. 'I'm afraid –'

'It's for research,' cut in Ace before he could get any further with his refusal. 'The Doctor's writing a book on the history of the area, and your help would be much appreciated. We'd include an acknowledgement to yourself and the church, of course, wording to be agreed at a later date. And there could be a small payment…'

'What are you looking for?' asked Baber, his eyes narrowing in suspicion.

'Anything I can get, basically,' she said.

Baber seemed to consider this for a long time. Ace could imagine the turmoil in the man's mind. Her request was reasonable enough, but there must *surely* be some reason that he could contrive to refuse her. At length the cleric shrugged and said, 'I have nothing to hide.'

'I didn't say you had,' responded Ace automatically, but Baber wasn't really listening.

'Research is the quest for truth,' he said with a faraway look in his eyes that Ace found disturbing and yet rather pathetic. 'I can understand that. This way, young lady.'

He led her to the church, opening the main wooden door with a big iron key about as long as Ace's arm. Once inside, he tapped a code into an electronic pad. Ace found the mixture of old and new amusing.

'A shame we have to keep the house of God like a bank vault,' said Baber. 'But there are some valuable things in here. And young people are always so keen to desecrate. Present company excepted, I'm sure.'

'Times change,' she said.

'Indeed,' nodded the man, switching on some lights. 'But God doesn't. And people think that makes him irrelevant, but actually that makes him more relevant than ever. It's old fools like me who get in the way.'

Ace couldn't believe that this was the same glacier-cold man as she had seen the day before. She followed Baber into the vestry, a musty, dank room than contained a single writing desk and a hard-backed wooden chair. 'Not a very comfortable place to do the Lord's work,' he said, with what passed for a smile. 'Many of the older parish records were destroyed in a fire during the 1830s,' the vicar continued, dragging a heavy oak chest towards the desk. 'The burning of stubble has always carried risks. However, some material was salvaged, and there are a great many other documents. Some school records were donated to us during the 1960s. They're all in here.' Baber opened the chest, and the damp smell hit Ace like a punch.

'Phew,' she said waving a hand under her nose. 'What a pong!'

The vicar departed with a smile, muttering something about lunch and the shipping forecast.

The chest was, indeed, a treasure trove. Had Ace's real purpose been straightforward historical research then she would have been busy. But since she was looking for something unusual, and she had no idea of what that might be, her search became a random trawl through registers, lists of landowners, and miscellaneous school records. She settled down to read a log of school punishments for the year 1907. It seemed the village lads had been regularly caned for a bewildering range of 'crimes'. 'Bad boys!' she exclaimed, her finger running over 'insolence', 'tampering with the school clock' and 'kicking a hedgehog'.

'Serves you right, Wally,' she said, noting that Walter Smith got two strokes for booting the defenceless creature. Then she thought of him, knee-deep in the mud of Passchendaele, screaming as shells exploded around him, and she dropped the book back into the chest.

Finally, Ace found something pertinent to her own interest in the village. It was an enormous ledger with rich, cream-coloured paper and thin, almost faded, gold edging. It crackled with imagined importance.

The book was some kind of census of the last few years of the nineteenth century and the first five decades of the twentieth. There was another volume beneath detailing the previous fifty years. As Ace read she found a year-by-year record of all of the people in the village, grouped together into families, with brackets indicating links that became more and more intertwined as the years rolled on. There were columns listing dates of birth, christenings, marriages, and deaths and, at the end of each yearly page, a note, in neat copperplate script, of the total village population. There were 506 people in 1894, 507 in 1895, 506 in 1896. Ace turned another handful of pages: 499 in 1917 (well, Wally and his mates were all away getting themselves shot in Europe, weren't they?), 504 in 1918, 507 in 1919 (wasn't there a great flu about then that should have made the population decline, not increase?). Ace reached the 1930s: 510 in 1936, 508 in 1937...

Ace heard the sound of footsteps moving quietly in her direction, and turned, startled.

'Oh, I'm sorry,' said Thomas Baber, almost dropping the tray and glasses he was carrying. 'I thought all this dusty work might be making you thirsty. Lemonade?'

Ace chuckled. 'Thank you,' she said. 'That's well thoughtful of you, Vicar.'

Baber came across to the desk and set the tray down, looking over Ace's shoulder at the ledger.

'Oh, I see you've found the parish population record.' He walked towards a small cupboard by the door and pulled out a similar-sized ledger, but this time the cover was newer, with fewer spots of mildew and damp. 'This is the most recent volume, begun by my late grandfather in 1954, continued by my father, and now by me. The record has much less relevance in these days of information superhighways and such technical nonsense, but I carry it on. I'm mindful of the importance of tradition, aren't you?'

'Sure,' said Ace, taking a grateful drink from her lemonade. 'Tell me, Vicar, what's the current population of the village?'

'About five hundred,' said Baber casually. Then he set the book down and checked on the most recent page, right towards the back. 'It was actually 513 on the thirty-first of December last year, but a couple of people have left the village since then. Why do you ask?'

'No reason,' said Ace quickly. 'Just curious. There was one other thing I was wondering.'

'Yes?'

'There are columns in these records for births, christenings, marriages and deaths. And there's also one other column. It hardly seems to be used, except every couple of years there's a date next to one of the names.' She pointed to the 1937 entry in her hand. 'Like here: Grace Partnoll, first of July 1937. What's all that about?'

'That column refers to people who have left the village for one reason or another. If you look at the next page you'll see it says that Miss Partnoll is no longer part of the village list.'

'Oh yes,' said Ace, flicking over the page. 'So it does…' She stood to give the vicar back his glass, glancing at the newer volume that he held. 'Has somebody just left?' she said, pointing to that day's date on the page, partly obscured by Baber's thumb.

'Yes indeed,' said the vicar. 'Mr and Mrs Tyley informed me just this morning that young William has left the village to go to London.' He sighed. 'Such a debauched place.'

'I come from London,' said Ace sharply, not sure if she was being insulted or not. She pointed to the small wooden cupboard which had contained the up-to-date register. 'I noticed when you got the new ledger out, it looked like there were some old photographs in there, too. May I have a look?'

'No, you may not,' said Baber, suddenly stiffening. 'I'm afraid that I really haven't the time to show you those. Anyway, they're family heirlooms, and have no relevance to your researches. And now…' He looked at his watch. 'I must ask you if you would be so good as to allow me to lock up.'

Ace shrugged, and closed the ledger, placing it carefully back in the chest. 'Thanks for your time,' she said.

'I hope you found what you were looking for,' said Baber, seemingly torn between hustling Ace from the church and maintaining a show of being the genial host.

'I've certainly got a few leads worth pursuing,' said Ace with a wicked grin, trying to remember the last time she had broken into a church.

The radio was turned up much too loud, but at least it rendered the taxi driver almost inaudible.

'Many people have accused you of pursuing vendettas, of concentrating on individual troublemakers at the expense of wider police work.' The female interviewer's voice was breathy and forward, obviously used to chasing after the stray morsels dropped by politicians and film stars.

'No, no,' responded the man, his slow, deliberate voice oozing cool authority. 'That would be unfair. You see, what you've got to realise, especially in Liverpool, is that one or two people *do* account for ninety per cent of the crime. It's a proven fact. To call them "troublemakers" makes it sound like they're teenagers who play their music too loud. In actual fact, I want to pursue the ringleaders, the kingpins, the drug barons, all the way into prison. And, if you've heard complaints, let me suggest to you that they're from the families of these thugs, not from the decent, law-abiding people of Merseyside.'

'If I can put another commonly expressed concern to you,' continued the interviewer, 'it's that you enjoy a high public profile, and –'

'Enjoy is not the right word,' interrupted the guest. 'I've never sought the interest of the media, but I've always been happy to respond honestly when asked about any subject.'

Damn him, thought Nicola Denman. She couldn't even escape

from her father in the back of a cab.

She leaned forward. 'Would you mind turning that off?' she asked.

'Whatever you say, miss,' said the taxi driver. 'He's got a point, though, hasn't he? That copper. I think we've tried to understand them criminals for far too long. Should just lock 'em up, and throw away the key.'

'Yeah,' said Nicola, bored and irritated. Thankfully, the taxi driver seemed to want to talk about the latest spate of burglaries in his area, and Nicola was content to grunt at the appropriate moments. Five minutes later the vehicle came to a halt.

'The Catholic Cathedral, miss,' announced the driver grandly.

Nicola scooped the required money into the man's hand, and set off at a nervous run. The huge building, part crown of thorns, part concrete circus tent, dominated the skyline, and she pushed impatiently through the crowds milling about its entrance. There was a row of confessionals off a small side aisle, which the visitors seemed instinctively to avoid, and Nicola headed towards these, letting the silence and the cool air wash over her.

She found an unoccupied booth, and sat down in a flurry of tired limbs and exhaled breaths. 'I'm not really a Catholic, right,' she began immediately to the face half-obscured by the mesh. 'So don't give me any Hail Mary nonsense. I just want to talk.' She paused, and the fragility of her feelings welled like a wound. 'I *really* need to talk to someone, OK?'

'I'm here to help in the name of God in whatever way I can,' responded the priest. He sounded young, but he spoke slowly and deliberately, as if to emphasise that he had all the time in the world, and that Nicola was the sole object of his attention. 'What troubles you?'

'It's my dad,' Nicola blurted out. 'Or rather, it's all because of my mum. She's dead, you see.'

'I'm sorry.'

Nicola caught a flash of blue eyes framed by pale skin. 'Yeah.

Well, Dad's always been very strict. You see, he's…' Nicola paused, unsure of what to say. 'He works in the legal profession,' she lied. 'He's very upright, very moral.'

'Those aren't necessarily bad things.'

'No, of course not. But, before she died, his strictness went hand in hand with his love. I never doubted then that they both thought the world of me.'

'And now?'

'I think we both feel very empty. She died years ago, and you'd think the void we feel would have gone away by now, wouldn't you?'

'No,' said the priest firmly. 'There are some trials in life that we can never recover from. I believe that God's grace is sufficient for us, but that it would almost be… disrespectful to live on as if nothing had changed.'

'Oh, but *everything* has changed. That's the point. As I grew up, he wanted me to be more and more like her. I don't even know who I am any more.'

'But does your father still love you?'

Nicola was crying now, and she did not respond for some time, the priest waiting patiently, his lips moving, perhaps in prayer. When she finally did speak again, her voice was thick with emotion and suppressed hurt. 'Daddy's love… Daddy's love can be a very frightening thing.'

Phil Burridge was not especially talented, but one skill he did possess was the ability to break into a house with the minimum of fuss and bother. And the vicarage was a particularly easy target, a huge tree dominating the back and affording easy access to one of the bedrooms.

The window was ornate, and composed of many small panes of glass, and Burridge pushed at one with a folded penknife. It shattered easily. He reached inside to twist open the window. With surprising agility for a man of his frame, he manoeuvred himself into the room from the big, thick bough of the tree, and then pulled the window closed behind him.

He glanced at his watch. Just after two o'clock. The girl would still be at school, teaching, and her dad would be… Doing vicary things in church, probably.

As he'd been led to believe, this was her room, all tasteful scatter cushions and impressionist prints. The bed was enormous, and the duvet clearly had been pulled straight before the woman had left for school. Burridge sat on it for a moment, wondering what to do. Hatch had told him to find something incriminating, something to link her to the Proteus bombing.

Burridge wasn't surprised it had come to this. He'd been suspicious when Matty Hatch had first become involved with the teacher, and now it seemed she'd been screwing the poor bloke in every way imaginable.

There was something wonderfully voyeuristic about breaking into someone's room, like reading an intimate diary. A woman's room, even more so. On an impulse, Burridge leaned across the bed and towards the pine chest of drawers to one side.

Rebecca Baber's knicker drawer was a delightful mess of scanty bits of brightly coloured silk and lace. Burridge thrust his hands into them.

He extracted a pair at random, pulling them over his face, thinking that he'd like to rob a bank like this one day, just to see if they'd dare put *that* on *Crimewatch UK*. Then he rooted through the other drawers, finding paperbacks, scarves, ballpoint pens, sports socks, a calculator, a single black stocking, and what appeared to be a year's supply of antihistamines. Right at the bottom, under an angora sweater, he found a small pile of gay porn mags, and a loaded handgun.

Phil Burridge tutted to himself. 'Oh, bad! That's gotta be worth two years in Holloway for a kick-off.'

The pants still over his face like a mask, Burridge patrolled the room, half blinded by floral satin. He opened cupboards and rifled clumsily through shelves. After five minutes of intense searching, only the computer was left, and Burridge had *no* intention of touching that.

Thinking he'd drawn a blank, he turned for the window, ripping the knickers from his face.

One of the framed prints caught his eye. Phil Burridge didn't know his Matisse from his Magritte, but, in the context of this room, a crooked painting *screamed* at him.

He turned the picture over, and taped to the back with thick masking tape was a small sheaf of paper. They were the plans to Proteus's head office, and lists of passwords and security alarms.

'Oh dear,' he said. 'We have been a *naughty* girl, Becky.'

CHAPTER 6
CITY SICKNESS

Nicola Denman took a deep breath, her hand resting against the pub door. She watched the sun creeping behind the smoke-grey clouds that peppered the horizon. Despite the noise that surged through open windows she felt more peaceful than she had in the cathedral. This was her world, for all its dirt. That other land, the place of forgiveness, was unobtainable.

For a few moments Nicola watched a gangling dog rummage through the rubbish in a side street. It seemed oblivious to the people passing by, methodically inspecting each dustbin in turn. Nicola saw its head bob up and down, and could hear an occasional snort of interest above even the rush of the cars and the dance music thumping out from the pub jukebox.

The dog turned to look at Nicola, its jaws flecked with saliva and cardboard shreds. A car turned on to the main road, the headlights briefly illuminating the creature's eyes. Startled, the dog vanished into the shadows.

Nicola pushed open the door of the pub. The air smelled of cigarettes and sweat, of perfume and salt-and-vinegar crisps. Some girls, stinking of alcohol, pushed past Nicola and towards the exit.

Nicola found her friends clustered around a small table in an alcove away from the bar. She sat down gratefully, mopping up some spilled drink with a beer mat. 'It's busy tonight,' she said. 'Mine's a vodka and orange. Loads of ice.'

One of the young women grunted and got to her feet, tugging a purse from a jacket pocket.

'You OK?' asked Tina, glancing up from the table with concern. She had known Nicola since school, and recognised the signs of tired anguish in her friend's face.

'Yeah. I'm fine. Just knackered, that's all.'

'Heard your dad on the radio this morning,' said Jane, who'd never been known for her tact.

'Oh, don't,' said Nicola.

'Let's get slaughtered, then,' said another friend, as she downed half a glass of white wine.

'There's this great place on Lime Street,' offered Jane.

'It's a dive,' said Nicola.

'Oh, go on,' said Jane. 'The lads there are just gagging for it. You could string 'em along, Nicks, get some free bevvies.'

'I don't think so.'

Jane delved into her handbag, pulling out some cheaply printed slips of paper. 'I've got free tickets…'

Nicola sensed that she had already lost the argument. 'Where'd you get them?' she queried in desperation.

'She's just a tart, love, didn't you know?' laughed Tina.

It had been a bad day in the Mother of Parliaments. The opposition had really laid into Defence Minister Hatch as he tried manfully to defend the government's recent relaxation of arms embargoes placed upon a number of unsavoury totalitarian regimes.

'Would the Right Honourable Member,' he asked one former friend and ally, 'like to be the one to tell voters in his own constituency, working in the shipbuilding industry, that their jobs are to be sacrificed to satisfy his lust for political correctness and ideological dogma?' That had set the cat among the pigeons. They came at him from all sides, probing and pushing and reiterating the same inane points over and over again until he lost his temper. Hands gripping the dispatch box tightly, he bellowed at them that he was a member of a government with a majority of one hundred and twelve, and what the hell did they think they were going to do about it?

Even the Speaker's voice had been drowned out by the near riot that ensued.

Now, pushing his way past television crews and lobby journalists outside the House, Hatch still felt that anger seething within him. It was a relief just to climb into the ministerial limousine and shut the door on the whole damn lot of them.

'Thought you were very good today, sir,' said his driver as he pulled away from Westminster and into Pall Mall.

'Thank you, Ian,' replied Hatch wearily. Not that he was particularly interested in what some civil service lowlife thought about *anything*, but politeness cost nothing.

'Straight home, sir?'

'No,' said Hatch. 'The Wellton clinic, Ian.'

'Right you are, sir.'

The oncoming twilight seemed to darken Hatch's mood, and they drove in silence towards the motorway. His driver knew well enough when to flatter him, when to ask a few questions, and when to shut the hell up.

Hatch had once overheard Ian Slater talking about him to some of the other government chauffeurs. 'Hatch is a twenty-four-carat bastard who wallows in his own crapulence,' Slater had said, with a straight face. Hatch knew praise when he heard it, and he decided there and then that the man could be trusted.

Ian Slater had been with Hatch when the politician negotiated a major Third World arms deal on behalf of Trevor Winstone. And Slater had accompanied Hatch on Spanish holidays with Shanks, the drugs and porn king of Liverpool. And Ian Slater knew something about the Wellton clinic and the reason for Matthew Hatch's frequent visits to the private medical research facility.

Most importantly of all, Slater knew where the bodies were buried. Literally.

Slater negotiated the M3 to Chertsey, and they reached the Wellton clinic shortly after 9 p.m. The light from the setting sun cast ominous shadows across the path of the car.

'I'll be about twenty minutes,' said Hatch, stepping out of the limousine. 'If my wife should ring, we're stuck in traffic, and I'm on the other line. Understand?'

'Absolutely, sir.'

Hatch strode towards the building, glancing back once to see Slater, cap down over his eyes, already fast asleep. The MP brushed through the reception area without a word, and marched into an office without knocking. A white-coated man smiled briefly as Hatch entered, immediately sweeping paperwork on to the floor to allow the politician to sit. The room was typically cluttered and, it seemed to Hatch, overlit.

'You said you had some news, Nick,' said Hatch.

'Indeed,' said Dr Nicholas Bevan. 'We're close to isolating the D47 gene. The next few days form the most important period in the entire project.' He removed a glass from a drawer, and poured the politician a whisky. 'Are you feeling all right, Matthew?' he asked.

'I'm fine,' said Hatch, passing a hand across his brow. It came away slick with perspiration. 'I'm sweating like a pig, that's all. The weather.'

'Our main concern now,' continued Bevan, 'must be to progress to the next phase of the fertility programme.'

Hatch picked up the whisky glass, and toyed with it in the harsh glare of the strip lights above his head. 'You know,' he said, 'I can remember when I first came to you, when I told you about the Hexen "curse". You said it was a scientific impossibility...' There was an ironic detachment in Hatch's voice.

'I said, if you remember, that the chance of there being a genetic strain that causes sterility in a group of human beings when they leave the area in which they were conceived was...' Bevan paused, searching for a tactful way of putting his conclusion. 'Well, it's unlikely,' he said at last. 'There are parallels in nature of course. The salmon, for instance, must spawn in the river where it was born...'

'Nick?' interjected Hatch. 'Do shut up.' He took another sip of whisky. 'How soon until we're ready to go? That's what I need to know.'

'Soon,' said Bevan.

'It's always "soon".'

'We've come a long way.'

Hatch snorted. 'I should think so: five years and getting on for two million quid.'

'Which reminds me…' said Bevan in a quiet voice.

Hatch stood, patting his pockets. He brought out a padded envelope, and tossed it on to Bevan's desk. 'There's eight thousand there,' he said. 'I can get more if you need it, but you'll have to give me a week or two. I've got a few monkeys on my back at the moment.'

'Yes,' said Bevan, 'I listened to the debate today. They're really after you this time, Matthew.'

'Well, I won't give them a chance to get me, will I? Anything else you need?'

'The usual,' said Bevan. 'Somebody from Hexen Bridge who's not sterile. Preferably female, because if the insemination technique works then it's safe to assume we can synthesise the actual sperm components. You got any strapping young Hexen lasses hidden about your person?'

'What would you say if I were to tell you I could supply one?'

Bevan was taken aback. He'd been looking for a live donor for some months, but Hatch had always resisted, citing family and other ties to most of the suitable candidates. 'In the age range? Fifteen to twenty-nine?'

'Just,' said Hatch.

'Then, I'd ask if you consider her expendable. You know how risky this procedure is.'

'And how painful,' said Hatch, with the beginnings of a cruel smile playing on his lips. 'Yes,' he continued, 'she's expendable all right.'

By the time the effects of the drug began to wear off fully, the sun was setting in the west. Shanks untied his captive, his strong hands moving with surprising dexterity over the knots. 'Make yourself at home,' he said, turning to leave with his female companion. 'Don't try to escape, though. There's twenty stone of prime-cut thug outside the door, and he's got orders to snap your spine in two if you so much as think about it!'

'Where am I?' the Doctor asked, still confused.

'You're on my home turf now, la,' said Shanks with a cheerful grin. 'God's own country. There's drink in the cabinet, and the remote control for the telly's lying around somewhere. I've got to go and see a man about the considerable amount of money he owes me.'

'Drug money?' queried the Doctor darkly.

Shanks tugged at the cuff of his jacket. 'That's libellous! I'm a respected businessman. If I weren't so busy, I'd take you on a guided tour.'

'Perhaps some other time,' said the Doctor, watching as the door closed behind Shanks.

The Doctor sat alone, gratefully savouring the still quietness and his limited freedom. Then he got to his feet, walking through the sliding doors and on to the apartment veranda. He remembered having been in the city one Christmas with Stephen and Sara. It seemed so long ago.

He reached the wrought-iron railings and glanced over the edge, feeling a momentary sensation of vertigo as the ground, twenty storeys below, seemed to rush up towards him. The Doctor stepped back, almost tripping over his own feet. 'You've lost one life that way,' he muttered to himself, and sat down on one of the flimsy canvas-and-metal chairs. He closed his eyes, and let his thoughts assemble.

The universe was an enormous jigsaw puzzle, with only the edges completed. Billions of other pieces sat in a huge pile, waiting to be sorted out. Order from chaos.

Hexen Bridge was at the centre of this part of the puzzle, but even the remaining pieces were out of reach.

The Doctor looked around the room. There had to be a

connection between Shanks and Hexen Bridge, beyond the obvious fact that he had been educated there. He strolled over to the television, and noticed that what he had taken to be a video recorder beneath it was in fact a computer terminal. A cable extended from the back of the machine and towards a telephone socket in the wall.

'Ah, the wonders of modern technology,' said the Doctor, kneeling. He looked closely at the machine, wondering if Shanks were devious enough to booby-trap the terminal, knowing that the Doctor would be drawn to it. He dismissed the thought with an irritated shake of the head. He was like a fish out of water, and it was making him paranoid.

Working as quietly as he could, the Doctor reconnected the computer, and switched it on. It wouldn't contain any information itself, but perhaps there was a way of looking at communications sent or received from within other rooms in the apartment, the electronic equivalent of picking up an extension phone to listen in on a private conversation.

The television's remote control would also operate the Internet terminal, but the Doctor couldn't find the device anywhere. A swift search of the cupboards revealed the computer's small keyboard, still in its original wrapping. The Doctor tore at the cellophane with his teeth, then plugged the device in.

He closed down the garish user interface and began tinkering with the underlying text-based operating system. In ten minutes he had written a stealth program from scratch. It was like using a clockwork toy to launch a space shuttle, but he hoped it would work.

Data from a science lab somewhere in the building was flowing over the screen. A sequence of formulae, followed by a starburst of unintelligible information.

The Doctor was searching his pockets for his notebook when the elevator began its noisy climb up the building towards the penthouse. He hastily switched off the terminal, and pulled the lead from the telephone socket. He turned, expecting to see his host returning, but instead he found himself facing Trevor Winstone and six men carrying wooden crates.

'Put them down,' said Trevor to his companions. 'And be careful.' He turned to the Doctor, and inclined his head to one side, curiously. 'You really *must* be his friend. Not many people hang around Kenny Shanks for long and live to tell the tale.'

'I obviously have a lucky face,' said the Doctor, sitting on the leather sofa, and then standing again quickly as something sharp stuck into his rump. 'Ah,' he said brightly. 'The remote control. We've been looking for that…'

'Great,' said Trevor sarcastically. 'If *Match of the Day*'s on later, I'll get the beers in. We'd better hang on for Kenny, though: his party trick is naming Holland's 1974 World Cup squad.'

The Doctor ignored Winstone and moved towards the pile of crates, now neatly stacked by the lift. 'A consignment of arms for Shanks's private army of thugs and drug-pushers, no doubt?'

'Hey, man, what can I say? It's my job.'

'He's a bully, and a rogue. A third-division crook with inflated ideas of his own importance.'

'Possibly,' replied Winstone, indicating that the men should leave. 'But in this life, it's sometimes difficult to choose your friends.'

'You're an intelligent man –' began the Doctor.

'Damn right I am!' exploded Winstone. 'And in Hexen Bridge that's a curse worse than meeting the hollow men.'

The Doctor gave Trevor a quizzical look.

'A stupid West Country legend,' he continued, looking almost embarrassed. 'The point is, I don't have to justify myself to you, or anybody.'

'Except, perhaps, yourself,' said the Doctor sitting and casually turning on the television. 'Ah, *Men Behaving Badly*.'

'What exactly is that supposed to mean?' asked Winstone angrily, moving to the television and switching it off.

The Doctor ignored Winstone's question. 'How does Hatch fit into all of this?'

'Why didn't you ask him last night when you had the chance?'

'He's a complicated individual, isn't he?'

'Deep as the Earth's core is our Matt,' said Trevor, his anger subsiding. 'Listen, if he wants you in on the deal then that's fine, but you'll get nothing out of me. I'm just the poor bloody errand boy, all right?'

'"Do not all charms fly, at the mere touch of cold philosophy?"'

'Any fool can quote Keats,' said Trevor, turning away from the Doctor. 'What do you expect me to do? Trot out some Shelley, or some Shakespeare? Why should I play by your rules?'

'You fascinate me,' said the Doctor gently. 'Most of those in Hexen Bridge have been stunted by the limitation of the genetic pool. It's like society running in reverse. But you, you're different.'

'No,' said Trevor quickly. 'No, I am not. I'm just the same as all the rest.'

Suddenly the Doctor felt he was getting somewhere. 'Have you ever wondered why Hexen Bridge is so isolated?' he asked.

'Nobody likes us. We're different.'

'Yes, but…' Once again the Doctor heard the elevator coming up, and he knew that the moment had gone. The doors opened and Shanks stepped out, accompanied by the woman in the white dress.

'Get me a drink, Marla, love,' he said. 'Make it a double. I need it after that palaver. All right, Trev,' he continued, clapping his hands together. 'You've got the stuff?'

'Behind you,' said Winstone, nodding towards the boxes.

'Great,' said Shanks enthusiastically. 'The rocket launcher an' all?'

'It's in the top crate.'

'And it can bring down a chopper from a range of three thousand metres?'

'It could bring down Concorde from that distance,' replied Trevor coldly.

'Excellent!' said a delighted Shanks. 'That I've *got* to see.'

'Won't the Chief Constable be a little upset about that?' asked the Doctor.

Shanks laughed. He sat beside the Doctor and placed an arm around his shoulders. The Doctor noticed a fleck of blood on the man's face, and a few stray spots on his cream jacket.

'I'd get that dry-cleaned, if I were you,' said the Doctor. 'Blood's difficult to remove. Cut yourself shaving?'

'Do you know what?' said Shanks, with a sickly grin on his face. 'I think it's about time I put you to good use.'

'I don't believe I'm doing this,' moaned Steven Chen, not for the first time. His face was like the skull of the moon against the blackness of the graveyard.

'Oh, don't be so *yellow*,' snapped Ace. A look of horror crossed her face as she realised what she had said. Steven seemed hurt and bewildered, but made no comment.

Ace paused, not sure if an apology would make things worse. Angry with herself, she clambered over the low wall that ran around the back of the churchyard, the torch beam flashing in random directions. She looked back at Steven regretfully.

'You're weird,' said Steven, pulling himself over. The moment had gone.

'Listen, sunshine, compared to the locals, I'm flippin' well normal,' said Ace. She strolled up to the side entrance, a small door of oak studded with iron. 'This should be impressive.' She pulled what looked like a small lump of putty from her rucksack, and pushed it gently into the lock.

'Please tell me that isn't what I think it is,' said Steven, nervously glancing around him, although the church grounds were deserted but for the trailing shadows of the yew trees.

'It isn't,' said Ace. 'It's much better.' She placed a flat metal disc, no bigger than a watch battery, on the end of her finger, and showed it to Steven. 'Miniaturised timer and detonator.'

Steven paled.

'And this,' said Ace, holding up what seemed to be a thick patch of fabric, 'will make sure we don't wake up the whole village.'

'Oh, good,' said Steven. 'I'm glad. I'm standing here, in the middle of the night, about to break into a church, and I'm thinking to myself: Steven, we mustn't wake up the whole village. Oh no. We –'

'Steven?'

'Yes?'

'Shut up. You're getting hysterical.' And with that Ace slammed the pad and timer on to the explosive, and pulled Steven to one side. A moment later the church shook slightly, but there was no noise. It was as if the entire building had just suppressed a sneeze.

'I don't believe it,' said Steven, through clenched teeth.

Ace returned to the door. 'Oh, *smart*!' she exclaimed. The blackened pad had fallen to the ground, its job done. A wisp of smoke issued from the keyhole. 'Poor Mr Baber'll have to buy a new lock, but it's better than blowing the door to bits.'

Steven nodded in mute astonishment, and watched as Ace heaved open the door. She parted the thick velvet curtain immediately beyond, and strolled towards the aisle. There was some sort of security keypad towards the main entrance, and she tapped in some numbers. 'This switches off all the alarms. I watched what the vicar did with his fingers. Very useful if you want to borrow someone's PIN number.'

'You're outrageous,' said Steven.

'I know,' said Ace, turning towards the cupboard and the trunk in the back of the church. 'I'm looking for some photographs. The Rev said they were family snaps, but you wouldn't keep your shots of Margate beach under lock and key, would you?'

Suddenly Steven glanced nervously down the aisle. 'What was that?'

'What?'

'I thought I heard something.'

'Relax. If it's one of the villagers, we just leg it.' Ace paused, listening at the wind that shook the trees that surrounded the church. She sighed. 'Nothing. You're just jumpy.'

'I've never done this sort of thing before.'

'Part of growing up where I come from.'

'Not round here, it isn't.'

Ace rooted through the cupboard. 'Ah, here we are,' she said, pulling a sheaf of photographs from a shelf. She arranged them on the low table, glancing at pencil marks on the backs to place them in order. 'Interesting,' she said at last. 'Hexen Bridge, as photoed by Reverend Baber, and his dad before him.'

Each one was an elevated shot of the village, showing the clustered cottages and surrounding countryside.

'This one dates back to the 1940s,' said Ace. 'Just after the war.'

Despite the age of the photograph, Steven could see what had interested Ace. The ground surrounding the village was stained a darker colour than the outlying fields.

'What is that?' asked Steven. 'A different type of soil? Or a glitch in the processing?'

Ace pointed to the next one, from the mid-1950s. 'Whatever it is, it's bigger in this photo.' The picture was taken from a slightly different angle, but the dark, amorphous shape had clearly spread further. 'And in this one it's bigger still, and less circular.' The first colour photograph showed what seemed to be dark arms, trailing away from the village and under the soil.

'And this one's the most up to date,' said Steven. 'The dark stain is so large the edge is almost out of shot.'

'No wonder Baber wanted to hide these,' said Ace. 'They're seriously weird.'

Steven scratched his head, completely lost. 'I suppose it could just be some geological feature. A bit like those Roman forts that you can only see from the air.'

'What, one that moves?' scoffed Ace. She took up the pictures again, her face sombre. 'Hexen Bridge is right at the centre of something dark and nasty. And it's getting bigger all the time.'

* * *

Shanks's men held the Doctor down, clumsily tying a blindfold around his head and strapping something to his chest. Every verbal protest was met with a punch. The Doctor could *feel* Shanks in the background, orchestrating matters, but the men worked in mute obedience, dragging the Doctor through interminable echoing corridors before bundling him into a vehicle.

The seat beneath the Doctor was uncomfortable and basic, the Doctor concluding that he was in a van. The engine coughed into life at the third attempt. An ear-splitting metallic scream followed that could only have been garage doors opening. The van lurched forward.

The Doctor tried his best to count the junctions and corners along the way, but there was little else to indicate that they were travelling. The interior of the van seemed to have been soundproofed, and Shanks's men sat either side of the Doctor in complete silence.

'I've always enjoyed mystery tours,' said the Doctor brightly.

There was no response beyond a snort of irritation from one of Shanks's men.

The van began to slow, and the Doctor felt movement around him. He was about to ask if the journey was over when the sliding doors opened with a crash, and the Doctor found himself falling through space.

There was a blurred rush of fresh air and noise, then the awful impact of concrete on the Doctor's back.

He lay on the ground, dazed, for some moments. Then he tugged at the blindfold, desperate to ward off unconsciousness. Eventually his vision cleared, revealing a clock face at the top of an ornate tower. It was seven minutes to midnight. From the noise, he seemed to have ended up somewhere in the city centre.

The Doctor tried to move, and his head throbbed angrily. He'd have been better off battling the Cybermen or the Daleks. Human beings seemed to specialise in this type of mundane torture.

Young people were moving around him, shouting loudly. Some stopped to look at the Doctor, but their voices were distant. Only occasional words filtered through the haze.

'...all right, pal?'

'Lousy tramp.'

'Look at 'im...'

The Doctor finally pushed himself upright. It felt as if his head would explode.

'Where am I?' he asked, sitting with his face in his hands.

He hadn't expected anyone to answer.

'You're on Lime Street.'

The Doctor sat bolt upright. He put a hand to his ear and found the tiny metal speaker placed there.

'Don't try to shift it,' said the voice in his head. 'It's the only thing keeping you alive.'

The Doctor stood up, a frantic terror filling him. 'Can you hear me?' he whispered.

'That's a big Ten-Four!' It was Shanks's voice.

'Where are you?' asked the Doctor looking around him, bewildered.

'Nowhere close,' said Shanks. 'But that's immaterial. I can see every move you make. Down to business. If you care to check your midriff, you'll find about four pounds of high explosives strapped there. Enough to blow you into a million pieces, along with anybody else within a couple of hundred yards. So don't be a hero, at least for the sake of the innocent clubbers around you, OK?'

The Doctor found the Semtex taped to his stomach, glancing all the while at the oblivious people who streamed past him. 'You think you can bully your way to success, Shanks,' he said in a calm, cold voice. 'But you will fail. I promise you that.'

'Yeah, yeah, whatever,' said Shanks casually. 'Thing is, Doctor, I need you to do me a favour, and seeing as you're in the area...'

The Doctor felt his throat tighten as he considered the limited options open to him. 'What do you want me to do?' he asked cautiously.

'Half a block down on your right you'll see a nightclub called the Pit. Apt name. Run by a villain from the top estates called Corkhill who needs teaching a lesson...' Shanks's voice trailed away, and the Doctor began walking in the direction of the nightclub.

'What do you want me to do when I get there?'

'Go in, you soft get!'

'Would you like me to have a dance or two?' asked the Doctor. 'Only, you see, I'm a little out of practice.'

'Have a look in your pockets.'

The Doctor found a passport-sized photograph of a young woman and a roughly wrapped parcel. 'See the girl, right?' said Shanks. 'Stick the packet in her handbag while she's not looking.'

'What does it contain?' asked the Doctor.

'Half a pound of cheese,' said Shanks sarcastically. 'Use your imagination.'

'It's drugs, isn't it?'

'Like I said, cheese. Now get on with it, I haven't got all night.'

'How am I supposed to get in? I haven't got any money...'

'One of my boys is working the door tonight. I could have got him to do this for me, but he's not the sharpest pencil in the pencil case, you know what I mean?'

'And what if this young woman isn't there?'

'Oh, she is, Doc. I've made sure of that.'

'What next?' asked Steven Chen.

'Well,' said Ace, 'the latest photo's a couple of years old. Let's see what the state of play is now.'

'And how do you propose we do that?'

'Come on, dumbo, where'd you think these photos were taken from? I haven't seen a helipad at the vicarage.'

Steven looked around him. 'The church tower?'

Ace nodded, and led Steven Chen towards the winding stone staircase, half obscured by another thick red curtain. 'Last time I did this I was being chased by vampires.'

'Really?'

'Oh yes.' Ace's eyes, briefly caught by the torchlight, were hard and resolute.

The steps were cold and smooth under foot, and Steven had to steady himself many times on a metal handrail that had been hammered into the outer wall. By the time he reached the very top, through a small trapdoor that led out on to the flat surface of the tower, Ace was already scanning the horizon with a pair of khaki-coloured binoculars. 'Gulf War issue,' she said without a glance in Steven's direction. 'Makes night-time look like the middle of the day.'

Steven gingerly grasped the castellated wall. 'I'm not very good with heights,' he said.

'Don't be a wimp,' said Ace. 'Anyway, if you fell off now, at least you wouldn't be able to see the ground before you hit it.'

'Thanks,' said Steven through clenched teeth. 'So, what's out there?'

'It's difficult to make out that black mark, but I think I can see the edge. It's almost out of sight, going well beyond the copse over there. Look.' She handed the binoculars to Steven.

He fiddled with the rubberised controls for a moment. The churchyard, village and fields were all shaded an artificial green, but, as Ace had said, the detail was remarkable. He could see a young fox skipping between the gravestones and a single light left on in one of the cottages that shone like a beacon. The line where the black Hexen mark ended, and the surrounding, normal soil began, was just visible. He scanned the periphery of the dark stain, noticing that where it bisected fields scarecrows had been placed, as if they were marking some sort of boundary.

'You noticed the scarecrows?' he asked nervously.

'Yep,' said Ace.

He tracked along the ascending hills, following the edge of the shadowy area as it dipped slightly towards Hexen Bridge and the river that ran through it. In a field where he had expected some scarecrows there were only two wooden crosses, gaunt against the darkness.

Steven removed the binoculars from his eyes, handing them back to Ace. 'I think we'd better get out of here,' he said.

The Doctor descended the steps carefully, feeling his way forward in the gloom. If he tripped and fell the explosives might detonate, burying him and everyone else in the club under hundreds of tonnes of rubble.

At the bottom, the Doctor found himself in what had once been the cellar of an imposing Victorian hotel. While the Gothic façade of the building above the ground had long since crumbled, the subterranean chamber, with its ornate arches and sweeping ceiling, did retain a hint of ancient grandeur. Kaleidoscopic splashes of colour flickered over the walls. Ambient rhythms pulsed out of the large speakers placed around the room, reminding the Doctor of the fractal symphonies of the Third Draconian Era.

The nightclub thronged with young people. They came together in great jostling groups in front of the sweeping arcs of the main bars, spread out over the dance floor, and crowded around the tables and seats and potted plants. The Doctor watched as white-suited bouncers pushed through the crowds, their jaws jutting like Ogrons'. The Doctor knew that at least one of these individuals was working for Shanks. In fact, for all he knew, the gangster might be watching the pictures from the club's closed-circuit cameras in the back of the van.

'Right, ravers,' announced the DJ at the far end of the room. 'This is the sound of Heroin Sheikh, and "My Body is a Temple".'

The Doctor looked around, bewildered and powerless. The girl's face was locked in his mind, but it would take a while to find her.

'Excuse me,' the Doctor said to a man who passed. 'I'm looking for...' he began. But the man's eyes were glazed and he seemed not to hear.

The Doctor concluded that the people serving behind the bar would be best placed to help him in his search. He turned, and stumbled straight into the young woman he was looking for.

'I'm sorry,' said the girl, reaching out to steady the Doctor. 'Clumsy of me.'

'My fault entirely,' noted the Doctor with a charming smile, doffing his hat. 'In actual fact, I've been looking for you. A mutual friend has sent me with something for you.'

The darkened interior of the van was filled with surveillance equipment. Light from a monitor splashed over Shanks's face, framed by a set of headphones.

'You're not supposed to talk to her!' shouted Shanks into a microphone, linked to the tiny receiver in the Doctor's ear. 'Just give her the packet!'

Shanks could see the Doctor on the screen in front of him. The little man glanced around, as if looking for the CCTV cameras. Then he and the girl disappeared behind a column. 'What are you playing at, Doc?' screamed Shanks into the microphone. 'I told you, one false move and the place goes up.' He turned to one of the men at his side. 'Get Dean to move in. I need to know what the Doctor's doing,' he ordered.

The Doctor put a finger to his lips, quelling the girl's surprise. With the piece of pencil lead under his nail, he scribbled on to a beer mat: 'Important. We are in danger.'

'Well,' said the Doctor brightly. 'I have a gift for you. But you mustn't unwrap it yet.'

'Go along with what I say,' he wrote.

'OK,' said the girl, the uncertainty obvious in her voice. The Doctor was just hoping that she'd humour him for a few moments. 'Who's it from?' she added lamely.

'Ken,' said the Doctor instantly.

'Ah,' said the girl. 'I remember Ken.'

Shanks switched off his microphone and cursed loudly. 'What's he playing at?' he asked rhetorically.

'Shall we detonate?' asked a man at his side.

'No,' snapped Shanks. 'That's not what I had planned. Denman has to *really* suffer.'

'So…?'

'So, has the Doctor passed on the merchandise?'

'Dean's not sure.'

'Plan B, then,' said Shanks. 'Tell Jane to move.'

The Doctor handed over an imaginary parcel. 'There you are,' he said.

The girl clearly considered the Doctor a harmless lunatic. 'Er, thanks,' she said, pretending to pocket something just as one of the bouncers burst through a crowd of people. He stared at them, mouthing something into a walkie-talkie, then swept past a moment later as if he'd not seen them at all.

'Now, I really must be going,' said the Doctor, raising his hat again.

He walked as quickly as he could towards the exit. He had gambled on the fact that Kenny Shanks hated his plans being interfered with so much that he wouldn't actually detonate the bomb; that the explosives were there simply to intimidate the Doctor, and to incriminate him later. But he couldn't rely on a man as erratic and violent as Shanks. He had to get out.

A young woman stumbled into him as she skirted the expansive dance floor. The Doctor reached out an arm to steady her. 'I do beg your pardon.'

'No worries,' said the girl with a smile.

'He *thinks* the package was handed over, boss.'

'Cretin!' exploded Shanks. 'I'm not falling for that song-and-dance. Get the law in there, now.'

* * *

Jane sidled up to Nicola cautiously, one hand in her pocket, resting on the package she'd lifted from the small man in the pale suit. It hadn't been difficult to steal the parcel from the man, but then it was Jane's pickpocketing skills that had first brought her to Shanks's attention. When Jane was twelve, she had started stealing old women's purses as a dare. She didn't need the money, but she craved the buzz.

Then one day she'd been caught by a plain-clothes security man running through the automatic doors of Marks & Spencer. When the police investigated her room, they found hundreds of wallets and purses, many of them still crammed full of money. Her friends had said she'd be sent to borstal, but Shanks got her off with a weak rebuke from a greedy magistrate.

She'd been paying him back ever since.

Nicola's back was turned, her handbag hanging half open at her side. Holding her breath, Jane pushed at the zip, then gently lowered the package into place. With a trailing hand, she pulled at the zip again, walking around in front of Nicola. 'Who was that I saw you with?'

'Oh, just some nutter,' said Nicola. 'Off his head.'

Jane was about to say something when she became aware of a commotion behind them. Uniformed figures were descending the stairs.

'Damn' she said. 'Looks like another raid.' In truth, she was just glad to be shot of the package – you didn't have to be Einstein to work out what it contained.

Nicola Denman swore under her breath. 'If Daddy gets to hear about this...'

'Oh dear,' said the Doctor, standing at the bottom of the stairs. Four policeman blocked his way.

'Stay where you are, shorty,' said one, putting a hand on the Doctor's chest.

'No, you don't understand,' said the Doctor, pulling his jacket open. 'I have a bomb about my person. You must clear the area immediately.'

The policemen were looking at the packages and wires strapped to the Doctor's torso with a mixture of incredulity and terror. The Doctor supposed that none of them had seen a bomb before.

'Are you mental or something?' asked one angrily.

'I really am most desperately sorry about this,' said the Doctor, tugging at the wires attached to the plastic explosive. 'But I do suggest you clear the area. *Now*.' The Doctor concentrated on pulling the wires from the detonator, trying to remember what Ace had shown him. He expected at any moment to feel the searing heat of an explosion, but nothing happened. As he removed the final wire and breathed out slowly, he heard a faint chuckle in his head.

The Doctor scooped the tiny transmitter from his ear, and looked at it closely. It was immediately knocked from his hands as he was grabbed by two of the police officers and bundled to the ground.

'You do not have to say anything,' stated someone standing over the Doctor as handcuffs locked around his wrists, 'but it may harm your defence if you do not mention when questioned something that you later rely on in court. Anything you do say may be given in evidence.'

'You're making a terrible mistake,' he spluttered as he was dragged to his feet. Around him he could see other policemen questioning the young people in the club. He noticed the young woman he had spoken to earlier. An officer was pulling something from the girl's handbag, and a look of horror was spreading across her face.

'That shouldn't be there!' the Doctor shouted across the club just as someone pulled the plugs on the music. 'That woman is innocent.' The Doctor tried to reach into his jacket pocket, despite the cuffs that bit into his wrists. 'Look, I was given a –'

One of the constables punched the Doctor in the stomach.

'I am not resisting arrest,' the Doctor said through gritted teeth.

'Yes you are,' said the senior officer. 'Bring the girl. And anyone else in possession.' The policeman's grip on the Doctor's arm tightened as he was propelled towards the club stairs.

CHAPTER 7
DOWN IN THE POLICE STATION AT MIDNIGHT

Phil Burridge left the vicarage as easily as he had entered, climbing down the tree and then heading for home. He stopped off at the Green Man on the way.

When finally he pushed open his front door he found the house in darkness. A lingering smell indicated that Cheryl had tried to keep a meal warm for him and then surrendered it to the flames. It was probably another lasagne. Phil Burridge hated foreign food. When would that stupid cow realise that you can't beat pork chop and chips?

A clock chiming the darkness of the sitting room reminded him of the time, and Burridge switched on his mobile phone, hoping to leave a message at Hatch's office.

'Damn and blast it,' he muttered. The signal was too weak, so he pushed his way towards the back of the house, wandering out on to the patio. The garden beyond was a tip, a rambling sprawl of rusted furniture and enthusiastic weeds. The clouds parted, allowing moonlight to splash down on to the path.

Burridge held the small phone to his ear, kicking aside an old wheelbarrow which hit the ground with a rending clatter. The recorded announcement of an answering machine interrupted the ringing tone, and Burridge paused, waiting to leave his message.

'All right, Matt,' he said, opening the garden gate and walking through. 'I did what you asked me to, and, yes, *she* is linked to *you know what.*' A grin stretched across his broad features. 'I've got what you need – I'll fax it to you tomorrow. Just give me a bell.'

Burridge terminated the call, and folded the mobile into his pocket. He'd wandered a little way down the hill, close to where some straggling trees hid in a chalky hollow. The air was clean and fresh here, and Burridge breathed deeply, waiting for his head to clear. When he was younger he could have handled ten or more pints in an evening, no problem. Now, it seemed, the merest sniff of alcohol made him muggy-headed.

For the first time Burridge noticed movement at the bottom of the hill. A bush was twitching frantically, as if an animal had become trapped. Burridge was not the sort of man to cringe at the thought of an animal suffering, but he was pragmatic: if a lamb was stuck there, well, he was just the man to put the creature out of its misery. And there was always plenty of mint sauce in the larder. He cautiously approached the twitching knot of thick brambles, but in the darkness it was difficult to see what was going on. Burridge reached out with his hands, gingerly parting the branches.

Without warning, something moved at his feet. Burridge glanced down, expecting to see a fox or a rabbit darting for cover.

The ground was moving.

Burridge leapt away in horror. A long strip of land, with the bush at its centre, was writhing. It was as if an enormous snake was struggling just below the dark soil.

His eyes now accustomed to the gloom, Burridge could see the true extent of the moving *thing*. It stretched from back towards his house, down to the bottom of the hill, right across a flattish piece of scrub land, and then out over the fields beyond. And suddenly Burridge saw that other patches of ground, far off to his left and right, were twitching and shuddering.

Obeying some wordless instinct, Burridge found himself trudging alongside the shifting earth, following the trail of the movement.

He walked for a mile or more, coming finally to a small meadow overlooking Hexen Bridge. The moonlight seemed to cut the field in two: a darker area, towards the village, and lighter ground beyond. There was frenzied movement at the intersection between the two.

A mass of tentacles and ill-formed limbs reared up from the dark soil.

Burridge stumbled closer. He glimpsed plantlike fronds and dripping, insect legs, mottled by what seemed to be... faces? And hands?

His stomach churning, he turned to run, and blundered straight into a human shape that smelled of straw and damp cloth. Phil Burridge let out a cry of surprise, staggering backward. Then he laughed.

It was just a motionless scarecrow, gaunt and impassive in the darkness. He must have become disorientated, and stumbled towards the edge of the field and into the shadowy manikin.

Phil Burridge turned away, and hands of straw and flesh flew towards his throat.

The Doctor was thrown into a police van that smelled of alcohol, urine and dogs. Other people were being bundled in and, through the mêlée, the Doctor could just make out the face of the girl. She had sad eyes, big and brown. The Doctor felt something he had rarely experienced during his travels through the cosmos: shame.

'That woman has not –' he began to say, but again he was forced into silence by a well-placed blow to his body.

'You her pimp, or what?' asked one of the young constables with a snarl.

The Doctor remained silent. There would be no reasoning with these people in the mood that they were in. As far as they were concerned, he was a criminal, a deranged man who had endangered the lives of innocent people. He looked across at the girl as the van doors banged shut. She was staring out of the back window, her eyes brimming with tears.

Two burly constables sat on either side of the Doctor, digging their elbows into his sides.

'I'll tell you everything I know about Shanks,' said the Doctor, which certainly seemed to capture the attention of the police officers in the van. 'But let the girl go.'

'No deal, sunshine,' said a man in an expensive suit sitting opposite the Doctor. 'Possession is nine-tenths of the law…' He guffawed loudly and his colleagues joined in with sycophantic sniggers. 'Right, Frank,' he shouted, banging the grille behind the driver's seat. 'Let's get these scumbags down to the shop and have some fun!'

Steven Chen pulled the thick curtain back across the stairwell. 'So, what's it all mean?' he asked, his voice echoing through the empty church like a bell.

Ace shrugged. 'Dunno. But it's well weird, and that's enough to interest the Professor.' She walked towards the side door, the torch illuminating the plaques and stone caskets that lined the wall.

'Maybe we should ask Reverend Baber about the photos,' said Steven, hurrying after her.

Ace snorted. 'What, and admit that we broke into the church? No thanks.' She reached the side door, and pulled it open.

Something stood in the doorway, something that had once been human, but had changed beyond all recognition. It was a stickman, a puppet stuffed full of straw and corn and grass – but the dark eyes, just visible through what seemed to be a mask of roughly stitched leather, were alive with a sadness that was human, corrupted by an evil that was not.

Two hands shot upward, spraying ears of corn. Ace glimpsed twigs and bone, wrapped with ill-fitting skin.

She slammed the door shut. Next to the archway was an ornate chair, and she jammed it up against the thick planks of oak. 'Give me a hand!' she exclaimed.

Steven was as motionless as the scarecrow had seemed, his eyes wide and uncomprehending. Only his lips moved. 'It's… It's…'

'Course it is,' snapped Ace as blows rained down on the door. 'Help me wedge this door shut!'

Steven shook himself from his reverie, and ran towards the baptismal font. The simple stone construction had an ornately carved top that resembled a fantasy castle's spired turret. With grunts of exertion, he heaved the cover into the air, rolling it towards Ace, who was trying to keep the chair in position. Steven wedged the font top between the door lock and a fluted stone column that ran up into the rafters.

'Can't you just blow that thing up?' shouted Steven.

'I didn't bring any more Nitro with me,' said Ace, just as a straw-covered fist punched through the wooden door.

'Turn out your pockets, sir,' said the duty sergeant. The Doctor was in the charge room, a red-bricked alcove next to the cells which held most of the people arrested at the club. The people around him whooped and hollered as if a trip to the police station was part of the evening's entertainment. Only the young woman was silent, her dark eyes blinking back the tears.

'I wish it to be noted,' said the Doctor, 'that Shanks tried to force me to plant some drugs on that young lady. She is wholly innocent. Somehow, Shanks must have taken the drugs off me and implicated the young woman.'

'So the drugs were yours?' queried the well-dressed CID officer. 'That'll send you down for a long time.'

'Handful of heartbeats to a Time Lord,' said the Doctor.

'What?' asked the man angrily. 'Turn out your pockets.'

'Of course,' said the Doctor with a smile. 'You'll have to bear with me, gentlemen, this may take some time.'

Nicola Denman was the first person to be taken to the interview room. She wondered if they were showing her preferential treatment – that an observant officer had already twigged who her father was – but the force with which she was propelled into the bare brick room belied any comforting thoughts of bias. In a way, she was pleased. Perhaps there was a way of getting out of this without Daddy even knowing.

It was the feeblest of hopes, but it was all that kept her going.

She watched as a couple of audio cassettes were unwrapped by a uniformed policewoman, the cellophane crackling like fire. Moments later the twin tape deck was running.

'DC Fielder questioning female suspect,' said the policeman for the benefit of the recording. 'WPC Murphy also in attendance.' He glanced at the big clock on the wall. 'It's ten past midnight, Tuesday the seventeenth of June.' He turned his tired eyes towards Nicola. 'Right, these are just some preliminary questions, but what happens over the next few hours depends on the quality of the answers I receive. Understand?'

She nodded silently.

'Name?'

She shook her head.

'Name?' The officer paused. 'Look, you're not helping yourself, you know. We've got enough evidence to hang you out to dry. The drugs in your handbag were dealer-quantities. We want to know where you got them from.'

'I've never taken drugs in my life.'

'That's not the question I asked.'

'They were planted on me. They must have been.'

'Really? By whom?'

'There was a small man in a white suit. I thought he was a bit weird.'

'He was carrying enough explosives to bring the roof down. Are you two working together?'

'I've never seen him before in my life.'

'Come off it!'

Nicola was close to tears. 'I'm telling the truth. I didn't even want to go out clubbing tonight.'

The WPC leaned across the table towards her. 'Do you want a lawyer? Is there someone in your family we can phone?' Good cop, bad cop.

'No,' said Nicola vehemently. 'Like I said. I don't want anyone to know.'

'Everyone will know about this, soon enough,' said the male officer, grinning. 'You can make it easier for yourself if you tell us who your supplier is. We're not so interested in you. It's the main channels we're interested in.'

'I've told you. I don't know anything about drugs. I'm not saying anything else.'

The man turned to the WPC. 'Better take her away and search her again. Send the next one in on your way out.'

The desk sergeant, one of the young constables, and the bemused CID officer watched as the Doctor completed his search through his pockets. He looked down at his worldly possessions. 'There,' he said proudly. 'That's the lot.'

The desk sergeant removed a brown, padded envelope from the drawer and gave it to the constable. 'You hold them up while I write them in the book,' he said. 'One yo-yo. Blue. One bag of...' He paused and looked inside.

'Jelly babies,' said the Doctor, brightly. 'Would you like one?'

The desk sergeant grunted loudly and carried on with his list. 'One Swiss Army penknife.'

'Very useful in a tight corner,' said the Doctor. 'Though I've never found a proper use for the implement that takes the stones out of horses' hooves...' He noted the black looks on the faces of the three policemen and fell silent.

'One teddy bear.' The desk sergeant raised an amused eyebrow.

'Sentimental attachment,' said the Doctor with embarrassment.

'One...' The sergeant reached out for the peculiar piece of electronic equipment the constable was holding. He looked at the Doctor quizzically.

'Oh, that's an etheric beam locator. Also useful for detecting ion-charge emissions.'

'I'm sure,' said the sergeant.

'Smart arse,' muttered the arresting officer.

The list continued. Eventually the desk sergeant reached for another envelope. The mound of objects on the desk in front of him was threatening to topple on to the floor. He held up the TARDIS key. 'What's this?'

'A key,' said the Doctor.

'To what?'

'A door.'

The CID man grabbed the Doctor by the hair and pushed his face towards the desk. 'Just you wait till I get you in them cells, pint-size.'

'May I remind you,' said the Doctor, between gasps of pain, 'of the 1982 Police and Criminal Evidence Act?'

'Some sort of lawyer, are you?' asked the sergeant, casting a wary look at the CID man.

'I have practised law,' said the Doctor, straightening himself up as the officer let go of him. 'Would it be possible for these matters to be dealt with as quickly as possible?' the Doctor asked. 'I'm keen to begin my confession.'

'All in good time, sir,' noted the desk sergeant. 'There are a few particulars I require first. Could you sign here to confirm that this is your property?'

The Doctor did so, his mark producing another angry exclamation from the two men behind him. The desk sergeant, however, had seen it all in his time. 'Thank you, sir,' he said, tipping the various items into the envelope. 'Now, may I have your name, please?'

'John Smith,' said the Doctor with a nervous glance at his feet.

'Thank you, Mr Smith.'

'Doctor,' corrected the Doctor.

'Thank you, Dr Smith. Address?'

'No fixed abode.'

'Occupation?'

The Doctor said nothing. How could he explain his lifestyle in words that these people would understand? Saviour of the universe? No... possibly not.

'Unemployed?' suggested the desk sergeant.

'I wouldn't say that, exactly. I was once a scientific adviser at the United Nations Intelligence Taskforce…'

'No gainful employment,' wrote the sergeant firmly.

'All right, Dr Smith,' smiled the arresting officer. 'You have been charged with possession of explosives with intent to injure. Your right to representation has been explained to you. Do you understand all of that?'

'Yes, yes,' said the Doctor quickly. 'That doesn't matter. Listen to me. I have only two things I wish to say at this time. Firstly, I can state, categorically, that the young woman is completely innocent, and she should be released instantly.'

'And the second?' asked the incredulous desk sergeant. The Doctor glanced around, but the woman was nowhere to be seen.

'I would like to speak to Mr Denman as soon as possible.'

The CID man seemed amused by this. 'I'm sure you'll appreciate how busy the Chief is,' he noted. 'And, I'm sure you'll also appreciate how little he enjoys being frigged about by toerags like you.'

'I think he'll want to speak to me,' said the Doctor. 'Tell him, I know everything there is to know about Kenny Shanks.'

In cell number 9, Nicola Denman sat hunched on a hard wooden bench, shivering. After the first – brief – interview, she had been taken into the cells by two women officers who had strip-searched her. When it was clear that she was still refusing to talk, the WPCs had thrown a rough woollen blanket at her. They took most of her clothes away.

The hours passed, slowly. Her hands idly tore at the blanket. She knew what she had to do.

There was a tube of lipstick on the floor, under the bunk. It was covered with dust and seemed to have been there for months. The colour was a sickly shade of mauve, and Nicola smiled as she ran a finger over the tip. It came away purple, coloured like a bruise.

She stood up and walked towards the cell door.

* * *

The Doctor had been in the interview room for three hours. His initial questioning had been with the CID man, Hill. But this had proved fruitless and frustrating for both parties. The Doctor had waived the right to be represented by a solicitor, but then parried every question asked of him and demanded, again and again, to see Denman.

After half an hour Hill had stopped the interview tape and threatened the Doctor with much physical violence. The Doctor had fixed the policeman with a cold stare and said, 'You're a better man than that, detective.'

'What?'

'You don't have to be so angry about everything. I know what you see every day. I know about the drugs, the violence, the child abuse, the death. I know there are days when it seems as though the whole world is divided into the police and everyone else, and that everyone else is a criminal. But it's not as black and white as that, you know.'

'I don't know where you picked up your degree in philosophy,' Hill had said, cynically.

'Vienna,' the Doctor had replied.

'Yeah. Right,' noted Hill, standing. 'To be continued…'

When Hill returned with a bacon sandwich and two cups of coffee, he had another officer with him. This one, called McMahon, asked the Doctor more or less the same questions as his colleague. And the Doctor gave the same replies. Eventually McMahon got tired, too.

'You realise that we've got enough on you to put you away for ten years?' he asked yet again.

'Yes,' said the Doctor. 'As I've already told you, several times, I don't care about that. I'll take whatever punishment you think is fitting. I would just like to talk to Mr Denman.'

'And suppose Mr Denman was here,' said a voice from the door behind the Doctor. 'What would you tell him?'

'I'd tell him that Kenneth Shanks is laughing at him.'

Denman walked past the Doctor to the other side of the desk, McMahon and Hill standing to allow him to pass. He sat down, facing the Doctor.

'Three sixteen a.m., Chief Constable Denman joins the questioning,' he said, for the benefit of the audio tape whirring away by the Doctor. 'So, you're Smith.'

'The Doctor. You probably don't remember me.'

'Should I?'

'I helped you put the chain back on your Raleigh Chopper in 1971,' said the Doctor.

'I was seven in 1971,' said Denman.

'I know,' said the Doctor. 'And you lived at Riverboat Cottage in Hexen Bridge with your father, Harold, and your mother, Lily. You also had a younger sister, whose name escapes me for the moment, but she died in infancy.'

Denman stood up. 'You're wasting my time,' he said and headed for the door.

'Then I met you again in 1984 or 1985. You had just joined the force. We had a walk by the river, close to the old wooden bridge, and you told me that one day you wanted to be Chief Constable of Avon and Somerset, but that promotion opportunities were limited in the area, and you might have to move. And my friend Tegan slipped on the bridge and injured her ankle and you carried her back to the school grounds.'

Denman paused. 'The Doctor...?'

'And you said, "If you're ever passing, drop in and say hello."' The Doctor smiled broadly. 'Hello.'

'You look nothing like the Doctor,' said Denman.

'You've changed a bit yourself in twenty-five years. Nevertheless, I *am* the Doctor.'

Denman returned to his seat and looked up at McMahon and Hill. 'Take a break for five minutes, lads,' he said and nodded towards the door. 'Actually, make it ten.'

'I'm glad you remember me,' said the Doctor as the two officers closed the door.

Denman reached across to switch off the tape recorder. 'It isn't going to help,' he said. 'I can't drop serious charges like these just because I've met you.'

'Those explosives were strapped around me by Kenneth Shanks. I was told to go to that club, or he would set them off,' said the Doctor.

Denman looked at the Doctor's face closely, as if searching for evidence of a lie.

'Knowing that piece of scum, I believe you. But...'

'Evidence?' said the Doctor sadly. 'Unfortunately, the communication device he gave me was lost when your officers arrested me.' The Doctor leaned forward. 'Hexen Bridge,' he said. 'Funny place.'

'Hilarious.'

'You know what I mean. Insular. Sinister.'

'Your point being...?'

'Are you sterile, Mr Denman?'

Denman looked as though he was about to hit the Doctor, and the Time Lord flinched. Then the policeman glanced away, clearly embarrassed.

'I'll take that as a "yes",' said the Doctor.

'If you must know,' said Denman after a moment's silence, 'ever since I left Hexen Bridge.'

'Interesting, wouldn't you say?'

'I'm not sure I follow you.'

The Doctor stood up and put both hands on the table in front of Denman, his fingers spread out like a spider's web. 'The taint of Hexen Bridge is very strong. Everything's connected, I'm sure. The school, the cleverness of the children, the lack of other villages around it...'

Denman laughed. 'You'll be telling me Jack i' the Green is behind it all next.'

'What?'

'A village legend,' said Denman.

'Tell me more.'

'There was a massacre.'

'When?'

'Seventeenth century. Judge Jeffreys and his black-shirts rode into town, rounded up every man over the age of fourteen and threw them into a pit in the village green.'

The Doctor nodded. 'I read something about this. Years ago. And Jack?'

'You don't talk about Jack in Hexen Bridge.'

'We're not *in* Hexen Bridge, Mr Denman.'

Denman paused, glancing around the room. 'Some say there's a force in the green,' he said at last. 'That he... it... controls the village.' Denman stopped and shook his head. 'Stupid country legends,' he said.

'Someone was telling me about the hollow men earlier,' said the Doctor.

'Yes, that's another one. Scarecrows. Good stories to frighten the children...'

'Shanks is planning to wage war against you, you know,' said the Doctor with another dizzying change of subject. 'I've seen the weaponry. Part of a huge consignment bought from a man called Winstone.'

Denman seemed unfazed by this revelation, nodding as if this was old news. 'With our beloved Minister of Defence acting as broker,' said the policeman. 'Of course, we'd never be able to prove *his* involvement. He's the uncrowned King of Not Getting Caught. Trevor, on the other hand, we could perhaps implicate, with your help.'

'Yes,' said the Doctor sadly. 'A pity. A man of great promise.'

'Oh, I know,' said Denman. 'I don't like trying to imprison my relatives.'

'Cousin?' asked the Doctor.

'Three or four times removed. So is Hatch. Still, the law shows no favours to kith or kin.'

'Indeed,' agreed the Doctor. 'I am very keen to help you. I think there's much more going on here than a bit of gunrunning. Hatch wouldn't involve himself in something so mundane.' The Doctor paused. 'But there are two conditions.'

'Go on,' said the policeman suspiciously.

'That the charges against me are dropped. I won't be able to help you pursue Shanks if I'm stuck behind bars.'

Denman nodded slowly. 'If you agree to testify against Shanks, and anyone else we can implicate, then I can recommend that to the CPS. And the other condition?'

'There was a young woman arrested at the same time as I was,' said the Doctor. 'She had drugs in her bag. Shanks tried to force me to put a package there, but I refused. He found another way. I give you my word that she is completely innocent. She should be released instantly. She must be terrified.' He removed a photograph from inside the sleeve of his jacket, where it had evaded the scrutiny of the arresting officers, and pushed it across the table to Denman. 'I have no idea why Shanks should want to hurt her.'

Denman glanced at the photograph, then jumped to his feet, the chair screeching against the polished floor. He ran from the room.

The Doctor stood up. The door was wide open. He walked out into the corridor, finding himself facing the desk sergeant.

'Can you tell me which way Mr Denman went?' he asked.

'Where'd you spring from, Dillinger?' said the sergeant.

'I was talking to the Chief Constable, and he suddenly –'

There was a cry of horror from further down the corridor.

The Doctor ran down the gloomy passageway, the sergeant at his heels. He found Denman crouched in a cell doorway, being forcibly restrained by other officers. He was shouting, hoarsely. Beyond him, some policemen were cutting down the body of a girl which hung limply from the ceiling.

CHAPTER 8

THE SOUND OF SOMEONE YOU LOVE WHO'S GOING AWAY AND IT DOESN'T MATTER

The scarecrow's hand pushed through the fractured hole. The fingers were formed from intertwined flesh and stick; the tattered arm of the shirt revealed stalks of corn, arranged as veins. Tiny rust-coloured leaves fell like blood when the hand snagged on sharp splinters of wood.

Steven Chen backed away from the doorway. 'What is that thing?'

Ace swung round, inadvertently blinding her companion with the torch. 'You've seen *Night of the Living Dead*, right?' She glanced around the dark church. Ill-defined shapes pressed against the windows along one wall. Twigs scratched against the stained glass. Ace ran into the small northern aisle, seeking weapons or an escape route. 'They don't seem to have got around here yet,' she said, pointing to the windowed arches that ran along the wall. She jumped on to a pew, peering through the glass at the churchyard beyond.

'Of course!' exclaimed Steven. 'That part of the graveyard is completely enclosed. The wall must be holding them back.'

'Give me a hand with this, then,' said Ace. At the far end of the aisle was a brass lectern in the shape of an enormous eagle with wings spread aloft. Ace glanced at the ornate Bible, open at Isaiah. *Those who hope in the Lord will renew their strength. They will soar on wings like eagles.*

Ace threw the book on to the floor. With Steven's help, she hefted the lectern into the air, and manoeuvred it towards the nearest window. With some difficulty they hurled it through.

The window exploded, raining coloured glass and lead on to the ground outside. Ace kicked at the hole with her boots. 'Come on!' she said impatiently, pushing Steven forward.

The side door of the church burst open.

'How is he?' asked the Doctor as his cell door opened slowly.

Hill stood, silhouetted in the light of the corridor. 'About as well as can be expected for a man who'll have to bury his only child.'

'Where is he now?'

'At home. Half the middle management in the region is with him. It's sickening.'

The Doctor nodded, encouraging Hill to go on.

'He's asked for you,' said the policeman. 'He wants to talk.'

The Doctor got to his feet. 'Responsibility for one's actions,' he said, marching towards the door, 'comes from the absolute belief in the validity of what one does. Do you understand?'

Hill stared back at him blankly. 'I don't think I understand anything any more.'

Hill drove the Doctor in silence through the leafy suburbs of Liverpool as the dawn skies grew brighter around them. Denman's house was a mock-Tudor-fronted building set within two acres of rich, rolling lawns. The Doctor strode up the gravel drive towards the front door and tipped his hat to a young-looking WPC. She instinctively moved to bar his entry, but then saw Hill behind, and the look of tired wisdom in the Doctor's eyes, and stepped aside.

The Doctor walked towards the living room, and found it full of men with glasses in their hands, standing around looking bewildered and anxious. The room was thick with their cigarette smoke and the sound of coughing.

'Right, all of you, out of here,' the Doctor announced. Amazingly, most of the men shuffled towards the door, as though they had been waiting for someone to take charge.

One man stayed with Denman. The Chief Constable was sitting on a beige couch, a look of crushed innocence on his face. The man with him stood and moved towards the Doctor, holding out a hand.

'Deputy Chief Constable Savage,' he said briskly.'And you are…?'

'A friend,' said the Doctor, moving past the man without acknowledging his outstretched hand. Hill, who had followed the Doctor into the room, gave Savage a respectful sideways glance but otherwise said nothing.

Denman looked up as the Doctor approached. The policeman had that same faraway look that the Doctor had seen in the eyes of men suffering from shell shock in the First World War, and on the faces of the victims of the sonic massacres in fifty-first-century Brisbane. Some things didn't change through time.

'You came,' he said, his voice thin and wasted.

'Of course,' said the Doctor, sitting beside Denman. 'You should try to get some rest.'

'I'm all right,' said Denman.

'No you're not.' The Doctor tapped the glass of whisky in Denman's hand. 'You should either drink that, or pour it in the sink. Don't sit there playing with it.'

'You're right,' said Denman, downing the drink in one. Colour began to flood back into his cheeks.'She was…' he began, but got no further.

'I know,' said the Doctor, as Denman crumpled into his arms. The Doctor held him tightly, as Denman buried his head against the little man's shoulder. Savage and Hill fidgeted nervously. 'Put the kettle on,' said the Doctor, and both men moved simultaneously to the door, their expressions mirroring each other's embarrassment.

Denman raised his head, his eyes red and swollen, his face wet with tears.'Why?' he asked, as if a simple answer to that question would make everything all right again.

'The message she left was quite clear,' replied the Doctor in a soft voice, remembering the terse words written in lipstick on the cell wall. 'That "they" were getting at you through her.'

'Shanks?'

'Yes. And she wanted to save you in the only way she could,' said the Doctor. He paused. 'You had a close relationship?'

'Yes. It was perfect.'

'No relationship is ever perfect,' stated the Doctor brutally.

He could almost see the memories passing across Denman's tear-stained face. 'If there were... problems, it was because of Hexen Bridge.'

'No,' said the Doctor firmly. 'You can't blame everything on your heritage. None of us can. We each have to accept a measure of responsibility.'

Denman shook his head against the gentle pressure of the Doctor's words. 'But I tried so hard to protect her.'

'Perhaps too hard,' said the Doctor. He sighed. It was too late for recriminations. 'Ah, look,' he said brightly, as Savage and Hill came back into the room. 'Tea.'

'And then, when she was fourteen, she broke her collarbone doing gymnastics at school,' said Denman, the trace of a smile playing at the corner of his mouth. He stopped. 'I'm sorry,' he said, 'I've got to take a leak. Help yourself to more tea.'

When he had climbed the stairs, Hill and Savage both looked accusingly at the Doctor, who continued to sip Earl Grey from a mug.

'What the hell are you playing at?' said Savage angrily. 'It can't be right, encouraging him to bare his soul like this.'

'I disagree,' said the Doctor.

'And you're an expert, are you?' countered Hill.

'As it happens, yes,' replied the Doctor. 'But that really isn't the point. He's lost the one thing in the world that mattered to him. To deny she ever existed would be to seal over a broken heart with an Elastoplast.'

Savage stood and paced the room. 'I want to know who you are, for a start,' he said, menacingly.

'Me?' said the Doctor. 'Oh, I'm just a traveller...'

From above them there came the sound of a flushing toilet and the heavy footfall of Denman descending the stairs.

'Now, where were we?' he said, arriving at the living-room door with a weak smile on his face. 'More tea?'

'Ian,' said Savage, 'for Christ's sake...'

Denman looked at Savage curiously. 'No tea, then. Something stronger?'

Savage shook his head in exasperation. 'Who is that man?' he demanded, pointing at the Doctor.

'That's the Doctor,' said Denman. 'He's going to help us catch Kenny Shanks.'

'And how the hell is he going to do that?' continued Savage.

'Breaking and entering,' announced the Doctor sharply.

'The man's mad,' said Savage.

'No,' cut in Denman. 'It's us that have been mad. We should have gone after Shanks *years* ago. It might have saved us a lot of grief – and a few lives.'

Ace and Steven sprinted into the churchyard, dwarfed by the gravestones and carved angels painted a sulphurous yellow by the approaching dawn. A wall encircled the area, beyond which glimmered the village's few street lights. The wind brushed through the yew trees, bringing the sounds of movement from within the church.

'I'll give you a bunk up,' said Steven, locking his hands together as he stood at the base of the wall.

'And then what'll you do?'

He paused, ignoring her question and glancing back at the church. 'Am I dreaming, Ace, or is this really happening?'

'It's all seriously real.' Ace pushed the torch into her rucksack, and threw it over the wall. It landed with a satisfyingly soft thud.

'How big's the drop?' Ace asked.

'Only one way to find out,' replied Steven.

'OK,' said Ace, placing her foot in Chen's hands. With a grunt he hoisted her upward. The wall, bleached by the elements, had crumbled in places, but the covering of ivy and grass held it together. Ace pushed her boot into a gap where the mortar had fallen away, and pulled herself on to the top of the wall. She reached down towards Chen. 'Grab my hand and...'

Her words trailed away. Back towards the church, a dark figure was tugging itself through the hole in the window.

'What's the matter?' queried Steven.

'Nothing,' said Ace hurriedly, looking back towards Chen. 'Just get up here. *Now.*'

Steven held on to Ace's arm. She could feel his pulse racing.

Behind him, the straw man stepped into the graveyard, and began trudging in their direction.

The sound of breaking glass, though muffled by a thick woollen sweater, seemed enormously loud in the darkened corridor of the office building.

Denman withdrew the sweater and reached carefully through the smashed pane, fumbling around for the lock. 'Damnation,' Denman said as the door refused to budge. 'Hang on.' He lifted a size-ten boot and kicked at the door. Once. Twice. Three times. Finally, it burst inward.

'Subtle as a bloody brick,' said Hill, shaking his head. 'Mr Savage told me not to let you do anything stupid, you know,' he said as the Doctor followed Denman into the office of Stanley Road Holdings, the front company for Shanks's organisation. 'My pension could be on the line here!'

Denman ignored him. 'The night watchman should be here around seven a.m.,' he said, checking his watch. 'We've got fifteen minutes at most.'

Hill moved to the window, looking down the eighteen storeys

to the car park below. 'Shanks is hardly going to leave anything incriminating lying around.'

'That remains to be seen,' said the Doctor, opening the filing cabinet closest to the door with a bent paperclip and a triumphant flourish. 'Ah!' he exclaimed with such excitement that Denman rushed across the office.

'Have you found something?' asked Denman.

'Yes,' said the Doctor, proudly. 'Files. Lots of them.'

Denman breathed deeply. 'Containing...?'

The Doctor opened the first green suspension file and took out a bundle of paper. He waved the sheets with delight at the two police-men. 'I had a feeling he wouldn't bother to hide it. There's nothing incriminating in this, unless you know what you're looking for.'

'Would you care to elaborate?'

Just as the Doctor seemed ready to, Hill turned back from the window. 'Time to get out,' he said quickly. 'Someone's coming.'

'Quick, out the fire exit,' snapped Denman. 'We'd better have got something important,' he told the Doctor. 'This is probably our only chance.'

'We've got everything we need,' replied the Doctor, stuffing the paperwork into his jacket.

Megan Tyley was the lightest of sleepers. It was both a blessing and a curse. When her children were young, she had never lost a minute's sleep through worry, as she knew she would hear the slightest cry of distress.

On the other hand, any noise from the street, whether it was a motorcycle accelerating, or cats fighting, would jolt Megan into sharp wakefulness. And then she would lie there, listening to her husband snore. In, out, in, out, in – long pause. She sometimes wondered if he'd ever stop breathing, there and then, while she was listening to him.

But the next breath always came, a rasping snort that went on for ever.

And when the snoring ceased to be amusing, she would turn things over in her mind, desperate for sleep. She would think of how she'd redecorate the living room, if money were no object; or what laws she'd pass, if she were in charge; or how she'd arrange the shelves at Safeway, if it were down to her.

And then she'd think of her children, and cry herself to sleep.

Now, as Megan Tyley sat bolt upright in her bed, the blood pounding with sudden wakefulness, her first thought was Billy.

No, Billy was... gone.

Megan Tyley got to her feet and shuffled over to the window. She stared across at the church which she cleaned once a week, the source of not a little pride.

Two people were clambering over the large northern wall, and she could just make out the smashed window behind them. Little vandals! They can't get away with that, she thought.

Enraged, she pulled on her dressing gown, and moments later she found herself in the street, marching towards the church. She couldn't remember coming down the stairs, or pushing open the front door. All she felt was an anger at the injustice, that these hooligans might escape punishment.

'Now, listen here!' she shouted as the two young people dropped down on to the ground. It was a girl and a boy. She thought she recognised the lad, but it was difficult to be sure in the semi-darkness. 'Just what do you think you're doing?' Her voice was loud enough, she supposed, to wake even her corpse-like husband.

The two vandals fled in opposite directions. 'Run!' shouted the unfamiliar girl as she passed.

Megan Tyley stood, rooted to the spot, her mouth hanging open. The girl had been telling *her* to run.

Something brushed against Megan's back, and she turned. A hulking, unreal figure was patrolling the shadows around the church wall. Its dirty, striped clothes were covered with leaves and stalks of straw.

The misshapen, lumpy head twisted uncertainly in her direction. It could have been a pumpkin covered in cloth, with a harsh red slit for a mouth, were it not for the eyes, deep within the face.

Frightened, powerless eyes. Eyes that had once been human. Eyes that cried out silently –

Mum.

'I don't get it,' said Hill, reading the page in his hand again. 'This is just… nothing.'

'On the contrary,' said the Doctor. 'It establishes a link.'

'What link?'

The Doctor took the paper from Hill's hand. 'This letter acknowledges an invoice for construction work carried out by one of Shanks's companies at the local water company's purification plant at the Garside reservoir.'

'So?' asked Hill.

'Look at the board of directors for Mersey Water PLC,' noted Denman with a triumphant snarl. 'Significant, wouldn't you say?'

'Matthew Hatch – non-executive director,' read Hill. 'I still don't see anything to get excited about, sir. Hatch has put some work Shanks's way. So what? We know they're mates. At worst we've got a bit of bribery and corruption – which we'd never be able to prove. We might wreck Hatch's political career, but Shanks is still fireproof.'

'Nobody's fireproof,' said Denman angrily.

'Gentlemen,' the Doctor said. 'You're all missing the point. Why do Shanks and Hatch have an interest in the city's water supply?'

'I don't know. It's not what I'd expect of Shanks,' said Denman. 'What's he playing at?'

'I'm not entirely sure,' admitted the Doctor. 'But I have some very horrible suspicions. I know that Shanks has scientists working for him, and they're not just developing narcotics. I suggest we take a look at that reservoir.'

* * *

They drove in near silence across the city. The sun was rising and the streets were filling with commuters. A main road took them through rolling countryside. Twenty minutes beyond Liverpool they saw the first road sign for Garside.

The car came to halt overlooking the reservoir, an enormous construction of swept white concrete. The sun was a ball of orange, floating on the still waters.

Denman rummaged around in the glove box, and found a small pair of binoculars. He scanned the purification plant on the other side of the reservoir, a simple block of a building, surrounded by fences. 'There's a Jag there,' he announced. 'It's Shanks's.'

'Are you sure?' queried Hill.

'It's my business to know,' said Denman.

The Doctor pushed open the door. 'We should find out what Shanks is up to.'

Hill, in the driving seat, turned to Denman. 'But Mr Savage said –'

'I don't care,' snapped Denman. 'If you want to arrest me when I come out of that building, you can. But I'm going to have that piece of vermin.' He got out of the car. 'If we're not out in half an hour, call for backup.'

Straggling pine trees had been planted in a strip around one bank of the reservoir. The Doctor and Denman kept to the shadowy undergrowth as they approached the building.

Shanks's Jaguar was just visible through a razor-wire-topped fence. A thick metal gate bore the Mersey Water Company's logo.

The Doctor and Denman skirted around to the back of the purification plant. An ancient deciduous wood terminated just short of the building. The bough of one particular tree extended over the fence. With surprising agility, the Doctor climbed up into the branches of the oak, stopping occasionally to give the puffing Denman a hand. Then, with great care, his feet dangling down on either side, the Doctor edged his way along the bough. He crossed the line of the fence, and began to lower himself towards the ground.

He dropped down, tumbling on to his side like a parachutist. Denman followed.

The two men walked across the weed-covered patch of land towards what appeared to be a fire exit. Denman raised his boot, ready to kick down the door.

'Oh, I think we can do better than that,' said the Doctor. 'A piggyback, if you don't mind?'

'Doctor, I didn't come all this way to muck about with –'

'A piggyback, please,' said the Doctor sharply. 'Or would you rather set off all the alarms inside this building?' He pointed. Above the door was a small box of white Perspex with an integral loudspeaker. Thick, insulated wires ran from that down to sensors on the door and frame, and back into the building.

The Doctor found a flat piece of flint on the ground, and then gingerly clambered up Denman's broad back.

'Oh, do keep still,' said the Doctor.

'I'm trying my best,' said Denman, swaying under the Doctor's weight.

The Doctor removed a couple of screws, revealing a simple red light bulb and a more complex box of electronics.

'If a fire breaks out,' said the Doctor, 'all these alarms are triggered. Lights flash, klaxons wail – and the doors automatically unlock themselves. It goes without saying that you can open these exits manually from the inside, but seeing as we're not, and –'

'Get on with it,' snapped Denman.

'So,' said the Doctor, 'what we've got to do is trigger the circuit that will open this door without setting off the actual alarm.' He rummaged through his pockets, and found a small spool of bare electrical cable. He bent a complex shape from the wire, and began gingerly inserting it into the fire sensor. 'And now something that doesn't conduct electricity...' He pressed a small black coat button against a switch.

There was a loud click from the door.

'*Et voilà*,' said the Doctor, moments before falling to the ground as Denman finally let go.

'Let's find Shanks,' said the big policeman, pushing his way through the door.

'No,' said the Doctor, brushing himself down with as much dignity as he could muster. 'Let's find out what he's up to first.'

'Which is?'

'Well,' said the Doctor. 'I think it will involve water, don't you?' And he swept past Denman and into the building.

They made their way towards the main purification and testing room. It was a functional construction of brick and metal, and contained a large number of circular tanks, connected by a complex array of thick tubing. A faint smell of ozone hung in the air. The place was deserted.

'What are we looking for?' asked Denman.

'Something that doesn't belong,' said the Doctor, scanning the room with expert detachment. 'There,' he announced at last, pointing to a gantry high up in the ceiling. A metal vat had been bolted on to an observation walkway, a twisted black rubber hose leading down into the water.

The Doctor made his way up the wrought-iron steps two at a time, Denman close behind. The walkway, slatted to reveal the tanks and the floor far below, swayed slightly as the two men approached the container. Between the vat and the tube was a small electronic box, a row of LEDs on the front. 'It's releasing a very precise amount of fluid straight into the water supply,' explained the Doctor. 'After this tank, it heads straight to the taps and toilets of Merseyside.'

Denman looked at the cylinder. 'It isn't very big,' he said. 'Surely it can't do much harm?'

'If it were a concentrated poison, it could kill thousands, even if diluted to one part per billion.' The Doctor noticed Denman's horrified expression. 'But I don't think this is poison. Even Shanks has little to gain from wholesale slaughter.'

'That's true,' said a voice, unexpectedly close.

Denman and the Doctor turned, and Shanks emerged from a shadowy area at the far end of the gantry. 'Took your time, lads,' he said as he walked towards them, a pistol held confidently in his right hand.

'You knew we'd come?' the Doctor asked, with a hint of resignation in his voice.

'Oh yeah. I've had someone watching you. And that office you broke into is riddled with sensors. You tripped so many of them the security desk looked like a Christmas tree.' He turned to face Denman. 'I'm sorry to hear about your kid,' he said. 'So unexpected.'

Denman snarled, about to hurl himself at the gangster, but Shanks pointed the gun straight at him.

The Doctor stared at Shanks.

'I'm nothing special.'

'Oh yes you are. You're very important. And that's the most frightening thing in the world.'

The Doctor shook his head, remembering how the sun had risen, all those years ago, in Hexen Bridge. 'Are you satisfied?' he asked. 'You're important now. You can end a man's life simply by giving orders.' His eyes burnt with disappointment, and Shanks glanced away momentarily. 'I hope you're pleased with yourself.'

'What's in the container?' asked Denman, through gritted teeth.

'Something Hatch's crowd have concocted,' said Shanks. 'It immunises people against CJD. Means they can go on munching burgers in patriotic safety.'

'I've heard no official announcement,' said Denman.

'Of course not, you divvy. This is all hush-hush.' Shanks tapped the canister with his gun. 'People are still so twitchy about BSE, Matt said it would take years to get this stuff passed.'

'So you're pumping it straight into the water supply, so that you can try it out on the populace?' queried the Doctor.

'That's obscene,' said Denman.

Shanks shook his head. 'You could say I'm putting something back into the community after all these years.' He smiled. 'I always told you I had a compassionate side.'

'Don't give me that crap,' said Denman.

'Funny you should mention that,' said Shanks. 'I was thinking of dumping you both in the sewage.' His eyes became cold and almost colourless. 'I can't think of a worse way to go.'

'I don't believe a word of it,' said the Doctor suddenly.

'What?' said Shanks.

'This tank doesn't contain a cure for Creutzfeldt-Jakob disease,' stated the Doctor firmly.

For the first time, Shanks looked ill at ease. 'That's what Matt told me.'

'And you believed him,' mocked Denman. 'I reckon he's been stringing you along all this time, Shanksy.'

'Don't call me that!' snapped Shanks, his expression revealing the shabby child, once scorned and still lonely, beneath the adult veneer.

'Your understanding of science is as loose as your morals,' said the Doctor. 'This is genetic material, but it has nothing to do with BSE.'

'What then?' queried Denman.

The Doctor stared at Shanks, trying to remember the rest of the paperwork he'd glanced at in the office. 'I have a suspicion that this substance is more mind-expanding than half a tonne of your drugs. How long has this fluid been pumped into the water supply?'

'I ordered that it be switched on as soon as I knew you'd broken into my office,' replied Shanks. 'A bit ahead of schedule, but I wanted to make a point. You and the copper have failed. The good people of Liverpool are already drinking this stuff.'

PART THREE
HAPPY JACK

CHAPTER 9
TWISTED FIRESTARTER

Matthew Hatch waited for the call from Phil Burridge. It never came.

Something was wrong. Phil would never let Hatch down, not even if there was a pint or a shag involved. He loved Hatch too much.

Hatch picked up his mobile phone and started dialling.

'Hello?' The voice at the other end sounded out of breath.

'Rebecca. Did I catch you in the middle of something important?'

'Matthew!' she said. 'No,' she continued with an embarrassed giggle. 'Actually, I'm taking the year-ten netball class. I've broken up two fights already.'

'Well, there you go,' said Hatch with little attempt to conceal his lack of interest. 'Listen, are you free tonight?'

'Free?'

'Yes.'

'I can't get up to London, Matthew, I've got school tomorrow.'

'What about halfway? That restaurant in Hungerford where we met last year?'

Rebecca paused. 'It's still a hell of a long drive back, Matthew.'

'I'll send a car down for you after school, and make sure you're back in your bed by midnight, in case you turn into a pumpkin or something.'

'In my *own* bed?'

'Probably,' said Hatch. 'The car will be at the vicarage by six.'

'OK,' she said with a sigh.

A wretched smile of satisfaction crossed Matthew Hatch's face and he terminated the call.

* * *

The Doctor stared at Shanks. 'Turn it off,' he said. 'You have no idea what you're pumping into the water supply.'

'I trust Matt,' said Shanks. 'I owe him.'

'You owe him *nothing*,' said the Doctor. 'He looked at you, and saw someone he could use. I'm told that's always been his way.'

'Don't try to reason with that piece of filth,' said Denman angrily.

Shanks turned to Denman and laughed. 'That's rich, coming from you. We're going to take you to the cleaners. Cop's daughter, busted for drugs, kills herself in the cells. Has quite a ring to it, eh?'

'You bastard,' said Denman. 'I'll make you pay for what you've done.'

'And there are some strange rumours about you and your girl,' continued Shanks. 'But I don't like to spread gossip. Anyway, you'll be suspended, your department will be investigated... All those cases you've got ready to bring against me will fall through.'

'I wouldn't be so sure,' said Denman.

Ignoring the exchange, the Doctor crouched down at the side of the vat, his hands moving over the keypad.

Shanks's gun waved back towards the Doctor. 'Stop that, Doc,' he said.

'No,' said the Doctor simply.

'Look, I'm warning you,' said Shanks, flustered again. 'Leave it alone, or I'll kill you.' Shanks turned towards the crouched form of the Doctor. It gave Denman the opportunity he needed.

The burly policeman threw himself at Shanks's legs, catching them in a perfect rugby tackle. The gun flew out of Shanks's grip.

The men hit the walkway as one. Denman was the first to respond, pummelling blows against Shanks's head with his fists.

The Doctor ignored the commotion, and concentrated on switching off the vat. He glanced up just as Shanks smashed his forehead against the bridge of Denman's nose. Denman twisted away, blood pouring from his face. Shanks powered his knee into the man's groin, scrambling to his feet, desperately seeking out the gun.

Denman charged at Shanks, head down like a bull. The drug dealer caught the brunt of the impact on his chest, and he flew backward, slamming into the handrail that ran along the side of the walkway. His legs flicked upward, his body pivoting around the low metal wall, and he disappeared from view, screaming.

Denman pulled himself to the edge of the walkway, and looked down. Shanks had landed on the edge of the enormous water tank, his head and shoulders bobbing beneath the water, his legs curled over the other side. It was obvious that his spine had snapped in two.

The Doctor's hands flickered over the keypad, his eyes narrowed in concentration as he watched the numerals blinking on the electronic display. At last, he switched off the device, the LEDs dimming one by one. He glanced across at Denman. 'I had to deal with this first,' said the Doctor. 'Every second could have been vital.'

Denman rolled on to his back, too exhausted to speak.

The Doctor stood up, and moved to the edge of the walkway. He looked into the water below, the surface still broken and rolling. 'Did it have to end like this?' he asked quietly.

'Yes it did,' said Denman, assuming that the Doctor was addressing him. He wiped away the blood from his upper lip. 'Him or me.'

The Doctor busied himself at the vat again, filling a test tube with the mysterious liquid. He placed a stopper on it gingerly.

'What is that stuff?' queried Denman.

'As I said, I'm not entirely sure. I saw a flash of DNA on the screen in Shanks's apartment.' He shook the test tube gingerly. 'My guess is that this activates certain dormant human genes. Those involved with the more esoteric or vestigial mental functions.'

'Like what?'

'It could be telepathy, or precognition, or just a trigger for mass hysteria. I'll need to do a full analysis, which will mean going back to Hexen Bridge.' The Doctor paused. 'Or…'

167

'Or…?' said Denman, pulling himself to his feet.

'I could go and ask Matthew Hatch what this material is.'

'Yeah, right,' said Denman. 'Forgive me if I'm sceptical.'

'You don't think it'll work?' queried the Doctor, seemingly surprised.

Denman laughed bitterly and struggled to his feet. 'You do what you want. But I've got some things to take care of.'

'Really?'

'Yeah. I've been thinking about that BSE laboratory that was bombed recently. There might be a link. After all, Hatch told Shanks it was all to do with mad-cow disease. I think I'll take a look – my last piece of official business. The vultures will be raking over what's left of my career by this time tomorrow.' Denman turned away. 'And Shanks's thugs will be checking up on him soon. Let's get out of here.'

Joanna Matson awoke to bird song and sunlight filtered through white cotton curtains. Bob was waking up, too. She trailed her fingertips over his chest, and he chuckled sleepily. There was less anger in him than usual, probably a result of their having had a blazing row in the kitchen last night, followed by an hour's vigorous sexual gymnastics in the bedroom. That always went some way towards a temporary healing of the eternal rift between them.

'Sleep well?' she queried.

Bob grunted.

Joanna paused, turning things over in her mind. Everything always seemed better in the mornings, but she knew that they'd made too many fresh starts down the years. None of them had ever amounted to much. 'Bob,' she said at last, 'we really ought to talk.'

'Whattabout?' he said through slurred lips, his eyes still closed.

'God knows we've had our ups and downs, but… well, they had this guest on *Danny Baker's Dozen* yesterday. A psychologist.'

'Bloody daytime TV,' muttered Bob.

'He made me think. You're sailing pretty close to the wind at the moment.'

Bob opened an eye. 'What do you mean?'

'This business with the Chens. Everyone knows that you were the one who –'

'Look,' said Bob sharply. 'Don't spoil the day before it's even begun, for crying out loud.'

Joanna sighed. 'I still love you. I'm just trying to look out for you – I'm the only one who will. You're too handy with your fists, Bob. If you don't sort out that anger of yours, you'll pay a terrible price.'

Bob Matson snorted and rolled over. 'Damn the consequences,' he said.

Trevor Winstone strolled past Shanks's secretary and into his office. Shanks had called earlier that morning to say he had to 'sort a few things out'. Winstone was to go ahead and meet their contacts on the local papers.

As expected, the journalists had lapped up the revelations about Denman and his daughter, just as keen to hear the hinted innuendos as the objective facts. Within moments, the hacks had been on the phone to editors, photographers, friends in the Smoke. The tabloids felt that they had made Denman a public figure, and so were happy to break him now he'd had his fifteen minutes of fame. Wapping editors always loved and loathed outspoken coppers in equal measure.

Winstone had returned to Shanks's office, but he still wasn't back. No one had seen Shanks all morning. Despite his impatience, Trevor settled down to wait.

When the phone rang, Winstone could hear the secretary's gasp of surprise in reception. 'He's dead,' she babbled, pushing the door open. 'Up at the reservoir.'

'What?' exclaimed Winstone.

'Drowned.'

'Shanks said he had some work to do,' said Winstone, having already guessed exactly what *that* meant. 'Why the hell didn't he take his bodyguards?'

The secretary stood open-mouthed, as if she was expected to answer the rhetorical question.

Winstone strode over to the nearest filing cabinet, pulling open the top drawer. 'Right, phone Matthew Hatch. Tell him that Shanks is dead. He can put two and two together. And then you'd better get clear of the building. Push a fire alarm button on your way.'

'Why? There's no fire.'

Trevor pulled a cigarette lighter from his pocket. 'There will be in a minute,' he said.

Ace had spent the morning walking around the village, searching for evidence of the scarecrows she and Steven Chen had encountered. However, once the broken window and door had been discovered, she thought it best to avoid the area around the church.

She found herself walking towards the school. The sound of children playing filled the village with whoops and cries of delight. The building was less sinister in daylight, a low weather-beaten wall ringing the playground of the lower school. Children teemed over every available square inch of boiling tarmac, playing hopscotch and tag and re-enacting unknown wars. Three girls were playing skipping games. They looked up as Ace's shadow fell across them.

'Hello,' said Ace brightly. 'I'm looking for Miss Baber. Do you –'

'What the hell do you want?' asked one of the girls, her angelic complexion changing in an instant.

'I just want to –'

'Go away!' snarled one of the others.

Ace was suddenly aware that the rest of the children had seen her. One by one, they were stopping their games and, en masse, were walking in her direction. Their eyes were bright and unblinking.

'You know, Miss Baber? Your teacher?' said Ace, a hint of uncertainty in her voice. She wasn't used to being freaked out by kids.

'We know who you are,' said one of the children. 'You ought to leave us alone.'

'I'm not leaving until I find the Professor.'

'Maybe Jack's already got him,' said a boy towards the back of the group, his companions murmuring in eager agreement.

'Who's Jack?' queried Ace.

'You'll meet Jack,' said a girl. 'Most outsiders get to meet Jack.'

'And you think "Jack" has the Doctor?'

'We *know* he sent the hollow men after you last night.'

'What?'

'The scarecrows.'

'How do you know that?'

The children surged towards the fence. 'We just know,' said one, teeth bared.

A bell rang out across the playground. A teacher had emerged from the school to call the children inside. Slowly the children dispersed, casting sour glances over their shoulders at Ace.

'Give our regards to Old Jack,' said a girl with a skipping rope. Her friends sniggered into their hands.

The Doctor and Denman stood in the lay-by, voices raised against the surging rush of the traffic.

'Look after yourself,' said the Doctor. 'You're no use to me floating face down in the river.' The Doctor wasn't sure if he could trust the policeman, but Denman was the only ally that fate had seen fit to provide him with.

'I owe it to my daughter to come back here and clear my name,' Denman said. 'I intend to do that, when the time is right.' He paused, his eyes focusing on some remembered event. 'When we travelled down to Hexen for the reunion, I told Nicola I wanted to deal with the past, face up to our heritage. That started with the death of Shanks... But it's not finished yet.'

'No,' agreed the Doctor as a juggernaut thundered by. 'The past rarely stays dead.'

'Once I've checked out the research labs, I'll catch up with you in London,' said Denman, opening the car door and settling behind the steering wheel.

'London's a big place,' warned the Doctor.

'And Matthew Hatch is a big man.' Denman turned the key in the ignition. 'I'll find him first, then find you.'

The Doctor raised a hand as the car swept on to the road, watching it weave through the traffic. Then he turned to look around, as if he hadn't been aware of his surroundings before. With great deliberation, he walked towards the roadside, and extended his thumb.

'How are... things?' asked Steven Chen, leaning against the war memorial.

Joanna Matson sat on the pale stone steps, her head in her hands and her back to the village. She sighed. 'You know.' She realised it was madness to meet in full view of everyone, but then Hexen Bridge was a place where secrets were common currency.

'I can imagine,' said Steven.

'He just can't see that the worse he becomes, the more likely I am to turn my back on him completely. He's reacting in the only way he knows how – by lashing out.'

Steven remembered the excrement posted through the door. 'He's out of control.'

Joanna nodded. 'I think you're right. I tried to warn him, but...' She glanced at the church, remembering Baber's sermon, and the argument it had provoked. 'Maybe we should stop seeing each other for a while. Just let Bob calm down a bit.'

Steven nodded. 'Yeah. I've got quite a bit on my mind right now.'

He caught something sinister flashing across Joanna's face. 'Don't worry, I'm not seeing anyone else, if that's what's bothering you,' he said.

'It isn't.'

'Don't lie,' snapped Steven. 'You're not very good at it.'

'Sorry,' Joanna said with a weak smile. 'I'm jealous, that's all.'

'You, and everyone else in this damn place.'

'That's Hexen Bridge for you. You've been here long enough to get used to it.'

Steven paused, as if struggling with the bitterness that was welling up inside him. 'But recently it's like someone's floored the throttle. The whole place is out of control.' He sighed. 'Maybe it's time to quit, before it consumes me, too.'

'Maybe,' said Joanna. 'But I'd miss you. It's people like you that keep this place sane.'

'My family are the only outsiders left.' Steven Chen glanced around. Something flickered on one of the hillsides overlooking the village, the sun catching glass or metal. 'You'd better go back to the pub,' he said.

Joanna nodded, and got to her feet, giving Steven an impulsive kiss on the cheek before returning to the Green Man.

Bob Matson put down the binoculars. He couldn't believe it. That shameless bitch was at it again, and in full view of the whole village.

He began the descent back down to the village. His hand was clamped so hard around the binoculars that his knuckles were white.

He fingered the Molotov cocktail lovingly. He'd give those slant-eyes something to think about.

CHAPTER 10

THE ST ANTHONY'S ESTATE CHINESE TAKEAWAY MASSACRE

The vintage Triumph Stag pulled on to the hard shoulder and the Doctor smiled, squatting down at the passenger window. 'Are you going anywhere near London?'

The driver, a man in his sixties, shook his head. 'Redborough,' he said. His weather-beaten face creased into a smile. 'But we can drop you near the M25, if that's any good?'

'It is. Thank you so much,' said the Doctor, climbing into the back with some difficulty.

'We don't normally pick up hitchhikers,' explained the woman. 'But I said to Robert, "This man looks respectable enough." '

'It's very good of you,' said the Doctor, relieved to be out of the choking fumes of the M6.

'We've been to the Lake District. It's our fortieth wedding anniversary.' The woman's smile became more tender as she glanced across at the man. He took a hand from the wheel and touched her arm gently. It was a warm and private moment, one that spoke of years of uncomplicated intimacy. The Doctor thought suddenly of Hexen Bridge, and Bob and Joanna Matson's sullen anger.

'It's lovely up there,' said the woman. 'Do you know the Lakes at all?'

'I spent a short time in Grasmere many years ago,' said the Doctor, remembering a holiday with Jamie and Victoria. 'It rained and rained and rained.'

'We've been going there for years. I'm Julia, by the way.'

'How do you do? I'm the Doctor.'

'A medical doctor?' she queried. 'Where did you train?'

'Glasgow,' answered the Doctor. 'Many, many years ago…'

'Oh yes,' smiled the woman. 'The accent's a giveaway.'

The still countryside passed slowly, the smooth growl of the Stag's engine blurring with the couple's discussion of Mrs Pearce's varicose veins and John Tomasson's rumoured affair with his secretary. Soon the Doctor fell into a deep sleep.

He awoke with a start just as the car pulled into a service station.

'This is where we'll have to drop you off,' said the man as the Doctor stretched and yawned.

'Thank you so much,' said the Doctor with genuine gratitude. He stepped down on to the tarmac, taking in his new surroundings before turning back to the couple. 'It's reassuring to know that there are still good people in the world,' he said.

Denman approached the research centre cautiously, guiding the car on to a patch of broken concrete edged by pale-looking buddleia. He switched off the engine, and breathed deeply to steady his chaotic thoughts.

Moments after he left the Doctor, Denman called an old friend who worked in the West Midlands. A final favour. The man had told him exactly where the laboratories were, and warned him about 'doing anything stupid'. Denman had ended the conversation with an impatient stab of his thumb. There had been too much talking.

There wasn't much left of the buildings, the main one a splintered mass of blackened brick and metal. The sun made myriad patterns on the shards of glass that littered the ground around the lab. Some of the outlying Portakabins had survived, though all the doors and windows were now held shut with metal bars and padlocks. The area was still cordoned off by long yellow and black ribbons of hazard tape that warned of toxic contamination.

Denman stepped from the car. The research centre was right on the edge of a benighted industrial estate, and the wind chased the litter over a desert of cement and tarmac.

There were two policemen patrolling the area, but they only seemed to be there only to keep away local children. Denman waited for one young uniformed constable to pass, and then he sprinted towards the main building.

One of the window frames had been only loosely boarded up, and Denman tugged at the planks of wood with rough, impatient fingers. Then he pulled himself through, dropping down into a room that smelled like the aftermath of a barbecue. He remembered one he had organised earlier that summer, exclusively for the officers pursuing Shanks. Denman had hoped that if they realised his interest in the case they would work still harder to put the man behind bars.

And Nicola had been wonderful, taking coats, handing out drinks, cracking stupid jokes with some of the younger officers. Everything his wife would have done, and more.

Denman lashed out at a blackened computer monitor with his foot, the slab of fractured glass at the front shattering.

On the far side of the room Denman noticed a filing cabinet that seemed largely unaffected by the fire. The metal was twisted and warped, but the drawers, with a squeal of protest, slid open.

'Jesus,' said someone behind him. 'What a racket.'

Denman spun round, fists clenched. It was Hill, his suit as immaculate as usual.

'Sir,' he added, apologetically.

'What the hell are you doing here?' asked Denman, his body still tense.

'I followed you. The grey Rover. Can't believe you didn't see me.'

'I've got a bit on my mind at the moment, laddy,' snapped Denman. 'You might have noticed.'

'Smoke?' offered Hill, pulling a packet of cigarettes from his jacket.

Denman shook his head. 'You haven't answered my question. Why did you follow me?'

Hill lit the cigarette and inhaled deeply. 'It's time you came back to Liverpool.'

'Really?' snorted Denman. He turned back to the filing cabinet. 'It can wait.'

'But Shanks is dead. What more do you hope to prove?'

'You know your problem, Paul? You never see the big picture. You're too busy rooting around in the dirt.'

'And how do you work that out?'

Denman pulled a sheet of browned paper from the drawer, and made a show of inspecting it closely. 'The same way I'm working out that the business with my daughter was no coincidence.' He swung round to stare at Hill. 'We were this close,' said Denman, his thumb and forefinger almost touching. 'And then suddenly –' He slammed the filing cabinet shut. 'I find my daughter framed with some of Shanks's drugs.'

'How do you know they were his?'

'It's obvious, isn't it?'

'Maybe,' continued Hill. 'But like I say, he's dead, and I don't suppose you'll find anything incriminating here.'

'And you'd know all about that, wouldn't you?' said Denman, his voice a choked whisper. 'You being in Shanks's pocket and all.'

Hill tried to speak, but his words were cut short by Denman's relentless stare of accusation. His eyes were like a dead man's.

'Don't deny it, sunshine. You didn't come here because you wanted to look out for me. You wanted to make sure I wouldn't find anything linking you to Shanks. Correct?'

Hill puffed on his cigarette nervously, but said nothing.

'You were the one who told Shanks how close we were to busting him. Right?'

'I swear I didn't know what Shanks had planned. If I had –'

'I don't want to hear it. You played your part in the death of my daughter. Can you live with that?' Denman had walked towards

Hill and was inches from the junior officer now. Denman could smell the expensive cologne on the man's temples. 'You saw Nicola hanging there. You watched as they cut her down.' Denman removed the cigarette from Hill's mouth and hurled it away. 'Can you live with that?' he repeated.

Denman turned away abruptly.

Hill cleared his throat, as if Denman's staring eyes had robbed him of the power of speech. 'What will you do?' he asked in a tiny voice.

'Follow the Doctor to London. Find Hatch. Sort things out. Like I said, there's a bigger picture, and it involves my past. Which you know nothing about.' Denman gestured at the filing cabinet. 'You say that there's nothing here to find?'

'No. Word has it that Hatch's CJD material came up from the south.'

' "Word has it"?' queried Denman. 'You watch too much TV.'

'What about me?' queried Hill.

'Oh, when I'm back, I'll take you to the cleaners, sonny, don't you worry about that.'

'But not…'

'Kill you? No. If my career is going down the toilet, I'll make damn sure yours is flushed so far down with me that you'll never see daylight again.' He turned for the door. 'That's justice, you see. Funnily enough, that's why I became a copper. Justice.' He glanced back at Hill. 'I don't know about you.'

Water dripped from taps and broken showers, pooling in sinks and dirty baths. In tumblers of cola, ice melted under the fierce glare of the sun. People sat outside bars and pubs, chasing away wasps as the early-morning breeze gave way to the glare of midday, and then to the stealthy approach of dusk.

Mounds of refuse rotted in backstreets, attracting mice and rats. Diluted bleach and the eventual rain could not disguise the smell that was rising from the city, the stench of death that grew as the water fell from the taps.

* * *

Wayne drummed his hands on the steering wheel as the rhythm of the song ricocheted around the inside of the BMW. It was 'Born Slippy', an old dance track, and its elegant, pulsing soundscape throbbed loudly over the bubbling voices of those in the car.

'Turn it up, Wayne,' shouted Jim.

'Eh?'

'One louder!'

'Right.' Wayne nudged up the volume.

> *Mega mega white thing*
> *Mega mega white thing*
> *Mega mega*
> *Shouting*
> *Lager, lager, lager, lager*

Wayne, Jim, Chris and Darren joined in, loudly. Wayne tossed Darren and Chris in the back two cans of Red Stripe from the plastic bag at his feet.

'Sound,' noted Darren as he attacked the ring-pull with relish.

When the song ended Jim reached over from the passenger seat to switch off the CD. The dirty BMW was plunged into a silence broken only by the occasional slurp from a warm beer can. Without the illumination from the car's stereo, darkness shrouded the interior. Fortunately, the sulphurous glow of the street lights was enough to help the drinkers find their cans.

'We having some scran, or what?' asked Chris to no one in particular.

'It's still chucking it down,' noted Darren, looking out at the thunder storm that raged overhead.

'It's only just around the corner!' exclaimed Wayne.

'I don't want to get my hair wet,' said Jim flatly.

'Ponce!'

Wayne ran his fingers over the CD cases scattered over the

dashboard. 'What do you want? More old stuff? Oasis? The Prodigy?'

'Got any Star Jumpers?' asked Darren.

'Naff off. Johnny *bleedin'* Chester. Wouldn't have him in the car.'

'He was all right till he married that Australian bird,' offered Chris. 'The politician. He's totally lost it now.'

'Them lot from Leeds – Amanda – are better,' said Wayne.

Darren half opened his side door and put one trainer on the sodden tarmac. 'I'm up for some curry even if you tarts are staying in here all night.' He took another swig from his can and then dumped it on the back seat, shutting the door behind him.

Through the rain-soaked windscreen, Jim watched his friend sprint around the corner. 'I'll bet that soft get doesn't even have the sense to bring me back a bag of chips.'

'Remember that party on Walker Road?' asked Wayne. 'Hippie Kev's house-warming?'

'Aye, when he copped off with Brenda the Gender-Bender?'

Wayne's laughter was like an explosion in the confines of the car.

He turned as a dark shape passed across the windscreen, moving towards the back door. 'Hurry up, Darren, I'm *starving*!'

The back door opened.

Chris stretched out a hand to pick up Darren's lager can. 'Blimey, that was quick,' he said. 'I didn't expect to –'

Sound flooded the car. A burst of noise uncannily similar to the rhythm they had just listened to. Rat-a-tat-tat. Burr…

'What –' Wayne tried to turn his head towards the back seat, but the windscreen and upholstery that surrounded him was already splashed with red.

Another roar of sound, and his shattered body jerked on to the steering wheel.

Eight minutes later Darren returned to the car with four Kam Ming takeaway curries in a carrier bag. People swarmed around the vehicle, shouting and screaming. He dropped the bag in the gutter, and pushed his way to the front. Inside the car were the bodies of his friends and the remains of his bullet-ridden lager can, still gently weeping its contents on to the bloodstained seats.

The question surprised the Doctor.

'I'm sorry?' he asked.

'I said, how many of these coins make one pound ten pence?'

The Doctor looked up from his coffee at the girl with the American accent. She held out a handful of coins to him with a disarming smile.

'That one, and that one,' the Doctor said. 'I'm afraid most of the meals in here are quite expensive.' He gestured towards the display above the counter. 'And full of animal fat. I'd avoid them if I were you.'

'Oh, it's for a phone call,' said the girl, sitting down beside the Doctor. 'I want to let a friend know that I've arrived. Hi, I'm Lisa.'

'How do you do?' said the Doctor. 'And you've reminded me: I must make a phone call to a friend of my own. She'll be very worried, no doubt.'

'You run away from home?' asked Lisa with a mischievous grin.

'Something like that,' said the Doctor. He stood and pushed the coffee cup towards the girl. 'You can have it if you like. I thought I wanted this, but in the end I didn't. Isn't that often the way with things?'

'Ugh, no thanks,' said Lisa, wrinkling her nose. 'I hate coffee. And, anyway, I thought you guys drank tea.'

The Doctor smiled. 'I must be going.'

'Tell your friend I said not to worry,' said the girl. 'You can look after yourself all right.'

'Yes,' said the Doctor. 'And so can she.' There was an anxious edge in his voice. 'Usually.' He tipped his hat to the girl, who gave him a little wave.

The Doctor stepped out of the fast-food restaurant, and into the sticky and uncomfortable evening air. As he walked from

Tottenham Court Road to Charing Cross Road, unanswered questions clouded his mind. He had hoped to use Shanks, to help the man rid himself of what he'd learnt and experienced at Hexen Bridge. Shanks was an outsider, after all. But the Doctor had failed: the taint was too strong. Shanks had died while blindly protecting Hatch. All the metaphorical and literal roads the Doctor trod seemed to lead from Hexen Bridge to the politician. For all Denman's cynicism, the Doctor knew that he had to talk to Hatch, face to face. He seemed to be the one with all the answers.

Finding Hatch proved comparatively easy. Ten minutes at the library just off Leicester Square, trawling through copies of *Who's Who* and surfing local government sites on the Internet, provided him with all the information he needed. Number 24a Velocity Crescent. It was, the Doctor thought, the first time he had found an adversary's location listed in public records.

Outside the library some workmen had a radio that played sugary pop music at an extraordinary volume. As the Doctor left there was a brief news report. Hatch was at Westminster, taking part in a debate on the latest defence review. There was a brief snatch of his voice, the man clearly annihilating the arguments of the shadow minister.

The next report concerned an outbreak of random violence in Liverpool.

Shaking his head, the Doctor gave some money to a man selling *The Big Issue* outside Tower Records, and headed for the Underground.

The Doctor reached Knightsbridge in a crowded tube train full of sweating office workers. Outside, it was no cooler. He hurried towards Hatch's home.

He stood on the opposite side of the street for several minutes, but the house seemed dark and empty. The Doctor knew that this was partly illusory. As Defence Secretary, Hatch's residence was a prime terrorist target, and it was almost certain that security cameras and policemen watched the area intently.

'Another spot of breaking and entering,' the Doctor said as he crossed over.

Bob Matson pushed the fuel-soaked rag deep into the bottle of vodka, grinning like a child. 'You think I've gone too far?' he laughed. 'You ain't seen nothin' yet.'

He walked down the slope towards the conservatory at the back of the Chinese restaurant. Somewhere a dog barked, and a car accelerated away from the Green Man. He just hoped Don Tyley was looking after the pub properly.

Obscured by bushes, Matson stood watching the waiters as they flitted around the diners, who were making inconsequential, silent conversation. He recognised some of them, but he was far beyond caring. He pulled the old Zippo from his pocket, flicking it open and lighting it with a single flourish, as he'd seen people in the movies do. Then he ignited the dripping rag, paused, and hurled it with all his strength at the pristine glass.

The bottle smashed through, spraying liquid that instantly caught fire. The room was suddenly full of screams and smoke, people overturning plates of finely made food in their enthusiasm for the exit. The starched linen on one table was already burning, and an elderly woman shrieked, holding up an arm consumed by flame.

'That's one in the eye for Johnny Foreigner,' said Bob Matson as he turned away, his laughter drowned by the cries of terror from within the restaurant.

'Don't move.'

The voice was soft, but filled with menace. The Doctor instantly raised his hands and spun around as a table lamp was flicked on, momentarily blinding him.

'You're quite a scallywag, aren't you, Doctor?' The Doctor blinked the pain from his eyes and focused on Trevor Winstone, who sat at Hatch's desk. He was holding a gun.

'I didn't think anybody was at home,' said the Doctor.

'Evidently. Thieves seldom do. And you on the school's board of governors, too… Think of the shame.'

The Doctor laughed out loud.

'What are you so happy about?' asked Winstone.

'I'm just thinking that on the last two occasions we've met, you thought I was about to die. I'm still here. That should tell you something about me.'

'Lucky?'

'Difficult to get rid of,' said the Doctor. 'Where's Hatch?'

'Haven't got a clue,' said Winstone. 'Up to some nefarious skullduggery, no doubt,' he said with an ironic chuckle. 'I got someone to ring him from Liverpool when I heard about Kenny. I bet Matt was really cut up about that. Then I got the train down.'

'First class?' asked the Doctor, as though interested in such trivialities.

'Of course,' said Winstone. 'By the time I got here, Matt was gone. His wife's leaving him, you know. And there's some scandal brewing, too. A couple of the papers have got hold of it. He's lied to the House. Bad times ahead for cousin Matthew, I reckon.'

'And you?'

'Oh, I'll survive,' said Winstone casually. 'I always do.'

'Do you know what we found up in Liverpool?' asked the Doctor angrily.

'Terrible housing, mass unemployment and rampant crime?' said Winstone. 'I blame the government, myself.'

'Shanks was contaminating the water supply,' continued the Doctor. 'I'm sure now that the genetic material unleashes mental powers – turns people into psychic batteries. Not everyone can cope with it.' The Doctor's eyes were dark and unblinking. 'As we speak, hundreds of people in Liverpool are being slaughtered. Men, women and children. Innocent lives lost. What's made the whole thing worse is that the area has just been flooded with weaponry. Tell me, where do you think this superfluity of arms originates?'

'I can't imagine,' said Trevor.

The Doctor sighed. 'Shanks wasn't clever enough to come up with the scheme to pollute the water supply all on his own.'

'No, indeed,' said Trevor. 'Bright lad, our Ken, but a very linear mind.'

'Hatch, on the other hand?'

'Remember what I told you in Giroland? Deep as the Earth's core.'

'The obscenity of what you people are doing staggers me,' said the Doctor with a furious anger in his voice. He leaned on the desk, almost shouting at Winstone, despite the gun still trained on him. 'Do you understand?'

'Nothing to do with me,' said Winstone, without blinking. 'I'm just a legitimate businessman.'

'An arms trader,' continued the Doctor, spitting the phrase at Winstone. 'A broker in death.'

'Your point being…?'

'Why?' shouted the Doctor.

'Why? Why is the sky blue? Because it is.'

The Doctor half turned, throwing up his hands in impatience. 'That's nonsense,' he said.

'Selling arms to Shanks's boys is no different from selling them to some bunch of Arabs in the Middle East. I sell metal tubes. Once they're out of my hands I don't care what the buyer does with them.'

'When you were six,' said the Doctor, slumping into a leather armchair, 'I visited the school with Nyssa. You sat on my knee and told me you wanted to be an astronaut. Do you remember?'

'Yes,' said Winstone. 'You told me a story about an astronaut who wanted to be in space so he could see the face of God…'

'But when he got there, he couldn't see anything but space,' continued the Doctor. 'Do you remember the moral of the story?'

'No.' There was an almost innocent curiosity in Trevor's voice now.

'The moral was,' began the Doctor slowly, 'that sometimes we do the right thing for the wrong reason, and sometimes we do the wrong thing for the right reason. But that right and wrong are always involved.'

'The money Matthew made from brokering the arms deals, and all his other projects, goes to an infertility clinic,' said Trevor suddenly. 'I don't know why I'm telling you this.'

'Because you want to,' said the Doctor. 'Infertility? I knew it. It's all to do with the village, isn't it? Once anybody leaves, they lose the ability to reproduce.'

Trevor nodded. 'You *are* smart. Matt wants me to kill you, you know.'

'But you won't,' said the Doctor.

'Won't I?'

'No,' said a voice from the blackness of the corridor. 'Because if you do, it'll be the last thing you *ever* do.'

'Chief Constable,' said the Doctor as Denman walked into the room, both hands around a pistol. 'How much of that did you hear?'

'Most of the incriminating stuff,' said Denman. 'Some idiot left the door open.'

'Ah, that was me,' said the Doctor brightly. 'I thought it was about time you got here.'

'Right, sonny,' said Denman moving closer to Winstone. 'You're nicked. Put the gun down and lie face down on the floor.'

Trevor smirked. 'I don't believe you have the authority to arrest me any more. Not after everything that happened last night.' He placed his gun on the table. 'In any case, that's all a bit hackneyed, isn't it, Mr Denman? What do you except me to say? "It's a fair cop, guv. You got me banged to rights and no mistake"?'

'How about "ow",' said Denman, punching Trevor in the face. Trevor toppled backward over his chair. Denman rounded the desk and kicked him savagely in the ribs. The anger that he had struggled to contain during the encounters with Shanks and Hill finally spilled over. 'Last night my daughter killed herself. She's dead because of people like you, you verminous bastard,' he said, kneeling down and punching Winstone again. 'Do you hear me? Nicola's dead.'

'I'm sorry,' wailed Trevor as the Doctor leapt over the desk and pushed Denman away.

'That'll achieve nothing,' the Doctor snapped.

'Except a lot of satisfaction for me,' said Denman, bunching his fists for another attack.

'You could break him in two if you wanted,' said the Doctor. 'But that won't bring her back. And it won't help us either.'

He took the gun from Denman's hand, then turned and picked up Trevor's discarded weapon.

'I'll take care of these,' he said, dropping them in a wastepaper basket. Then he turned his attention back to the wounded Winstone, still rolling around on the floor, clutching his bloodied face and weeping in pain. 'Get up,' he said.

Trevor stood, shakily.

The Doctor handed the man a blue-spotted handkerchief, then turned to Denman, who was still red-faced. 'The BSE centre?' the Doctor asked.

'Nothing. Nothing but a bombed-out shell.'

'Never mind,' said the Doctor. 'Now, this infertility clinic…'

'You think it's significant?'

The Doctor walked to the window and looked out at the road. The street lights were just flicking on. 'A taint,' he announced suddenly, turning back towards Denman and Winstone. 'Sterility once you leave Hexen Bridge. Tell me about Jack i' the Green.'

Trevor began to laugh, spitting blood from his mouth. 'A stupid folk tale,' he said. 'Judge Jeffreys killed all of the men of Hexen Bridge because he was possessed by Satan, who lives under the village green. Or something. I stopped believing in that stuff about the same time was I stopped believing in Father Christmas. And God.'

'And yet everyone from Hexen Bridge has a darkness to their character,' said the Doctor.

'Haven't we all?' asked Denman.

'Not as dark as some of the things I've seen recently,' continued the Doctor. 'Where's this clinic?'

'Surrey,' said Winstone.

'I think it's time we paid them a visit.'

Bob Matson pushed his way through the copse, hoping to return to the road and stroll back into the village. Whatever noise was coming from A Taste of the Orient was lost to the enveloping whisper of the leaves and the stillness of the night.

Bob chuckled to himself. Joanna and the Chink thought they could get the better of him, but he'd shown them now. And there were even worse things he could do.

He reached for a hip flask of Scotch, and drank as if in celebration.

The wind whispered through the darkness and the trees, rustling leaves and… Was that footsteps? Bob shook his head. He knew that no one had followed him from the restaurant – the people there had other things on their minds – so he was in the clear. And no one in Hexen Bridge would dare to confront him anyway. He ran the Jack in the Green pub; despite the new name, that still counted for something.

A twig snapped. Something was moving through the undergrowth, over towards the road.

'Who's there?' cried out Matson, his voice a clear and strong challenge in the still evening air. 'Come on out, or I'll –'

The snapping twig.

He'd assumed it was someone blundering through the trees, their feet trampling around willy-nilly. But what if the twig was actually part of –

'No,' he said under his breath. 'You can't send *them* after me…'

And what if the whispering leaves weren't the summer zephyrs patrolling the hillsides, but the noise from one of… *them*… stalking him?

Bob Matson ran now, blindly searching for the road. He could see its silvery-white trail through the stunted trees, and forced himself forward, overweight limbs pumping hard.

He burst out on to the welcome tarmac of the road, breathing heavily.

'Thank God,' he muttered, bent double with exhaustion.

Another rustling noise caused him to look up.

The scarecrows stepped out on to the road, forming a line. Different faces, but all with the same, dead expression, stared back at him. Reflecting his terror and confusion.

And then Matson realised that he was on the road just beyond the village boundary. And the scarecrows were a cordon between him and the only place he had ever considered home.

Jack had expelled him from the village, and Robert Matson was utterly alone.

CHAPTER 11
HATFUL OF HOLLOW

'And for madam?'

'Madam will have the same as what I'm having,' said Matthew Hatch briskly. The waiter nodded and turned to leave just as Rebecca arrived back at the table.

'Sorry I was so long,' she said breathlessly.

'I've ordered for you,' noted Hatch as he watched a young couple move towards their table. He tutted, and glanced back at Rebecca with a look of annoyance on his face. 'Time was when you had to be dressed to get in this place. That man was wearing jeans.'

'Call the manager immediately!' said Rebecca. 'You know your trouble, Matt? You're a snob. Always have been.'

'Nothing wrong with that,' noted Hatch. 'There are too many ignorant plebs in the world. We need a good cull every now and then to thin them out.'

'We haven't had a decent world war for a while,' noted Rebecca with a smile, sipping her vodka and lime.

'It's not for the want of trying,' continued Hatch.

He'd forgotten how much he enjoyed these sparring encounters with Rebecca. For all her acquired sophistication, she was still a vicar's daughter from the sticks, fascinated by powerful, dangerous men. And as dirty as they came.

She licked her red lips and said softly, in not much more than a whisper, 'You're bad.'

He stared into her eyes and lifted his glass of wine in a toast. 'Here's to badness.'

Steven Chen had met Ace earlier in the day, and they had walked the lanes around the village in near silence, grateful to be away from the claustrophobic madness of Hexen Bridge. Ace had spotted a pall of smoke drifting over the cottages, but Steven had said it was probably farmers burning away the stubble from their fields.

As evening fell, Ace and Steven sat on a wooden stile, high up on the hills. The darkness that covered Hexen Bridge seemed to seep up from the ground, swallowing cottages, trees and sky. They felt, rather than saw, things moving in the shadows all around them.

'It's time we got some answers,' announced Ace suddenly.

'Who from?' asked Steven, rubbing his arms against the sudden chill in the air.

'Who here seems to have the best idea of what's going on? The vicar. Let's confront him with what we know.'

'What, and tell him we broke into the church?'

Ace got to her feet. 'Come on.' She strode down the hillside towards the church, Steven following somewhat nervously in her wake. When she reached the vicarage she banged loudly on the door.

Baber pulled it open almost immediately, as if he had been expecting someone. His face fell. 'Oh, it's you. What do you want?'

'I'd like to ask you about the photographs of the village.'

The look that crossed the man's face was a contradictory mixture of relief and horror. 'You've seen them? But I expressly forbade you –'

'We saw the photos,' interjected Steven, 'and we were chased from the church by…' He paused, realising how ridiculous it all sounded. 'Scarecrows.'

Baber nodded. 'I had my suspicions when I opened the door this morning. Even the villagers wouldn't dare destroy the fabric of the church.' He looked around nervously, but the darkness that filled the lane was unmoving. 'You'd better come in,' he said.

* * *

'You know, the cost of that meal would have fed a whole village in Africa for a month,' said Rebecca as they climbed into Hatch's car. Ian Slater opened the door for her, and closed it as she settled in.

'Remind me to send a plane over to Bongo Bongo Land a.s.a.p.,' said Hatch, with a trace of irritation.

The car drove off, and they sat in silence for several miles before a trace of concern crossed Rebecca's face. 'We're going the wrong way,' she said, leaning forward and tapping on the glass behind the chauffeur.

'Short cut,' said Hatch dismissively.

'No it's not,' said Rebecca. 'We're heading back to London. Matthew, I haven't got time for all this, I've got school tomorrow.'

'Sod school,' said Hatch, looking away from her and out of the window.

'Look,' she said angrily, 'you can't just snap your fingers and have me come running every time you feel like it. If you think you're going to get your leg over tonight, matey, you've got another think coming. Now get your slave to turn this car around and take me home. Right now.'

Hatch turned back to her, a quizzical look on his face. 'You're sweating. Are you all right?'

'No,' said Rebecca after a brief pause. 'I feel awful. I think I'm coming down with something.'

'It could be the drug I put in your coffee,' said Hatch.

'You what?' shouted Rebecca.

'Shhhhh,' said Hatch, putting a finger to his lips. 'You just sit back and relax, and I'll take you somewhere where they'll make you feel much better.'

'We could have been killed last night,' said Ace. 'I think the least you could do is tell us what the hell is going on.'

Baber stared down at the carpet, as if there was a message somewhere in the Axminster. A cup of coffee was going cold on a table at his side.

'From what Ace has said,' continued Steven, more diplomatically, 'it's as if you wanted her to investigate further.'

Baber sighed. 'The darkest secrets are those we want most desperately to share.'

'Meaning?' snapped Ace.

'Everyone in the village is trying to cling to the past. But it's not working. We all feel it. Something is happening, something new and terrible. "Things fall apart; the centre cannot hold", as Yeats put it.'

'Jack?' queried Steven.

Baber nodded. 'Jack has always been here. But he's waking up, and it's terrifying me.'

'But Jack's just a legend,' said Steven.

'No,' said Baber. 'My father realised that Jack exists. It's possible his father knew before him. That dark patch in the photographs – you only really notice it from the top of the church tower.'

'Yeah,' said Ace. 'We know.'

'He started taking the photographs. I suppose you could call it a cry for help. He couldn't just go around talking openly about Jack. Not in Hexen Bridge.'

'Why not?' queried Ace.

'The register you saw,' said Baber. 'The traditions that surround it, the monitoring of the populace. It's inextricably linked to Jack.' He gulped down some coffee, seeming not to notice its temperature. 'The vicar of Hexen Bridge is one of Jack's children, you see. Perhaps more so than most.'

'So that lad who you said has gone to London…' began Ace, remembering the register in the church.

'He's still here,' said Baber. He turned to Steven Chen. 'But you wouldn't recognise him.'

'So Jack sits under the green and turns people into… Into the living dead?' asked Ace.

Baber dodged the question. 'I've said as much as I know.'

'How do we stop him?'

'Jack? You can't stop Jack!' exclaimed Baber, with unexpected vehemence. 'We're *all* his children. He could kill us all, just like that.' He snapped his fingers. 'You and the boy might be safe. You don't belong here.'

'I didn't feel particularly safe last night,' admitted Steven.

'I've said too much already,' added Baber hurriedly.

'You've told us *nothing* that we didn't already know,' said Ace, anger rising in her voice.

'Then condemn me as a coward if you wish,' said Baber. 'But that's better than being damned by Jack.'

Ace got to her feet. 'Come on, Steven. It's time we paid our respects to this Jack.'

'And how do we do that?' asked Steven. 'Get a shovel and start digging up the green?'

Ace turned to Baber. 'Well?'

Baber, still slumped in his chair, glanced up, but did not reply.

'Look,' said Ace, 'if we see Jack, we'll tell him you had nothing to do with it.'

'You seem to be treating this very casually,' observed Baber.

'That's because I know we're going to nail the scumbag.'

'Really?' His voice betrayed amusement.

'Yeah. I've done this sort of thing before.'

Baber shook his head. 'You haven't. The only thing we can do is pray that Jack sleeps again.'

'But Jack's this big black stain, right? He's growing all the time. That's what those photographs show.' Ace paused in the doorway. 'Get real, mate. He's not about to have another kip.'

'Then the fate of Jack's children is in your hands,' announced Baber sadly.

It was closing time at the Green Man. With both of the Matsons nowhere to be seen, Don Tyley had struggled on his own behind the bar. It had been an awful night, the clammy air thick with tension. There had been three or four messy brawls within the

195

pub as people pushed and jostled around the bar to get served, and the police had been called. Not that Stu Minton, returning from the fire-damaged Chinese restaurant, had done much other than tell his second cousin Dave to leave his third cousin Jimmy alone. Then he'd stayed for a pint himself and had ended up in the middle of yet another pushing-and-shoving match over who was the better pop group, Fractured Spirit or the Unlicensed Virgins.

Now, finally, Don had been able to close the door on the last customer. Little Josie Luston had hung around the bar until everyone else had gone, flirting with him. Time was when Don would have taken her around the back and given her a good seeing to. But then he thought about his son, only a couple of years her junior, and what had happened to *him*, and had ushered the girl out of the pub with little ceremony.

He pulled the heavy bolt at the top of the door into place and breathed a deep sigh of relief. Tomorrow, he thought, he'd have a few words with Bob and Joanna about leaving him alone, at the mercy of the regulars.

Thump.

Don turned suddenly, startled by the loud noise behind him. His heart thudded in his chest, but there was nothing there. He took a pace or two closer to the back door, but that was closed, as it should be. 'Anyone there?' called Don, his voice trembling slightly.

Idiot, he thought. If there is anybody there, they aren't going to answer, are they?

The thump came again, less heart-stopping this time as Don was facing in the direction of the sound. A few feet away he could see that the trapdoor hadn't been shut properly, the wind causing it to flap upward. 'Daft thing,' he said with a sigh of relief. 'Fancy scaring me half witless like that.' He moved towards the hatch, but found himself wondering what had caused it to move in the first place. Don scratched his head.

Sighing, he threw open the heavy oak trapdoor, and stepped down on to the wooden rungs.

On the third step, Don reached out and flicked on the light. Bob had never bothered to have anything stronger than a sixty-watt bulb in the cellar, but even this dim light brought a sigh of relief from Don. There was no one skulking about in the cellar, lying in wait to steal the takings or murder Bob and Joanna in their beds.

At the foot of the stairs Don took a long look around the beer kegs and stacked crates of bottles. The cellar was filthy and smelled of damp. Bob really should get something done about it.

Something moved.

Don snapped his head to one side, but felt only a gentle breeze on his face. He walked forward and found himself looking at a sheet of green tarpaulin that covered most of one wall of the cellar. Don had been down here many times and this bit of the cellar had always been stacked with crates. Now they had been moved, recently, too, by the look of the drag marks in the dust on the floor.

Don walked to the tarpaulin, which was rippling slightly from the breeze behind it.

Behind it?

Don pulled back the sheeting, and found an opening carved into the cellar wall, and a tunnel beyond.

'Funny place for a hole in the wall,' he said to no one in particular. His voice echoed off into the distance of the concealed passageway. There was a light flickering somewhere in the distance. Now more curious than frightened, Don took a few tentative steps into the opening, stooping slightly as his head scraped along the curved roof of the tunnel. After fifty feet the passage widened into a chamber. A breeze scurried down from another tunnel, at the far side of the cave.

Mounted on one wall was a rusted oil lamp, its flame fading as the wick was almost burnt away. Don picked up the lamp and shook it. Immediately it glowed brighter as some of the oil came into contact with the flame. The orange glow from the lamp reminded Don of his childhood, and winter evenings in front of the fire. Don and his brothers and sisters, watching television while their parents screamed at each other in the scullery. Happy days.

His attention was caught by something wholly unexpected. A mirror, set into the rock about twenty feet away. Don stepped closer, wondering what on Earth this place was. He estimated that he was right under the village green.

He looked into the mirror.

And screamed in terror.

Standing before him was not his own reflection, but a large man with mad eyes, anachronistic clothing, and bloodied hands. His expansive face bore a quizzical expression. 'The demon Hatch is known to us,' said the apparition. 'And Robert Matson visits when 'is weak spirit is fortified by drink. But, stranger, what dost thou want with Jack i' the Green?'

Up on the village green, covered by the dark blanket of night, Josie Luston had found what she was looking for in the drunken shape of Martin Price. As Josie lay back on the bone-hard mattress of grass and wriggled her arms from her leather jacket, Martin was trying to tug his T-shirt over his head.

'Gimme a hand then, Josie, I'm too bladdered,' he said with a mixture of anger and frustration.

'Do it yourself, boy,' she said with a giggle that sent a spasm of rigid anger up and down him.

'What are you laughing at?' he asked furiously, pinning the still-chuckling girl to the grass as he knelt astride her.

The scream that emerged from the Green Man caused both of them to sit up in embarrassment.

They both looked towards the pub. Its lights still blazed like a beacon in the night, and the door flapped open in the gentle breeze as Don Tyley sprinted away from the building, shrieking in terror.

'I don't get it,' said Steven. 'Baber didn't tell us how to find Jack.'

'You weren't listening,' said Ace. 'All that stuff about Jack's children. He must have meant the school.'

'But the legends say that Jack's under the green.'

'Yeah, but he's growing, right? And anyway, like you said, we can hardly start digging for him. I think the Matsons would have something to say about that.'

They trudged the lane towards the school in silence for some time, Steven jumping at every rustle from the hedgerows.

They heard the sound of a car engine just as the school came into view. 'Someone's coming,' said Steven.

'And fast, too,' said Ace. 'Better get off the road.'

They stood on the verge, the arms of the hedge prickling their backs. Two huge globes of light turned the corner, the headlights of the car dazzlingly bright.

'Who the hell is that?' asked Steven. 'They're driving like a lunatic.'

'They should have seen us by now,' said Ace, moving even further away from the road.

Instead of following the curve of the corner, the car's nose pointed in their direction. The engine screamed still more loudly as the accelerator was stamped to the floor.

'Christ,' said Ace. 'They're going to hit us!'

CHAPTER 12
UNFINISHED SYMPATHY

St James the Less was silent. Whatever voices Baber had once heard here – whatever answered prayers he had witnessed, or revelations he had received – had long since passed into memory. Now there was just the hard stool under his bent legs, and a church full of emptiness.

Baber continued his prayers, but it was as if he was shouting into an infinity of nothing.

'My God, my God, why have you forsaken me?' he cried. The rough canvas that covered the broken stained-glass window twitched, as if his words were enough to shake the church's foundations. But it was just the wind, patrolling restlessly through Hexen Bridge.

Baber sighed. At theological college he'd read about what St John of the Cross had called the dark night of the soul, but back then it was just words, an abstract concept. He had studied hundreds of miles from Hexen Bridge, and his faith had never seemed more alive.

But the dark cloud of unknowing had swallowed him almost as soon as he returned to his birthplace, to the church his family had watched over for centuries. God might be the Lord of the whole Earth, but even he seemed to draw the line at Hexen Bridge.

Baber remembered the conversation with the young girl, Ace, and her friend. The weight of the dark secrets of decades had pressed him down, threatening to snap him like a twig. And yet… Some part of him wanted to share the burden, to bring the shadows into the light and see them fade. The girl was overconfident… But perhaps she did hold the key, along with that mysterious Doctor whom everyone spoke about, but no one could describe.

Should he have said more? Had he said too much already?

He paused, a sudden brightness stabbing into his soul like pillars of sunlight through storm clouds. So used was he to unrelenting depression that he barely recognised the glimmer of hope that – quite without prompting – gripped him.

Baber got unsteadily to his feet, rheumatism nagging at his joints. For all his cries into the shadows of eternity, searching for the unknowable Light in the dark of the world, he felt better now than when he first came into the church. And he could not find any explanation for it.

Baber managed a smile as he turned to the sheet held in place over the shattered window. It was twitching again, the wind billowing it like a sail.

Baber leaned down to pick up a tiny sliver of glass that Megan Tyley had obviously missed that morning. He cradled it in his hand, a small red tear, still sharp enough to cut if not disposed of properly.

He straightened, remembering the tears the organist had shed back in the early 1980s when they had finally found the money to clean the old pipes. He had chosen to play 'Jesu, Joy of Man's Desiring' first, and as his hands moved over the keys he had –

The covering over the broken window surged again, this time concentrating on a single spot as if something were trying to push through.

Baber wasn't scared. He could barely feel his pulse increase as the finger of twig came through like a knife, slicing down in a long arc.

There was a rush of metal as the car flew off the road and into a ditch, its engine shrieking as the wheels lost their grip on the ground. Ace darted out of the way just in time, but there had been an audible thump as the vehicle passed Steven, whose body rolled on to the tarmac road.

Ace got to her feet, feeling for bruises, and then ran to Steven's side. A gash had opened up over his forehead, but he seemed otherwise unhurt. He muttered something, staring in disbelief at the motionless car, which had twisted part-way on to its side, the bonnet held fast by a thick hedge.

Ace ran up to the driver's door and yanked it open. 'What the bloody hell –'

The driver was Joanna Matson, her face still partly smothered by the inflated air bag. She had made no attempt to free herself and hung limply in the seat belt, her arms trailing at her side.

The engine was still screaming, the impact seeming to have knocked the gear stick into neutral. Joanna's foot was clamped down on the accelerator.

Ace reached in and turned the keys, removing them from the twisted steering column. The radio, which had been burbling out an inane Sugar Coma ballad, gave an indignant snort of static and died.

Joanna Matson stared ahead, seemingly unaware of anything that was going on around her. Ace shook her shoulders. Hard. 'Oi!' she shouted, in the older woman's ear. 'What are you playing at?'

At length Joanna looked up. Tears had transformed her mascara into panda eyes. Brightly coloured lipstick had smudged, turning her lips and one cheek into a jagged slash of red. She opened her mouth to speak, but said nothing until Steven approached the car, hobbling.

'Steven,' she said, her voice finding something of the tone of a shocked schoolteacher. 'What are you doing with this common tart?'

The scarecrow creature pulled itself through the canvas in a clatter of spidery limbs. Its eyes stared at Baber. Accusing him.

Even Baber had to look away, and he stumbled backward as another scarecrow came through, one shoulder studded with splinters of glass and lead.

'I only told the girl what she already knew,' announced Baber loudly.

The figures paused for a moment, rocking their heads from side to side as if trying to pinpoint the source of the unexpectedly strong declamation. Then, thickly wadded hands outstretched before them like grim somnambulists, the two scarecrows strode down the side aisle.

Baber was at the door. 'Anyway,' said Baber, in a quieter voice, 'perhaps it's for the best that it should all end now. I can only carry the blackness in my soul for so long.' Despite the bravery of his words, Baber knew then that he wanted to live, that life itself was a thing to be treasured. Simple animal self-preservation took over.

He flung open the inner door just as the first scarecrow lunged, and knocked it off balance. Baber turned to run – the main door was almost within his grasp – when the second creature swung out an arm.

Baber felt sticks and straw and brambles smash into the side of his face, drawing blood. He collapsed to his knees, before being jerked back on to his feet by strong hands that gripped his shoulders and throat.

'Tell me more about Jack i' the Green,' said the Doctor as Denman drove his car through the London suburbs.

'Like he said,' noted Denman, jabbing a thumb towards Trevor Winstone, 'it's hard for an outsider to understand.'

'I've lived with a *knowledge* of the evil in Hexen Bridge for longer than either of you,' said the Doctor cryptically. 'I just never knew the *reasons*.'

'It's because we're all damned,' said Winstone, shaking his head. 'No hope of redemption.'

'Everyone has that,' said the Doctor. 'It's what characterises humanity. You are born, you live, you are terrified by death, and obsessed with guilt and the desire for rationality. And you are redeemed by…' He paused and turned to look at Denman who, he noticed, was crying. 'Love,' he said at last. 'It's all you need.'

'Has anybody ever told you that you sound like a hippie?' said Winstone cynically.

'Yes,' said the Doctor. Again he turned to Denman. 'Stop the car,' he said. 'Now.'

'What?'

'Stop the car.'

Denman pressed his foot down on the brake pedal.

'Give me a five-pound coin,' the Doctor added, looking back and forth between Denman and Winstone. After a momentary pause, both men produced handfuls of loose change. The Doctor took a bright brass-coloured coin from Trevor, and opened the car door. 'Wait here,' he said.

Thomas Baber didn't even cry out as the scarecrows dragged him towards the village green. He knew that the grassy area would be writhing with tendrils and roots, and that they were waiting for him. Jack i' the Green was notoriously intolerant of disobedience, and his limbs twitched in the glorious moonlight.

The Doctor returned to the car and handed the coin back to Trevor.

'What was all that about?' asked Denman.

'I wanted to talk to Ace,' said the Doctor sadly. 'But there's no reply at the Green Man. I suppose it's very late, but I'm worried.'

'I'll never get used to that name,' said Denman, angrily. 'Why does everything have to change? Why can't anything stay the same?'

'An inevitable process,' said the Doctor, before fully catching the meaning of Denman's words. 'What did it used to be called?' he asked. But he already knew the answer, just as he had *always* known. It had been right before his eyes, every time he had been in Hexen Bridge.

'Jack in the Green,' said Denman and Trevor simultaneously.

'And they altered the name recently?'

'Last year,' replied Trevor. 'Bob Matson said they wanted to reflect a change in the village.' He looked at the Doctor curiously. 'Does it mean anything?'

'It reminds me,' said the Doctor, 'that it's later than I thought. I have to talk to Hatch. Urgently.'

Ace felt bad about smacking Joanna in the face, but it seemed to have done the trick. Natural colour was returning to her cheeks, and her eyes were less fixed than before.

'Sorry,' said Ace, 'but no one calls me "common" and gets away with it.'

Joanna nodded heroically, trying to hold back the tears. 'I just thought... You and him... I saw you both together and I lost it.'

Steven Chen knelt at her side. 'What the hell are you playing at, Jo? I thought we'd sorted everything out. Ace and I aren't going out or anything.' He smashed his fist into the side of the written-off car in frustration. 'You could have killed us!'

'I know. I can't explain it. It was like this anger surged up inside me, and I just couldn't do anything to stop it. I was so... jealous.'

Ace took a few steps away from the car, in case she lost her temper again. She stared up at the night sky and breathed deeply. She'd heard of road rage, but this was ridiculous.

She glanced back at the car. Joanna and Steven were talking in hushed, lovey-dovey tones, his arm around her shoulder. Ace pushed her fingers at her throat and made gagging noises, for the benefit of no one in particular.

Something stepped out on to the lane, a mass of dark shadows, twisted into vaguely human form. It turned in the direction of the wrecked car.

A stuffed scarecrow face stared implacably back at Ace.

Ace turned back to Joanna and Steven. 'We've got compan –'

The windscreen shattered, spraying glass like water droplets.

A second stickman had forced its way through the hedge and on to the bonnet of the car.

Joanna screamed, cleaving the still night air, then lapsed into choking. Its hands already around the woman's throat, the scarecrow pulled itself through the windscreen.

'That's Hatch's car,' said Denman as they drove up to the Wellton private clinic. The Doctor could see the chauffeur running from the ministerial limousine and towards the brightly lit building entrance.

'We've arrived, and to prove it we're here,' said Trevor with a chuckle as he sat forward and followed the Doctor's gaze. 'A bit of advance warning for Matt. You think he'll be pleased to see us?'

'I was planning to ask him that,' said the Doctor, getting out of the car and rushing towards the building. Denman followed close behind, dragging the handcuffed Winstone with him. Beyond the deserted entrance hall were a series of anonymous corridors, but the Doctor made for the main stairwell, with the footsteps of the chauffeur echoing somewhere ahead of him. 'Research-and-development labs,' the Doctor called over his shoulder to Denman, who was just beginning to climb the stairs. 'Quick as you can.'

At the top of the stairs the Doctor found himself in another long corridor. To his left a pair of fire doors were still swinging. 'This way!' the Doctor called as Denman and Winstone emerged into the corridor behind him. They ran through the doors, then through another pair. And found themselves in a brightly lit operating theatre.

The first thing that Trevor and Denman saw was Rebecca Baber on one of the white leather couches. A gag had been stuffed clumsily into her mouth, and she wore a pale slipover operating gown. She struggled against her bonds, her eyes wide with panic.

Behind her stood three men. One was Slater, the chauffeur, holding a lethal-looking knife; another wore a surgeon's mask and gown. The third was Matthew Hatch, smirking, a gun in one hand.

'Doctor,' said Hatch brightly. 'We've been expecting you.'

The Doctor moved into the room and cautiously approached the operating table. 'For goodness' sake, Hatch, this is serious.'

'Indeed,' said Hatch, turning his attention to Denman and Winstone. 'You couldn't even carry out my instructions?' he asked Trevor angrily.

'Well, you know, I tried,' replied Winstone, holding up his handcuffs apologetically.

Denman took a pace forward, snarling like an animal, but Hatch turned the gun in his direction. 'I really must have a word with my colleague the Home Secretary about you, ex-Chief Constable,' noted Hatch. 'Search them for weapons,' he told Slater, who moved quickly towards Denman and Trevor.

'How did I know,' said the Doctor, 'that whatever devious and overcomplicated plan you were hatching, if you'll pardon the pun, it would involve someone being tied up?' He peered more closely. 'It's Miss Baber, isn't it? Good evening.' He doffed his hat.

'Very amusing,' said Hatch as Slater finished his search of the two men.

'They're clean,' he said.

'Good,' continued Hatch. 'If they move, you know what to do.' He turned back to the Doctor. 'You shouldn't have interfered, Doctor,' he said sadly.

'Couldn't help it,' noted the Doctor. 'It's my job.'

'Interference?'

'Hmm.' The Doctor ignored Hatch, and walked around the table to the silent surgeon. 'How do you do?' he said holding out a hand. 'I'm the Doctor.'

'Nicholas Bevan,' said the surgeon instantly. 'Erm, a doctor of what, exactly?'

'Oh, this and that,' replied the Doctor. 'What's your speciality? Genetics?'

Bevan cast a nervous glance at Hatch and then back at the Doctor. 'You've heard of me, perhaps?'

'No,' said the Doctor. He leaned over the operating table and gave Rebecca a reassuring pat on the head. 'Don't worry, my dear,' he said. 'We'll have you out of there in a jiffy.'

'If you hurt her…' began Trevor, his voice overwhelmed with emotion. The chauffeur gave a menacing flick of the blade, and Trevor shrank back towards the door.

'She's more interested in monkeys than people, Trev,' said Hatch. 'Has she never told you?' He pushed the Doctor away from the table. 'She's screwed me up one time too many. And, family or no family, nobody screws with me.' Hatch smiled. 'Pardon *my* pun.'

'Not even Jack i' the Green?' asked the Doctor quickly.

Hatch spun around, his eyes ablaze. 'What dost thou know of Jack i' the Green?' he asked, his voice guttural and rough.

'Not as much as I'd like to,' said the Doctor. 'I'd really like to meet him. Could you arrange that?'

'Old Jack don't be needing the likes of 'ee,' said Hatch.

'Are you all right, Matt?' asked Bevan.

Hatch turned his head slowly towards his friend. 'Fine,' he said in his own voice. 'Why do you ask…?'

'*Jack*,' said the Doctor. Hatch's attention snapped back to him. 'I want to talk to Jack. Are *you* Jack?'

'I am he, and he is me…'

'…and we are all together,' continued the Doctor.

'Don't play games,' said Hatch. 'I have the cure, Doctor.'

'What are you talking about?' shouted Denman, but the Doctor shushed him to silence.

'The cure?'

'The final obliteration of Jack's taint,' said Hatch, as though that explained everything.

'The people of Hexen Bridge cannot reproduce outside of that environment,' stated the Doctor. 'And you've isolated the mutated gene that controls that.'

Hatch smiled. 'We took genetic material and ova from Rebecca, made certain changes to the DNA, and synthesised a serum.'

'So you'll be able to fill the world with little Hatches?' queried the Doctor. 'I'm delighted for you, if somewhat horrified for everyone else.'

'You don't understand. Sterility is only part of the problem.' Hatch tapped the side of his head. 'We humans have so much potential up here that we simply do not use.' He smiled a grey smile. 'Like Jack, I abhor waste.'

'And the drug we saw in the water supply in Liverpool liberates untapped psychic ability,' said the Doctor.

'Yes. We've combined a concentrated version of that drug with the new serum.'

'You mustn't use it,' said the Doctor. 'Jack will destroy you.'

'Doctor,' said Hatch softly. 'You're making a habit of being too late. I took the drug ten minutes before you arrived. I now have the power of the universe flowing through me!'

There was a sudden crackle in the air, like the release of static electricity. The Doctor's skin felt prickly and hot. 'You've used alien technology,' he said.

There were worried looks on the faces of Trevor and Denman, and even Slater was relaxing his grip on the knife.

The vibration increased until it began to pound like an industrial piston. The air around Hatch was glowing. His skin was a spectral pale, his eyes burning fire across the room and into the Doctor's mind.

'*I am he and he is me.*'

The others fell to their knees, clutching their heads, screaming. Rebecca Baber thrashed wildly against her restraints, her eyes bulging.

The Doctor resisted for as long as he could, his face a mask of pain. By the time he crumpled to the floor, overwhelmed by the assault, Denman, Trevor, Slater, Rebecca and Bevan had long since succumbed to Hatch's power.

The humming died away. Hatch stepped over the bodies and walked out of the room.

PART FOUR
MAD JACK'S EYES

CHAPTER 13
THE VACANT ZONE

Ace threw herself at the scarecrow, dragging it away from Joanna. Her fingers dug deep into the creature's eye sockets, stabbing into the cloth and the rotting vegetation beneath. At least, that's what Ace told herself it was. When she pulled her hand free, her fingers were wet and coloured reddish-brown.

In the car, Joanna was screaming. Steven stood rooted to the spot, his mouth hanging open.

Ace rolled free of the scarecrow, aiming a kick up at the creature's head. There was a satisfying thump of impact – Ace imagined the brain rolling around inside the cloth-covered head – and the creature stumbled backward, arms flailing.

Ace looked down the road. More scarecrows, cross shapes against the rising sun, were lumbering slowly towards them.

Joanna was babbling hysterically.

'Get her out of the car!' shouted Ace.

'Then what?' asked Steven.

'Run!'

They ran.

A hundred yards down the road, Ace looked back. The scarecrows had stopped beside their fallen colleague, pulling the creature to its feet. It was an almost pathetic sight.

Ace grinned. Then she remembered that she was being chased through an English village by killer scarecrows and that wiped the smile from her face. 'I think we've got their attention,' she said, breaking back into a trot after Steven and Joanna.

'Jack's sent them,' wailed Joanna. 'We're all going to die.'

'Not if I can help it,' said Ace with a grim determination, glancing at Steven. 'Come on, let's get to your parents' place. We should be safe enough inside.'

Steven grimaced. 'I'm glad you're so confident.'

'I'm not, I'm optimistic,' replied Ace, honestly. 'But *they* don't know that.'

The harvest had begun.

The stickmen dragged the weak and vulnerable from their beds and on to the green, where alien fronds reached out hungrily. Jack ate what he could, and what he could not eat, he *used*. His hollow men then turned to the wicked and the arrogant.

Jack i' the Green was a kindly father, longing to shower gifts upon his children. Now, at last he could – the gifts of death and screaming insanity.

All the while the black stain grew, tentacles pulling themselves from the ground, flailing blindly in the air, then burrowing down again. The scarecrows marched relentlessly as Jack expanded, reaching out towards the surrounding villages.

Bob Matson woke with a start. It was as if he'd had a sudden dream of falling from a great height, but the only images that penetrated his fogged unconscious were of the stickmen and the spreading black stain.

That hadn't really happened, had it? He hadn't really been... expelled?

The mattress beneath his back was thin and hard, the sheets provided little warmth.

Bob Matson sat up on the park bench, the dirty pages of newspaper falling from his legs like layers of sloughed skin.

Where the hell was he?

Matson looked around him at an unfamiliar expanse of short grass and flower beds. Beyond the park were tall buildings and countless rows of red-brick semis. A feeling of claustrophobia, such as he had never experienced in Hexen Bridge, washed over him.

He *had* been banished. He remembered now with grim clarity

the flight from the scarecrows that had pursued him until he was well clear of the village. And, if his dream was to be believed, he'd been granted only a temporary stay of execution.

He was so alone.

He pulled the shirt collar up around his neck and stared at the first light of the rising sun, shivering.

Eventually the noise, the incessant ringing in his ears… faded.

Denman picked himself up from the floor, cradling his throbbing head and swallowing down the feelings of nausea. He was surprised to find himself the last to wake. The Doctor paced the room while Trevor sat, minus handcuffs, comforting a clearly distressed Rebecca Baber. Hatch's chauffeur and Bevan, the surgeon, were closely questioning the Doctor about their employer.

'Multiple personality disorder?' asked Bevan. 'I've seen similar cases.'

'No,' said the Doctor. 'Nothing so simple.'

Denman tried to get to his feet.

'Ah, welcome back to the land of the living,' said the Doctor brightly.

'We've got to get after him,' said Denman in a slurred voice, and promptly fell down again. The Doctor helped him to stand.

'We've been unconscious for over two hours,' said the Doctor. 'It's almost dawn. I hardly think another ten minutes is going to make any difference. Hatch will probably be in Hexen Bridge by now. So, just take your time. Psychic energy is a very potent weapon.'

'You talk as if you've seen this sort of thing before,' said Bevan incredulously.

'Oh, I have,' said the Doctor. 'Several times.' He moved across to Trevor and Rebecca and squatted down beside them. 'And how are you, my dear?' he asked.

'Bloody sore,' said Rebecca angrily. 'Do you know what that man did to me?' she shouted, pointing at Bevan.

'I told him how painful and undignified the process of extraction was,' said Bevan defensively, 'but Hatch insisted.'

'I think it would be best if you both left now,' said the Doctor addressing Bevan and Slater, nodding towards the door. He watched the men leave with grim detachment.

'They're in it up to their necks,' said Denman, his words still having to force themselves out of his mouth. 'You can't just let them go…'

'You're *all* in it up to your necks, Mr Denman,' said the Doctor slowly. 'But I cannot afford to be distracted – not by you, your families, even Hatch. Only Jack i' the Green concerns me now.'

The scarecrows surrounded the village, a chain of debased humanity. A line of the creatures stretched across the main road into Hexen Bridge, but they parted respectfully as Matthew Hatch approached.

He felt like royalty. Or some kind of god.

He parked the car in the centre of Hexen Bridge. People were being dragged from their homes and on to the green by the stickmen, and then held in place as Jack consumed them. Their screams did not penetrate the airtight tranquillity of the Mercedes.

Hatch got out, shutting the door behind him. He didn't bother locking the car. With scarcely a glance at the villagers, swamped by foliage and frond-like limbs, Hatch strolled into the Green Man. The door was hanging open in the breeze.

The pub was in quite a state. Stools had been smashed, and broken glass was strewn across the damp floor. The body of a young girl was jammed into one window, as if she had tried to escape from something, only to slit her throat on the jagged glass.

The body twitched. A stickman was trying to pull the corpse through what was left of the window frame.

Hatch walked behind the bar, his fingertips brushing over the mahogany case of impaled butterflies. As he busied himself with the trapdoor, paper-dry wings fluttered under glass.

'You said you'd seen psychic energy like that before?' asked Rebecca as Denman drove them through the dawn into Wiltshire.

'Yes,' said the Doctor. 'At a place called Little Hodcombe.'

'I know Hodcombe,' noted Trevor. 'It's about twenty miles from Hexen Bridge.'

'What happened?' asked Rebecca.

'Oh, the usual nonsense. Alien reconnaissance probe crashed there in the seventeenth century. Became walled up in the local church and was mistaken for the Devil. Finally revived in the 1980s, and tried to kill everyone. That kind of thing happens to me rather a lot, you know.'

Denman gave a snort of derision from the driving seat, but Trevor and Rebecca in the back were transfixed by the Doctor's story.

'You defeated it?' asked Trevor.

The Doctor nodded. 'It was destroyed. The link with its human conduit was severed when the poor man was killed, and the craft blew up. It was quite a sight. We stayed for a few weeks. Tegan, Turlough and I.' The Doctor paused, as if wondering how much of this made sense to complete strangers. 'Well, first I had to get Will Chandler back home to 1643. And what a right how-do-you-do *that* turned into. Anyway, after I'd brought Jane back to 1984 –'

'Jane Hampden?' asked Rebecca.

'Yes. Lovely girl. She asked a lot of questions, too!' The Doctor looked up to see if Rebecca was going to interrupt him again, but she remained silent so he continued. 'Anyway, being in the local teaching community, she helped to get me on to the board of governors at the Hexen Bridge school. I've kept an eye on the village ever since.'

'So you've known about Hexen Bridge for a while?'

The Doctor was rummaging for something in his pockets, a

distracted look on his face. 'Centuries.' he said simply. 'Until the incident at Little Hodcombe, I'd almost forgotten about Hexen Bridge. I first stumbled across the place back in 1971 –'

'That wasn't centuries ago,' said Rebecca, but the Doctor seemed not to hear.

'– and when I discovered the Malus creature just a few miles down the road... Well, I hoped there wasn't a link. But the psychic powers exhibited by Hatch seem to prove a connection.'

Rebecca shrugged. 'If you say so.'

'I should pop in and see Jane when all this is over,' announced the Doctor suddenly.

'She taught at Hexen Bridge for a term when I was there,' said Rebecca. 'I idolised her.'

'I'll bet not many of the other children did.'

'No,' said Trevor. 'She was an outsider. We tolerated her for her intellect, but despised her for not being one of us.'

'The story of Hexen Bridge in a nutshell,' said the Doctor, settling back in his seat and humming to himself.

Hatch stood before the ancient mirror in the cavern under the green, staring at quicksilver clouds that gradually formed a reflection. The body was his own, even down to the Paul Smith suit and manicured fingernails, but the face was constantly changing. In a blur it encompassed young and old, male and female – the souls Jack had devoured over the centuries.

The eyes were a constant, burning flame. The eyes of Jack i' the Green himself.

'Yes?' snapped the figure behind the mirror, momentarily taking on the sun-cracked face of a nineteenth-century farm worker.

'All is prepared. Everything is in place.'

'Everything?' A young girl's face, framed by dark bunches of hair, was incongruous atop a male torso.

'The killing fields in Liverpool have been seeded. We will travel there and feed.'

'Everything has gone as planned?' asked an old woman, eyes blank with cataracts.

'The full force of mankind's madness is being unleashed in that place.'

Jack's face stabilised for a moment: a balding man wearing old-fashioned spectacles. 'Then shall we feed.'

'Indeed. Our enemies cannot stop us now.'

Jack became a blur of faces. 'They still live?' spat the creature.

Hatch nodded dumbly. 'I – I couldn't kill them. I... I was weak.'

Jack calmed, the image settling on that of a tall man with eighteenth-century clothes. His thin, pockmarked face broke into a toothy smile. 'Come, sir, Jack awaits 'ee. Thou shalt never feel the weakness of thy flesh again.'

Matthew Hatch swallowed deeply, reaching out for the mirror. His fingers brushed the metal surface, feeling the cold of the emptiness of space.

The mirror parted like water, sucking his hand inside.

Closing his eyes, Matthew Hatch pushed his way through the mirror.

And screamed.

'There's one thing that bothers me,' said Trevor Winstone suddenly.

The Doctor's eyes snapped open. 'Only one?' he asked. 'Dear, dear. A *lot* of things are bothering me.'

'What did Hatch do in the clinic? The light, the noise...'

'A form of psychic energy. Not a rare phenomenon, but unusual in humans. Unless aided.'

'By...?' asked Rebecca and Trevor together.

The Doctor looked at Denman, as though the policeman would immediately produce the answer. 'Haven't got a clue,' said Denman, returning his attention to the road.

'It's Jack, isn't it?' asked Rebecca.

'You tell me,' replied the Doctor. 'You've lived with the

knowledge all of your lives.'

'These are things that aren't talked about,' said Trevor, turning and looking out of the window at the countryside flying by.

'No one likes us, we don't care,' said the Doctor with a soft chuckle. 'Oh come, now. It's too late in the day for secrets.' He looked at the sun, rising high into the sky. 'Metaphorically speaking.'

'But Trev's right,' said Rebecca. 'Hexen Bridge is different.' She shook her head. 'Nothing is clear any more. Every question throws up another question.'

'But the answers we do have lead to Hexen Bridge,' said the Doctor.

'I still can't understand how Hatch finding a cure for his infertility can have any impact on the outside world.'

'Jack's awakening,' said the Doctor, as if that explained everything.

'What?'

'How else could one man spread Jack's taint beyond Hexen Bridge?'

Denman seemed interested now. 'If he wants to populate a brave new world, sterile or not, it'll take him a long time,' he said.

'Hatch said the cure for infertility was just part of it,' pondered the Doctor. 'The answer is obscure, but it has something to do with Jack's taint, Hatch's new powers, and the substance introduced into the water supply on Merseyside.' The Doctor withdrew a test tube from his pocket. 'I was able to do a quick analysis of it while you were all unconscious.'

'And?' asked Denman.

'Jack *needs* this,' said the Doctor mysteriously. He shook the test tube gingerly.

'Jack's just a myth,' said Trevor suddenly, though his nervous eyes belied the strength of his words.

'You think so?' said the Doctor sharply. 'A myth with a predilection for human bodies and souls.' His eyes looked beyond the scared humans and out into the cosmos. 'Hakol,' he said slowly, 'is a place of nightmares.'

'Sorry?'

'It's in the star system Rifter,' said the Doctor. 'I'm starting to see what Jack is.'

'What?' asked Denman, braking suddenly. The car came to a shuddering halt.

'Something terrifying,' said the Doctor. 'I've watched entire planets reduced to lifeless husks by creatures like this.' He stared out of the window, watching the traffic that sped past. His forehead was creased with worry. 'A Hakolian invasion takes place in three stages. Firstly, a reconnaissance probe is sent to a likely world to check for psychic energy. If that is found in high enough measure, a battle vehicle is dispatched. The probe and the war creature are designed to function in tandem during the second stage, enslaving numerous individuals and destroying any potential opposition. They feed on hate and fear, channelling the psychic energy of the indigenous population. The bloodshed rises to a crescendo. Only when the conflict is over will the Hakolians arrive in person.'

'So that thing in Hodcombe you told us about...?'

'The Malus?'

'Yeah,' said Trevor. 'That was the probe?'

The Doctor nodded. 'The psychic energy released by a minor skirmish between Royalists and Cromwell's Parliamentary forces in 1643 woke it up for a while. It assessed the area, found the surrounding life forms to be full of superstition and fear, and thus suitable for the people of Hakol. It sent an invasion signal, and became dormant again. Waiting. Forty years later the battle creature arrived. Only it missed the target by a few miles, and fell on Hexen Bridge.'

'Jack?'

The Doctor dodged the question. 'You know, I always meant to go back and find out why the Hakolians didn't invade Earth after we destroyed the Malus, but I never got around to it. A mistake on my part.' He paused, as if unused to admitting failure. 'We know that the reconnaissance probe malfunctioned at some stage. The battle vehicle, what you call Jack i' the Green, never joined with the Malus. The Hakolians must have assumed that one or both were destroyed. Perhaps they quietly abandoned any idea of conquering Earth, on the assumption that if the creatures who lived there were strong enough to defeat either their probe, or their war machine, then it wasn't worth the effort.' The Doctor beamed delightedly. 'See, there's normally a simple explanation for everything!'

'So, Jack is a… machine?' asked Rebecca.

'It's partly a living thing, just like the Malus. A creature with enormous psychic power. Ultimately, the Malus was able to convert that mental energy into a number of actual physical manifestations. Who knows what Jack is capable of…?'

Trevor scratched his head. 'But why is Jack waking up? If he – it – hasn't received any orders to invade…'

'Ah,' said the Doctor. 'Good point.' His fingers formed a steeple in front of his face, deep in thought. 'Either Jack is malfunctioning, too – blindly carrying out its original instructions, just as the Malus did…'

'Or?'

A dark look crossed the Doctor's face. 'What if Jack's orders have been revised? The intent – to destroy and invade – would remain the same, but the means would change.' He swung around to Denman. 'Put your foot down,' he said.

They approached the Chinese restaurant from the rear. Even from a distance they could see that something was very wrong with A Taste of the Orient. An enormous hole gaped in the glass and metal of the conservatory, and scorch marks stretched up the walls of the main building.

'Fire,' said Ace, as the smell of burning hit her. 'Looks like it's been put out.'

'I know who did this,' said Steven with a snarl, giving Joanna an ominous glance as he led them into the restaurant.

Inside, the damage was surprisingly light. A spent fire extinguisher lay on a large patch of charred carpet. Tables had been overturned, and one wall had suffered some damage. Steven bent down to pick up a blackened piece of glass. A partly charred paper label still clung to it. He held it up to Joanna.

'A vodka bottle,' he said bitterly. 'Now, I wonder who in Hexen Bridge would have one of those.'

Joanna looked away, tearfully.

Behind them, someone moved over broken glass.

Ace and Steven spun around.

'Steven?' said a voice from the darkness.

'Mother?'

'I was so worried,' said the small woman, flinging herself into his arms. 'You must come with me quickly. There has been a fire.'

'I can see that. I should have been here!' Steven looked at his mother closely. 'Are you all right?'

'Yes, but Mr Luston and his wife were badly burnt, and your father is ill.'

'Is he in hospital?'

'No, he is in the kitchen. We... We don't want to leave the building. Something's happening on the green.'

They found Mr Chen sitting on a chair, a thick pillow behind him. Both hands were covered in bandages, and his face ran with sweat. He appeared to be dozing fitfully, giving an occasional gasp of pain.

'He belongs in a hospital,' Ace told Steven.

'I belong in the grave,' said the old man, his eyes snapping open. 'But not yet.'

'Father,' said Steven, kneeling at the man's side, 'what happened?'

Chen reached out a hand towards his son. Through the strands of bandage his skin was blackened and raw. 'We have kept the spirits at bay for so long,' said the old man. 'But now…'

'I know, Father, I know,' said Steven.

Ace moved to the kitchen window and looked out into the street. 'Company,' she said.

'How do they look?' asked Steven.

'Like a gang of Millwall bootboys, out on the town,' said Ace, moving back from the window. 'They're after blood.'

As she spoke, heavy blows began to rain down on the door.

CHAPTER 14
SACRIFICIAL BONFIRE

'Oh my God!'

Denman's sudden cry cut through the low murmur of conversation in the car. The Doctor, Trevor and Rebecca looked up. A neat row of motionless scarecrows stretched across the road, marking the outer boundary of Hexen Bridge.

'Welcoming committee?' ventured the Doctor.

'I doubt it very much,' said Denman, changing gear and slamming his foot to the floor. With a squeal of protest the car shot forward, smashing into the line of manikins. One bore the full impact of the car, somersaulting on to the bonnet, then the roof, in a blur of straw and cloth. The creature landed on the road behind, a sickening mess of torn limbs. Rebecca and Trevor turned in time to see the thing pick itself up and resume its sentry position, apparently unharmed.

'Let's hope it's as easy to get out again,' said the Doctor.

To their left, on the village green, they could see alien tendrils writhing hungrily as the people of Hexen Bridge were consumed by the alien mass that pushed up through the earth. A pair of scarecrows crossed the road in front of the car, dragging a screaming man by his legs.

'That's Mr Tyley,' said Rebecca, reaching instinctively for the car door.

'Look out!' shouted the Doctor as Denman swerved to avoid the scarecrows. A telephone pole loomed massively in front of them.

Time slowed as they impacted. The Doctor felt a dizzying surge of forward momentum, then the tight constriction around his chest as the seat belt did its job and the whiplash as he was thrown backward into his seat.

The heartbeat of silence after the crash was ruptured by Rebecca, who was shouting incoherently. The Doctor looked to his right and saw a smear of blood, staining the cracked windscreen. Denman was slumped in the driver's seat, a deep cut above his nose.

'We've got to get clear,' said the Doctor, throwing open the door and unsnapping his seat belt. 'Help me with Mr Denman,' he said as Trevor pulled himself from the car. The Doctor glanced towards the green and saw the scarecrows dropping Tyley into the cavernous maw of Jack. The scream was shrill and inhumanly loud.

The noise cut off suddenly. The stickmen turned towards the car.

Inside A Taste of the Orient, Ace and Joanna moved cautiously through the restaurant towards the glass conservatory as Steven and his mother helped Mr Chen out of the kitchen. The front door of the restaurant reverberated with unfeeling blows.

Ace had taken a meat cleaver from the kitchen, and she hefted it nervously in her hands. She took a couple of hesitant paces on the charred carpet. It crunched under her feet. 'Crispy deep-fried rug,' she said. 'Nah, that'll never take off.'

Without warning a straw-and-skin hand smashed through the glass inches from her face.

For the first time since she was ten, Ace let out something close to a scream. An arm followed the hand through the jagged glass, but got no further as Ace brought the full weight of the cleaver down, burying itself in the scarecrow's tweed jacket. She could almost imagine the creature's terrible, silent pain, but she felt no pity. Only anger.

'Stitch that, Worzel,' she said as the creature made a fruitless attempt to pull its arm back through the blackened glass. Another arm crashed through the conservatory wall and flailed around, helplessly searching for the source of its torment.

Ace and Joanna turned and ran back into the main building. The Chens had gathered just outside the kitchen. 'It's the straw-suckers, and they're not happy,' announced Ace. 'Let's try the stairs.'

They walked into the hallway, the sound of breaking glass behind them telling its own story.

The front door, to the left of the stairs, shook visibly, then ruptured completely, stopping the group in its tracks. The scarecrows poured through, masklike faces impassive, eyes burning with wordless hatred.

'Come on,' shouted Ace. 'Back to the kitchen!'

The car's engine was on fire, and the Doctor knew that the heat would soon ignite the petrol tank. He and Trevor struggled with Denman's unconscious body. The Chief Constable was a large man, and his big boots kept catching in the churned-up earth around the wrecked vehicle.

Rebecca stood some distance away from the burning car, watching the scarecrows nervously. The two stickmen who had dragged Don Tyley to his death had been joined by a number of others. Each seemed as unique as any human: one was tall and slim, with a twisted, misaligned head; another was squat and heavy-looking, a bloated stomach constantly disgorging straw. Another was like a child, its oversized face locked in a leering mockery of some playground game.

'They seem to be frightened of the flames,' Rebecca exclaimed, her voice momentarily blotting out the terrifying rending noises as the fire bit into the buckled metal of the car's bonnet.

The scarecrows were shambling around dumbly, trying to reach out for the humans, but shrinking back as the burning sparks flashed high into the air. 'Straw men,' said the Doctor through gritted teeth.

'They haven't thought about going *around* the car,' said Trevor.

The Doctor snorted. 'Jack seems to leave them with very little intelligence. These psychically controlled creatures are just puppets.'

With an apocalyptic thunderclap of noise, the car exploded, showering the green with pieces of metal and glass. The blast hit the Doctor and the others in the back, a fist of oily heat that hurled them to the ground. They were just beyond the range of the bullet-fast shrapnel.

The scarecrows were not so fortunate. One or two had been completely consumed in the fireball, leaving only black twigs and corn in their wake. Another burnt like a human torch, head and arms flailing through angry red flames.

The other stickmen fell back, as if in superstitious awe, watching as the burning scarecrow collapsed to the ground in a rain of dark flesh and bone.

The Doctor turned to Rebecca and Trevor. 'Wake him up,' he said, pointing at Denman. 'Then get some petrol – you saw what fire did to these creatures. And find Ace. Tell her to leave the big picture to me. She'll understand.'

'What are you going to do?' asked Trevor, wiping some of the soot from his face.

'I have a pressing engagement with Jack i' the Green,' said the Doctor. 'Matthew Hatch, too.'

'Where will you find them?' queried Rebecca.

The Doctor pointed to the inn that for centuries had watched the dark heart of Hexen Bridge. 'The Green Man,' announced the Doctor. 'Formerly the Jack in the Green.' He sighed. 'It's obvious when you think about it, isn't it?'

The kitchen door shook, the wooden panels bulging. Cracks started to trail across from the hinges.

Steven Chen and Ace looked around the room for something that they could wedge against the door, but the cupboards and work surfaces were fixed to the floor.

'Come on!' shouted Ace, as much to herself as to her

companions. 'There's got to be something we can use.'

'The fridge?' queried Chen, pointing at the freestanding unit.

'Oh, great,' said Ace sarcastically. 'If things get nasty we can offer them a lager!'

A large split appeared in the door. Mrs Chen cried out, as if she felt every impact herself.

'Got any better ideas?' snapped Steven. He pulled the plug from the wall socket and began pushing the refrigerator towards the door. Ace helped, rocking it from side to side. Vegetables spilled out on to the floor, and Steven Chen kicked them away impatiently.

A scarecrow hand smashed through a door panel, tearing at the splintered wood.

With a cry of triumph, Ace and Steven pushed the fridge against the door.

There was a crack of bone and twig from behind the refrigerator.

'Now what?' asked Steven.

Ace scanned the hanging utensils and huge chest freezers that dominated the kitchen, pulling another cleaver and an enormous serrated carving knife from a wooden block. Joanna Matson stood at the side door that led outside, tugging bolts into position.

A dark shape appeared in the small frosted pane of glass high up on the outer door. Joanna screamed. 'We're trapped!'

The figure knocked at the door. 'Let me in! Please!' It was a human voice, edged with panic. 'They're coming for me.'

Without thinking, Ace ran towards the side entrance.

'Stop!' Steven pushed her arm away from the locks. 'You don't know what that is.'

'It's the Reverend Baber.' The voice from outside was a pleading whine. The faintest impression of a face could be seen through the glass. 'If you don't let me in they'll kill me!'

From the other end of the kitchen, the inner door shook under repeated blows.

Ace shoved Steven to one side. 'It's the vicar. We've got to let him in.'

'No!' Joanna's shout was unexpectedly loud in the confines of the kitchen. 'That's not him!'

As she spoke, a straw-filled hand smashed through the glass in the door.

'My head hurts,' said Denman, sluggishly. 'What happened?'

'We got lucky,' replied Trevor as he led the policeman through a twisting patch of trees towards the open field beyond. 'The Doctor wants us to find something to burn them with.'

Denman seemed to be having difficulty focusing on his surroundings. He rested for a second by a gnarled old oak, and patted it lovingly. 'I used to bring my wife down here when we were first married,' he said with a faraway look.

'Oh God, not the life story,' said Trevor, cuttingly. 'Come on, we've got work to do.'

Ahead of them stretched a field of billowing wheat, leading towards White's farm. Rebecca was crouching down beside a five-bar gate. She looked up nervously as they approached.

'Get down,' she hissed, letting out a sigh of relief. 'The whole area's crawling with scarecrows.' She gave Denman a close look as though his glazed eyes held some secret wisdom. 'Are you sure you're all right?' she asked.

'No,' said Denman flatly. 'But I'm not going to lie down for a bunch of walking rag men.'

'That's the spirit,' said Trevor sarcastically. 'Come on, there are some outbuildings beyond this field. There's bound to be some fuel there.'

Thomas Baber's face lay somewhere behind the scraps of cloth and the trailing veins of corn, but it had been hideously transformed. Only the dark, glowing eyes spoke of the remnants of a human intelligence – a spark of life corrupted beyond words and reason.

'In,' sighed the creature, Baber's strong voice replaced by what sounded like the moan of winter winds. 'Let me in.' Long arms of branch and bone extended into the kitchen, searching for human life. The nails on the hands were like bramble thorns. With a terrifying rending sound, the creature pulled itself through the small window, a space through which no human could climb.

'We're trapped,' repeated Joanna Matson, the word a grim mantra. 'There's no escape from them.'

'The wine cellar!' exclaimed Steven Chen, running across the room to a trapdoor set into the floor. 'It's small, but it's our only chance.'

Ace looked at the wooden hatch with suspicion. 'Is that going to be any stronger than the doors?'

Steven Chen shrugged. 'I don't know. But I don't see we've got any choice.'

Chen's father had already struggled back on to his feet, wincing against the pain. 'It will delay their attack a little. And time is always precious,' said the old man, his voice a harsh whisper.

'Yeah, but we'll be caged like rats,' persisted Ace. 'Once we're down there, there'll be nowhere else to go.'

Steven Chen had already pulled the hatch open. 'You can stay here and be butchered if you want,' he said.

Ace looked around the room again, and saw for the first time another window, high up on one wall, above the ovens. 'I'll try to get out. Get some help.' She gestured towards Steven's parents. 'You're right, you've got to try to protect them for as long as possible.'

Steven's father was wheezing as he made his way down the wooden stairs into the cellar.

Ace handed Steven the meat cleaver. 'Don't know if this'll come in handy, but…'

Steven took the implement, watching as Joanna Matson climbed through the hatch. 'I'll do what I can,' he said.

With a resigned shrug of the shoulders, Steven disappeared down into the artificial twilight of the cellar, pulling the trapdoor over his head.

The Baber scarecrow hit the floor with a thud. Its head moving almost sadly, it shuffled towards Ace, angular hands outstretched.

Ace leapt for the window.

The first barn was empty, but the second contained a weather-beaten tractor and a cluttered array of rusted equipment. The stone tiles were thick with grease and dust. Towards the back the floor was cleaner, dominated by towering bales of hay.

Rebecca started pushing through the clutter of old feed bags and plastic crates, looking for a can of fuel. 'I'll check up there,' announced Trevor, swiftly climbing a ladder to the hayloft.

A scream from Rebecca stopped him five rungs from the top.

He slid back down and ran across the barn. Denman and Rebecca were staring at the stickman form of a scarecrow, lying abandoned against the wall. Beside the scarecrow were the badly burnt remains of an old Guy Fawkes effigy. Its head, made from a football, was blackened and scarred from the flames of the previous year's bonfire. An old navy-blue woollen jumper covered a childlike body and limply splayed legs.

Trevor glanced back at the bulky form of the scarecrow. 'Is it…?' he began.

'Let's find out,' said Denman, pulling a pitchfork from the hay. He strode towards the scarecrow, his movements betraying the terror beneath his determination.

'Be careful,' warned Rebecca, backing away slowly.

Denman thrust the fork into the face of the scarecrow. The metal prongs sank into the rotting straw. He twisted the wooden handle, and most of the face staved in, releasing a sickly-sweet aroma. With a sigh of relief he removed the pitchfork and turned back to Trevor.

'No sweat,' he said. 'It's a *real* one!'

Denman laughed as he weighed the pitchfork in his hand, turning his attention to the Guy. 'I suppose I'd better deflate this little man, just in case,' he said with a wry grin, pushing the fork prongs towards the football-shaped head.

The fork pushed through the perished rubber easily, but came to a jarring halt as it hit something hard beneath. Denman half turned in surprise. 'Wha–?'

The doll-like creature knocked the pitchfork away, then flew at Denman's throat with talons outstretched.

The Doctor stepped into the pub through the open front door. Things were quieter on the green now, as if the scarecrows had taken most of the easy targets in the vicinity, and were moving further afield – which was worrying enough in itself.

The Doctor imagined what was going on, elsewhere, as the stickmen burst into houses. He could almost hear the screams of terror. The sound of bones breaking, like bundles of twigs.

In the Academy, his always-active imagination had been one of his greatest gifts, the one attribute that drove him on to greatness and doomed him to mediocrity. Now it was a curse. The Doctor shook his head, looking around the public bar of the Green Man.

In a scene of quiet devastation, the butterflies were little pockets of movement and light. His eyes wide in amazement, the Doctor approached the display cases. Within, the creatures had revived, despite the pins that kept them impaled on small squares of cork. Their legs flapped in anger at their new imprisonment, futile wings beating together.

'Jack kept you here,' whispered the Doctor. 'Now Jack is releasing you.'

Without warning, the ground shook.

The Doctor ran to a window, and saw that the green itself was... *writhing*. The ground squirmed and bucked as great threads of evil twisted beneath it.

The floor beneath the Doctor's feet shuddered again, and then became still. He returned to the cabinets, noticing a large split in one of the glass covers.

A rainbow of butterflies poured out, a fast-flowing stream of light in the cloying gloom of the Green Man. Moving as one, the creatures flapped over the counter, and disappeared out of sight.

The Doctor walked behind the beer pumps. The trapdoor was open, and the insects poured down into the basement.

Intrigued, the Doctor followed.

The cellar was dark and smelled of hops. The tarpaulin covering had been pulled away from the tunnel entrance, revealing a dark mouth of natural stone. The butterflies flowed down it, encouraging him on.

Water dripped from the walls of the tunnel, and sonorous murmurings from all around indicated that this was the heart of Jack – and that Jack was still moving. The passage widened into a cave, dominated by an ornate mirror. The butterflies streamed into the mirror, passing straight through and vanishing from sight.

The Doctor stood before the frame of gold. There was no reflection. Over his head, the last few insects fluttered through the mirror.

The Doctor breathed deeply, knowing that this was where everything started – and, hopefully, where it would end.

He stepped through the mirror.

CHAPTER 15
CEREMONY IN A LONELY PLACE

Rebecca picked up the fallen pitchfork and brought its full weight down on the scarecrow's back. The prongs bit deep into the mass of straw, but the little creature clung tenaciously to Denman, slowly throttling the life from him.

Rebecca shouted for Trevor, but he was nowhere to be seen. She turned in panic, and found what they had been looking for: a can of diesel fuel. She fell to her knees, her hands scrabbling at the cap, rusted solid with age. After four attempts, Rebecca finally got the top to move. The can squealed in protest.

The pungent smell of the fuel hit Rebecca full in the face, and for a moment she felt dizzy and overwhelmed. Then she remembered Denman, and heard the choking rattle of his breathing. She turned and hurled the can at the stickman.

This time the blow was unexpected, and it knocked the creature away from Denman. The policeman collapsed in a heap, clutching at his own throat as tightly as the stickman had.

The terrifying little creature rose to its full height. Its eyes, deep in the now exposed face of vegetation, screamed vengeance. Rebecca got to her feet, crying out at the stinging pain in her knees, bloodied by the barn floor. All she could think about was her mother's childhood tales of Jack's implike children.

A hiss of outrage emerged from the creature. It moved with great deliberation towards Rebecca, hands outstretched, stick-fingers clicking as they closed in a fist, then opened again.

'Go away!' screamed Rebecca.

Somewhere an engine kicked into life with a low growl, but Rebecca was unable to tear away her eyes from those of the stickman.

'Please,' she said in a hoarse whisper. The machine noise increased.

The creature was only inches away. She could feel its breath on her cheeks.

The roar of the machine cut through her stupor.

Rebecca looked up just as the creature turned its head.

The tractor bore down on the manikin, the silver blades of the hedge cutter spinning.

There was a swish, then a dull thud of impact, and a red mosaic formed on the barn wall, spattering Rebecca's face with blood.

The whirling blades began to slow as the tractor stopped. Rebecca put her hands to her face, and they came away smeared scarlet.

'You took your time!' she shouted angrily, the terror that had rendered her incapable of movement now exploding like steam from a valve.

Trevor jumped down from the tractor seat. 'You ever tried to manoeuvre one of those things?' he asked, stepping across the barn towards the prone figure of Denman.

'Is he all right?' asked Rebecca.

'He's alive,' said Trevor, kneeling beside the policeman. He looked back at the diesel can lying on its side in the centre of the barn. 'And you found some fuel, too. Well done.'

'Ohmygod.' Rebecca rushed to the can. Only a small amount of the precious fluid had spilled out. 'Right,' she said, trying to stop her hands shaking. 'We've got a weapon.'

On the other side of the mirror, Matthew Hatch stood, waiting for the Doctor. At least, the man resembled the politician in outward appearance, but his eyes were alive with an unfathomable alien intelligence. Hatch's usual scorn was as nothing compared with the outright contempt that dominated his features now.

'Hatch?' asked the Doctor, his voice swallowed up by the cathedral expanse of the dark phantom world behind the mirror.

Hatch – Hatch's body – took a step closer. 'You should not have survived the transition.' He lapsed into silence, as if searching out some long-buried piece of information. 'The Doctor,' he said at last, nodding to himself. 'A problem.'

The Doctor smiled. 'I'm delighted that you remember me.'

Hatch continued to observe the Doctor, his face twisted in a grin of amusement. 'Hatch is no longer here.'

The Doctor shook his head. 'No, he's in there, somewhere. You're just using his body.'

Hatch laughed. 'He thought my hold on him was slight. He believed he could use *me*. How pathetic.'

'*You* used his infertility, his fears and passions…'

'Humans are full of fear and passion.'

'The clinic?'

'I offered Hatch a solution.'

'And now?' The Doctor's questioning, though softly spoken, was relentless.

'Hatch has ceased to exist. What you see before you is a hybrid.'

'Of what?'

'A human being and Jack. To be in my presence is to taste my madness. You have entered Jack's domain.'

The Doctor looked around him. The void was ever-changing, sparkling with light and skewed images. 'Can't say I approve of the decor. Anyway, I don't suppose "Jack" is your real name. How should I address you?'

'Lord Jack i' the Green will suffice,' said Hatch, imperiously. 'Or God. Pleased to meet you…'

The Doctor laughed. 'You're a machine, an organic robot. Like the Malus: a simple vehicle, no more worthy of respect than the car that brought me here.'

'You know of the Malus?'

'Know it?' The Doctor's eyes narrowed. 'I *destroyed* it. As I shall destroy you.'

Hatch laughed, and the dark abode crackled with purple and

blood-red splashes of light. 'You shall not,' said Hatch, with sure finality. 'You have no idea where to begin. You know *nothing*.'

'I know that you were built by the people of Hakol, and that you followed the Malus to Earth.'

Hatch nodded. 'Jerak is an experimental battle vehicle.'

'Jerak – Jack i' the Green.' The Doctor nodded. 'Fascinating. And you landed here in, what, the 1680s?'

'The year of our Lord 1685,' came a voice from behind the Doctor. A tall man strode through the turbulent mental landscape. His tunic and leather boots were caked with mud.

'And you are?' queried the Doctor.

'John Ballam, blacksmith.'

'What happened when Jack came?' asked the Doctor.

The black vista behind Ballam peeled back to reveal a view of the village green. Not that there was much greenery to speak of. The entire area had been excavated, laboriously, by hand. The pit was dark with muddy water and blood. And filled with bodies.

Ballam pointed to the scene, as if that were explanation enough.

'Who was responsible for that?' queried the Doctor, his voice numb with outrage.

'Baron Jeffreys of Wem,' said John Ballam, his voice hushed. 'Or so we believed.'

The Doctor spun back to face Hatch. 'Well?'

'Oh, come,' said Hatch. 'These vermin can be of no concern. I had travelled long and far to this world. I needed replenishment.'

'So you corrupted Jeffreys, and fed off the mental energy of the terrified villagers?'

'Jeffreys needed little corrupting,' said Ballam, under his breath.

Hatch licked his lips at the memory. 'The meal was adequate. I drained what I could. From what was left, I fashioned my first followers. My limbs, in a world I was still not strong enough to dominate.'

'The scarecrows,' said the Doctor. 'You searched the psyches of all those dead people, and found something that you could defile.

Legends of wicker men and corn dollies, of pagan sacrifices to nature and the seasons. You based your reign of terror on mere stickmen to scare away birds!'

Hatch clicked his fingers, and John Ballam vanished from sight with a scream, the vista behind him folding up like a map. 'I *am* Hexen Bridge,' said Hatch. 'They are *all* my children, and they owe their survival to me. Any father can do as he wills to his children.'

'No,' said the Doctor. 'Children will always have their independence.'

'Not the children of Jack,' said Hatch. 'We are all together.'

'Yes, the taint of infertility ensured their dependence, didn't it?' said the Doctor. 'They could only reproduce if they stayed in the area. You expelled the unruly and the exceptionally gifted, so that you would remain undiscovered. You controlled the population that remained, harvesting individuals here and there…'

'They slaked my thirst. And now that thirst, that hunger, is all-consuming.'

'But why the experiments to counteract the taint?'

'Can you not guess?' Hatch smiled. 'There is a flaw even in the psychic technology of the Hakolians.'

'You mean the sterility is… an accidental side effect?'

Hatch nodded. 'There is no civilisation in the galaxy that can better the Hakolians' grasp of the psychic sciences. But, like all technologies, there are flaws. And sterility, though allowing me dominion over the village, is a by-product, a deficiency inherent in the mind-manipulation process.'

'I know that Hakolian technology is entirely reliant on the mental energy of the slave creatures,' said the Doctor, deep in thought. 'That much was obvious from Little Hodcombe. But if their slaves become sterile, then each conquered planet will in time die…'

'When the Malus malfunctioned – when normal linkage was impossible – my orders were revised.'

'You already had a cure for infertility, but it was localised,' suggested the Doctor. 'Your ambitions were far wider. You wanted to use human technology to find a *complete* cure.'

'When the people of Hakol conquer the Earth, the humans will provide all the energy they will ever need. The Hakolians will remain here for ever. They have no need for other worlds.'

'Rubbish!' The Doctor turned to face Hatch, his eyes blazing. 'They only know how to invade, how to destroy. Even the Terileptils turned against the Hakolians, aghast at their continual butchery!'

The Doctor stared deep into the man's eyes, searching for traces of Hatch, but saw only the alien terror of Jack i' the Green.

Steven Chen put a comforting arm around Joanna Matson's shoulders. Joanna dropped her head on to his shoulder, as a baby sister might as a thunder storm passed by. The constant hammering of the scarecrows on the trapdoor overhead sounded like an industrial machine.

A small split appeared in the wood, sending a spear of light into the darkness. Mr Chen said something to comfort his wife, but the words were drowned by the beating fists.

'The hatch is very strong,' said Steven, in as upbeat a voice as he could muster. 'Has to be. We walk over it all the time.' All the same, he gripped the cleaver in his hand more tightly.

Joanna mumbled something into his jumper.

'Sorry?'

Joanna looked up. 'How about cracking open a bottle of plonk? I'd prefer to face death drunk.'

Steven shook his head, a movement redundant in the gloom. 'Don't give up.' He hugged her tightly. 'How did you know that wasn't really Baber at the door?'

'Baber's an old stickler.' She paused, an eternity in the unquiet darkness. 'Or was, rather. Apparently it's incorrect to call someone the Reverend Something. He called it a "vulgar Americanism" once. He was either Mr Baber, or the Reverend Thomas Baber.

Never just Reverend Baber.' She laughed, a fragile, liquid sound. 'That creature gave itself away. Or maybe it was what was left of Baber.' Steven was about to speak when Joanna's voice cut through him like a knife. 'Christ, Steven, do you think we'll end up like that?'

As she pulled herself through the window and started shinning down the drainpipe at the rear of the restaurant, Ace suddenly remembered a holiday to an Outdoor Pursuits centre in Dawlish. She had been thirteen, and was grateful to be away from school. Each night the girls would climb down from their first-floor dormitory, after lights-out, and go into town. There was one particular pub where the barman clearly didn't give a stuff about serving underage hooligans. Most of the other girls chickened out after the first night, but for Ace, and Gillian Sweeney and Julie Smart, it was a regular dare.

Ace dropped the last six feet to the ground, grateful to be away from the Baber creature, and turned to find herself facing three statuesque scarecrows.

'Oh great,' she muttered, flattening herself against the restaurant wall.

Ace looked left and right. The scarecrows stood between her and the road. 'Great,' she repeated, taking a step towards the nearest manikin and holding the kitchen carving knife in front of her. 'Come on, then,' she shouted. 'I haven't done in anyone's knees for months.'

The nearest scarecrow inclined its head slightly to one side. Then a straw hand shot out, and grabbed Ace by the neck. Its two companions moved closer.

Suddenly Rebecca Baber and a man Ace did not recognise ran from the trees behind the restaurant, waving their arms and brandishing home-made torches. As the pressure on Ace's throat decreased she could see the reflection of the flames in the eyes of the scarecrow. And something else. Terror.

'Get them,' Ace managed to croak as the man closed in on the scarecrow holding her. He thrust the torch forward and, as the creature tried to back away, it released its grip. As she fell, Ace grabbed on to the scarecrow's stick legs, pulling with as much strength as she could.

The scarecrow crashed down on top of Ace, winding her.

'Get clear!' Rebecca shouted.

Ace rolled away, kicking at the scarecrow despite the pain and the shock. She glanced back and saw a torch being applied to the creature as it made a desperate attempt to stand. The fire bit into it immediately, and it collapsed backward, burning like a tinderbox. As the flames spiralled upward Ace looked for its two comrades, but they were nowhere to be seen.

Ace went to stand, wobbled, fell, then tried again. 'What kept you?' she asked no one in particular, then pointed a finger towards Rebecca. 'Whose side are you on?' she said menacingly.

'Not those things,' replied Rebecca, giving the still-burning scarecrow corpse a disgusted glance.

'Fine,' said Ace, her hands on her knees as she remained bent double, trying to forget the sickly pain at the pit of her stomach. 'Who's your friend?'

'This is Trevor,' said Rebecca.

The man was walking towards the hedgerow, torch held high above his head. 'Nothing here,' he called. 'I'll see if I can give Denman a hand out front. You sure you'll be OK?'

'I'll be fine,' said Rebecca. She gestured towards the restaurant. 'Who's in there?'

'The Chens and Joanna Matson,' replied Ace. 'They're in the cellar.'

'Then let's go and see if they need rescuing.'

The Doctor watched as the landscape around him blurred in a rush of images. He saw children at Hexen Bridge school, being taught harsh lessons in the way of life in the village. He saw the appointed elders, in masks and cloaks, dragging troublemakers away for conversion. Impassive scarecrows stood guard, and as the Doctor watched, decades wheeled past. He saw Jack itself, a bloated, shapeless creature of darkness, tunnelling through the very earth under Hexen Bridge, swelling and growing with every sacrifice, with every punished misdeed.

'Being a human is hard enough,' said the Doctor. 'The burdens you have pressed down on the shoulders of these people are unbearable!'

Hatch laughed – and this time the laugh was very like the politician's own. 'I sort the wheat from the chaff, if you'll pardon the pun.'

The Doctor watched the colour bleed from the shadows around them. 'Tell me,' he said, 'why *do* you need Hatch's body? Aren't the tentacles good enough?'

'Do not provoke me,' said Hatch, bunching his fists, as if to strike.

'Temper.' The Doctor tutted. 'I'd hate to see centuries of patient planning ruined in a day.'

Hatch paused. 'You need know only that I am the plague carrier. Where I go, madness will follow.'

'Ah, I see,' said the Doctor, leaning on his umbrella. He was sure he hadn't carried it into the mirror with him, but it seemed that Jack's splintered psyche had provided it anyway. 'You will carry the dark side of the taint: the instinct to murder, to brutalise, to destroy…'

'My mere touch will bring insanity and death.'

'Which Jerak will feed on?'

'Do I not deserve the richest pickings?' said Hatch. 'I can feast on anyone I wish. But countless humans, riddled by the taint – and yet not rendered sterile by it…? A mere meal becomes a banquet!'

'And you've "seeded" Liverpool in order to release psychic energy and destruction.'

Hatch nodded. 'We have liberated true humanity – the evil essence of the people of this planet.'

'Yes, you see, that's quite a problem, isn't it?' said the Doctor. 'The people of Hakol rely upon fear and terror – and these things are most naturally found in primitive, superstitious societies. They have always been limited as to what planets they can invade.'

'Now the people of Hakol can unleash primitive terror in any race, anywhere in the galaxy.'

'You've changed your tune,' observed the Doctor. 'Now, you've been very good, telling me what's going on like this. But I suppose our cosy tête-à-tête must come to an end.'

'Indeed it must. I will consume you, Doctor. You have entered my domain of your own free will. No one ever leaves.'

'If you say so,' said the Doctor with a cautious smile.

Steven had become so used to the sound of the scarecrows pounding on the trapdoor that he did not immediately realise that the noise had stopped. He turned to Joanna, huddled at his side. 'Do you think…?' he began.

There were moans and cries from the kitchen above them, and then the sound of something heavy being overturned. Steven's parents held each other in the semidarkness.

Someone hammered on the wooden hatch. 'Oi!' came a familiar voice. 'You lot OK down there?'

'Ace?' asked Steven.

'Yeah. Open up.'

'Prove it!' shouted Joanna, her voice ringing in the enclosed space of the cellar.

'What?'

'Prove it,' she continued.

Steven got to his feet, staring upward at the trapdoor. 'It could be another trick.'

'Oh, don't be such a plonker.' The voice from the kitchen sounded genuinely exasperated. 'What do you want me to do? List Charlton's greatest triumphs, 1975 to date?' A pause. 'Well, *that* shouldn't take very long…'

Steven climbed the stairs to the hatch, and pulled back the bolts.

Blinking in the bright light of the kitchen, he could just make out a hand reaching out for him.

And beyond that was Ace, smiling. 'Come on,' she said, helping him out.

Rebecca stood behind Ace, eyeing the room nervously.

'Don't mention Rebecca's father,' Ace whispered. Steven gave her an ominous look, then turned to help his parents and Joanna from the cellar.

'It was hell in there,' he said after a moment. 'We could hear banging and shouting...'

'Sounds like my local Chinese restaurant every Saturday night,' said Ace quickly. 'Let's have a look outside.'

They walked to the side door. The village was eerily quiet, the screaming from the green seeming to have stopped. 'Can't see any scarecrows,' said Ace.

Two men walked down the lane towards the restaurant, carrying sputtering torches despite the brightness of mid-morning. The larger, bearded figure Steven recognised as Chief Constable Ian Denman; from Rebecca's reaction, the other, younger man could only have been her infamous childhood sweetheart.

'We've seen them off,' said Denman briskly as he made his way into the kitchen.

Ace raised her eyes heavenward. 'And they won't be coming back, right?'

'Well...' began Denman.

'Cobblers, matey,' said Ace. 'They're evil, and they'll be back. Haven't you read any H.P. Lovecraft?'

'And you have?' asked Trevor.

'I've been around,' said Ace. 'The Doctor says that ancient evil can be found everywhere. It exists because it *is* ancient, and it *is* evil. There's no other reason.'

'Which reminds me,' said Trevor. 'The Doctor's gone off after Jack.'

Ace couldn't suppress a grin. 'He's back?' she queried.

'Yeah,' said Trevor. 'He's at the Green Man.'

'Then I'd better get after him,' said Ace. 'He'll need my help.'

'No,' said Trevor. 'He said he wanted you to leave the "big picture" to him.' Trevor made no attempt to conceal his puzzlement. 'He said you'd know what he meant.'

Ace grabbed a torch from Denman, her eyes bright. 'Yeah, I think I know.' She turned to look at the others. 'We need to make some torches, split up, and sort these scarecrows out. They'll be making for the boundary. The edge of the stain.'

'How do you figure that one, then?' asked Steven, watching as Trevor completed fashioning a makeshift torch from a piece of wood with a rag soaked in petrol.

'Jack is the main picture, right?' explained Ace. 'The scarecrows are just his bootboys. It looks like most of them have gone back to their sentry posts. And, if the church photographs showed anything, it's that the edge of the stain is important.'

'Have you seen my father?' queried Rebecca, picking up on what Ace had said.

'No,' answered Ace, before anyone else could reply.

Steven glared at the young woman, but said nothing.

'I'm up for that,' said Denman with a dramatic thump on the table.

Ace nodded at the man's enthusiasm. 'I suppose someone ought to check the Professor's OK,' she said. 'I'd do it myself, but I reckon I'm going to be a bit busy killing scarecrows for the next few hours.'

'We'll find the Doctor for you,' said Rebecca, although, in truth, Trevor looked less than thrilled at the prospect of meeting Jack i' the Green. 'All my life I've been terrified of Jack,' continued Rebecca. 'Now it's time to find out what he is.'

'Steven? Joanna?' asked Ace.

'I'm with you,' said Joanna immediately.

Steven couldn't hide his surprise. 'Since when have you been brave?'

'I'm not,' said Joanna, as if surprised at the strength of her exclamation. 'But we can't just wait here and do nothing.'

'That's the spirit,' said Ace. She turned to Steven. 'What about your parents?'

Mrs Chen put a calming hand on Steven's arm. 'We'll be safe here,' she said in a tired whisper. 'The spirits of this place have always been good to us. Just be careful.'

Steven hugged her. 'We'll be back before dusk,' he said. 'Make yourself torches, try to lock the doors, and don't let anybody in, no matter how plausible they sound.'

'Right,' said Ace as she headed for the door. 'I think I'm going to enjoy this.'

The black soil was expanding all the time, like an ink blot flowing over the fields. The ground shook as the alien creature pushed its tendrils far out into the countryside. What had once taken decades or centuries was now visible to the naked eye.

Ace, Denman, Steven and Joanna watched the dark stain from their vantage point behind a clump of trees. Numerous scarecrows trod resolutely just in front of the ever-growing alien mass, each one no more than five yards from its companion. The protective cordon of abused humanity stretched over the arcing hills and out of sight.

'I'd like a closer look,' whispered Ace. 'That Jack thing must be vulnerable at the edge of the stain.'

Steven nodded, remembering again the photographs that had cost Baber his life.

'Even with our torches those scarecrows are too close together,' said Denman.

'Then we'd better shift them,' said Steven. 'A diversion. Who's with me?'

'Listen, lad,' said Denman. 'This isn't the time to impress anyone with pretend –'

'You chicken, then?'

Ace opened her mouth to interrupt the argument, but Steven was already gone, bounding over the blackened earth between them and the edge of the creature. Denman swore, and set off after him.

'Men,' said Ace bitterly.

'Yeah,' said Joanna. Her eyes widened in concern as Steven and Denman approached the line of scarecrows, shouting and waving their sputtering torches. Immediately the scarecrows deviated from their slow advance in front of the alien mass, and moved as one towards the humans.

Denman and Steven ran off, a small group of stickmen following. A gap was left in the cordon, the other scarecrows resuming their diligent march.

'Now's our chance,' said Ace.

The mirror parted like water as Hatch emerged into the tunnel.

He turned and used the rippling reflection for its proper purpose, straightening his tie and his hair. He walked back up the tunnel towards the Green Man's cellar, whistling tunelessly. He strode out of the pub and spent a moment looking at the village green, now quiet and still. A smile played at the corner of his mouth.

'Did I miss all the fun?' he asked.

If there was a reply, there was no one else around to hear it.

He crossed the green, his feet seeming to sink into the ground with each step, then springing upward, escaping the power of the earth that threatened to drag him down again.

At the far side, Hatch paused and looked around, trying to remember where he had left his car. Arriving in the village seemed like a lifetime ago.

He began to walk towards the eastern boundary, and passed the

Chinese restaurant. Something made him stop. A voice in his mind seemed to say *There is life here. Seek it out.*

The front door of A Taste of the Orient was cracked but locked shut. The conservatory at the back was ruined. The pungent smell of fire still hung in the air.

Fire. His mind filled with images of burning flesh.

He approached the kitchen, smelling out life as keenly as a bloodhound. The lights had been switched off and the shutters drawn. In the corner of the room two thin flames flickered in the darkness.

'We were beginning to think that no one was left alive,' said a female voice.

Hatch took a step closer and saw the Chens squatting down, their torches held out defiantly in front of them.

'It's Mr Hatch,' said Chen, standing and lowering his torch. 'Don't be afraid,' he told his wife, and encouraged her to do the same. 'Sir, there are evil creatures everywhere,' he continued in a terrified whisper.

'We do not know what they want with us,' said his wife. 'We mean no one any harm.'

'I know,' said Hatch with apparent concern. 'These are bad times for the little people.' He moved forward, and grasped both of them by the arms. 'But do not be afraid. Your deliverance is at hand.'

Hatch turned and left.

Later, when he passed the area in his car, the Chens were on the road in front of the restaurant, attacking each other with knives.

Trevor and Rebecca crept closer to the green, keeping in the shade of the overhanging trees that edged the lane. The surrounding area was deserted and quiet except for the occasional shudder of the earth itself. Something lived, breathed and grew beneath their feet.

Something trying to rouse itself from centuries-old slumber.

At the edge of the green, Trevor tested the ground with his foot. He almost sank in to his knees. 'It's alive,' he shouted, scrambling backward towards Rebecca. His hand grabbed hers just as the ground beneath them ripped apart, a huge organic fracture like an underwater creature opening its mouth to draw in plankton.

They tumbled blindly into the darkness of the earth, screaming as they fell, their fingers clasping together. And then, with a thump, they hit the ground.

'Oh God oh God oh God,' breathed Trevor, trying to shake the terror from his mind. 'You OK?' he asked moments later into the darkness.

All he could hear in reply was Rebecca crying beside him. The nails of her hand, broken during the fight with the tiny scarecrow, still dug into his palm.

'Are you hurt?'

'No,' she sobbed. 'I'm frightened.'

'You and me both,' he replied, trying to stand. They were in a hollow cavern beneath the green. Above them, the pale sunlight still poured through the pulsing crack in the ground, illuminating the smooth rock walls around them. They could feel the floor moving sinuously beneath them.

'What are you two up to?'

Rebecca and Trevor gave a simultaneous terrified cry and spun around to find themselves facing an ornate mirror. Within this, in a misty, rippling lack-of-reflection, they saw the Doctor's face.

'Where are you?' asked Rebecca.

'It's a bit difficult to explain,' replied the Doctor sadly. 'Not in this dimension, in any real sense. Do I take it you found Ace?'

'She and Denman and a couple of others have gone scarecrow baiting.'

'Ah, yes, that sounds like her,' said the Doctor. 'Listen to me, I haven't much time. Hatch is the danger. He is a plague carrier. He's infected himself with a mutant strain of the Jack gene and a version of the psychic drug released in Liverpool. You must stop him. But don't touch him, or you'll become infected yourself. And don't let anyone else touch him, either.'

'Then how do you suggest we stop him?' asked Trevor.

Deep in the mirror, two men in peasants' garb appeared before the Doctor could reply. They grabbed him, dragging him backward as the mist swallowed them up.

'Balls,' said Trevor angrily.

'What do we do now?'

'Discover a way out of here, I suppose,' said Trevor as they turned, to find themselves facing more scarecrows.

Ace and Joanna sprinted towards the tendrils and misshapen limbs that writhed and penetrated the earth at the edge of the stain. They hurled their torches before the scarecrows even realised that they were there.

The flames bit into the alien fronds immediately. The ground beneath them writhed and bucked.

Somewhere, Jack was screaming.

The scarecrows stopped their implacable advance, their arms falling limply at their sides. Trevor and Rebecca exchanged nervous glances as they backed away from the creatures.

'What's happened to them?' asked Rebecca as they made their way into a tunnel cut into the dark rock of the cavern.

'Dunno, but, whatever it is, I don't fancy hanging around until it *stops* happening to them.' Trevor turned and broke into a run. 'Any idea where this tunnel goes?'

'No,' said Rebecca, racing after him, 'but that's where I'm going.'

Moments later they emerged into the cellar of the Green Man. With scarcely a glance behind them, they scaled the ladder, and ran from the pub.

The village green was heaving like a storm-ravaged sea, dipping and climbing.

'Come on, then,' said Trevor, running towards Phil Burridge's Land Rover, still parked in the undulating car park. 'We've got to find Hatch.'

* * *

Ace and Joanna hurled their final torches at the thrashing creature. The scarecrows guarding the edge of the stain were beginning to move in their direction, although their movements were even less co-ordinated than before.

'Let's go,' said Ace. 'We've done as much as we can here.'

Joanna needed very little encouragement, bolting across the field and away from the shambling stickmen. 'What next?' she asked between deep breaths as they ran.

'Back to the restaurant,' said Ace. 'Get some more torches.'

'And then?'

'We come back here, and we torch that thing again. And we keep doing it until we get a result!'

The ground reared up in front of them like a living thing. A smooth-skinned tentacle, as thick as a man's body, pushed through the soil. It twitched and flailed blindly.

As it scythed through the air towards them, Ace pushed Joanna away.

The huge grey limb slammed into Ace, throwing her to the ground.

Trevor hot-wired the Land Rover and they set off after Hatch. They caught sight of his car less than a mile down the road.

The limousine was travelling slowly, like a hearse. Trevor stamped on the accelerator, drawing level with the car, then twisted the steering wheel savagely to one side and pulled on the hand brake.

The Land Rover cut in front of the Mercedes a few yards short of the cordon of scarecrows that was guarding the only way out of the village. Hatch was forced to stand on his brakes, and his car screeched to a halt.

'What now?' asked Rebecca, as her eyes met those of Hatch.

'His move,' noted Trevor, making sure that the Land Rover doors were locked.

Hatch left his car with the motor idling and strolled to the front of the Land Rover. The scarecrows angled their heads towards the vehicles, their expressionless cloth faces merely adding to the incongruity of the moment.

'Becky, Trev,' said Hatch in a catlike purr. 'Hi. What's been happening?'

Trevor revved the engine. 'Got a bone to pick with you, Matt,' he said. 'You've been hanging around with some *very* bad company.'

Hatch was ignoring him. Instead he was looking at Rebecca, staring deeply into her eyes. His own were glowing.

All Rebecca could see was light. Light as sharp as a pinprick, boring into her brain like a drill. A diamond-tipped drill that twisted through flesh and bone and skull and promised only death and burial in an open grave where worms and beetles would crawl over her putrefying skin, gnawing the flesh from rotting bones.

'No!' screamed Rebecca as the light became as bright as a thousand suns. 'Stop it!'

Trevor was trying to say something, but his voice was too distant for the words to make sense.

Suddenly she turned to him and smiled. Her hand found the handle. 'It's all right,' she said, pushing open the door. 'This is a safe place.'

Hatch threw himself at Rebecca, like an animal pouncing on its prey. He grabbed her by the scruff of the neck, throwing her to the ground. Hatch was astride her before Trevor could even move.

Scarecrow hands smashed through the window and held Trevor motionless in the seat. Forcing him to watch.

Saliva dripped from Hatch's lips. 'Kiss this,' he said, moving his mouth to Rebecca's, and pressing down.

CHAPTER 16
WILDER

The Doctor was dragged through a wooden door and into a room thick with shadows and whispering voices. Chaotic rows of peasants stood either side of him, their dirty faces etched with excitement and loathing.

A stooped figure with matted hair and a rose-red face staggered from the crowd. He opened his toothless mouth, a guttural cackle bubbling from his throat.

'Hang 'im!' he cried. 'Hang 'im up, and cut 'im down.'

The impatient arms of the Doctor's captors pushed him past the sniggering wretch as the rest of the crowd began to bray like hounds eager for the kill.

'Ignore that buffoon,' said a voice to the Doctor's left. ''Tis just Henry, the village idiot.'

The Doctor turned to find himself facing a man in black robes, holding a Bible in his hands.

'And you are…?'

'Forgive me,' said the man. 'I am Silas Baber, of Master Blackwell's chambers.'

'You're a solicitor?'

'A barrister,' said Baber brightly. 'Thy barrister.'

'Then this is a courtroom?' asked the Doctor. Another shove propelled him towards what appeared to be a dock. 'Or, at least, someone's subconscious representation of a seventeenth-century assizes. I take it this is Jeffreys's courtroom?'

Baber nodded. 'Take my advice. Plead guilty. Throw thyself upon the mercy of the court.'

'I'll certainly consider it,' said the Doctor as a gathering hush settled upon the room. 'Fee fie foe fat, I smell the blood of an 'autocrat,' he said under his breath as an usher entered grandly.

'Please be upstanding for the honourable judge,' said the usher, grasping both lapels and puffing out his chest.

Jeffreys appeared behind him, with his retinue guard, who stationed themselves menacingly around the room. A well-dressed man strode towards the dock.

'This court is now in session,' announced Jeffreys. He sat, and watched keenly as the court settled. 'Be this the prisoner, Master Jowett?'

'Aye, Your Honour,' said the man, his lip curling with disdain. 'A travelling man, not o' these parts.'

'Master prisoner,' said Jeffreys. 'Dost thou know the charges thou facest?'

The Doctor shrugged. 'Insurrection? Treason? Libel and slander? That kind of thing?'

'And more,' said Jeffreys. 'How dost thou plead? Guilty?' He paused, licking his fat lips. 'Or not guilty?'

'I'm sorry,' said the Doctor. 'I don't understand the question. Don't I get a third option?'

'Silence!' screamed Jeffreys, as a murmur spread through the courtroom.

'Jack be nimble, Jack be quick, Jack jump over the candlestick,' said the Doctor, glancing towards Baber, who was shaking his head. 'May I address the court?'

'Contempt!' said Jeffreys, hammering his gavel against the ornate desk.

'I have contempt for no one in this court,' said the Doctor, catching the blazing alien eyes of the judge. 'Except for Jack.'

'Who be this Jack?' said Jeffreys slowly. 'What right dost thou have to make charges against him?'

'*J'accuse*,' said the Doctor simply, and plucked the Bible from Baber's hand. 'I swear by Almighty God that the evidence I give shall be the truth, the whole truth, and nothing but the truth. Can you handle the truth, Jack?'

'Master prisoner, thou speakest words that have no meaning,' noted Jeffreys, amused. 'Art thou a simpleton?'

'I have been accused of that often enough,' said the Doctor. 'However, I do not recognise the authority of this court to pass judgement on one man. I put it to you that it is not me that is on trial here, but all of us.'

A gasp came from the assembled crowd.

Baber crossed the floor towards the judge. 'My Lord, I humbly apologise for the conduct of my client.'

Jeffreys nodded. 'He wastes the court's time with his dribbling nonsense.'

'Time is relative and abstract,' noted the Doctor, stepping down from the dock. Neither Jowett, nor any of the other men, moved to stop him. 'This charade is an insult to my intelligence, Jack,' continued the Doctor. 'I want to see you, and I want to see you *now*!'

'Thou art as mad as the moon, prisoner,' said Jeffreys.

'And thou art a coward,' added the Doctor. 'Show yourself, Jack.'

Jeffreys said nothing.

The Doctor turned to the jury, twelve men dressed in peasants' rags. 'Gentlemen,' he said, 'you have all, in your time, committed crimes. Terrible crimes. Who among you will cast the first stone?'

'I shall,' said the foreman, the huge figure of Long John.

'You?' asked the Doctor. 'A child molester and rapist... I've read the old chronicles of your deeds, John Ballam. Your heart is black and evil. But it's Jack that makes you as bad as you are. All of you.' He stopped and addressed the crowd. 'All of your lives, throughout the centuries, you have lived like rats in a hole, blinking, terrified at the outside world. Hexen Bridge is your prison, and Jack i' the Green your jailer. He won't even show himself to you because he knows the moment that he does, he will lose you. Somewhere within each of you there is a remnant of humanity struggling to get out. Help it fly free. Help *me*.'

'Be there blackness in my heart, also?' The Doctor was surprised to hear the question coming from the judge.

'Yes,' he replied sadly. 'You more than anyone should know that.'

'Jack plans to free the world,' said Long John, a confused look on his face.

'He plans to *enslave* the world,' shouted the Doctor angrily. 'And you're all party to that.'

'But we did not know,' said Baber sadly.

'Well, you do *now*. So do something about it!' The noise in the courtroom rose to a crescendo as the Doctor ran back to the dock and stood on the dais addressing them all. 'The greatest evil in the universe isn't the monster from outer space,' he said. 'It is the dark space within us all. Shine a light on *that*.'

'We shall hear more,' noted the judge.

Ace shook her head groggily, momentarily aware of the loamy aroma of the soil beneath her. She pushed herself up on to her elbows, then managed to roll her protesting body away just as the alien limb impacted against the protesting earth.

The creature dipped beneath the ground for the last time, like a Jules Verne sea creature slipping below the heaving waves.

The quaking motion that rippled the field became less pronounced as the alien creature retreated, or took stock, or did whatever alien blobs do when attacked by resourceful women bearing torches. Ace was about to let out a cry of delight when she remembered the scarecrows.

She got to her feet just as a pair of stickmen made a clumsy but effective grab at Joanna. The woman's scream was choked off by a fist of hay.

Ace hurled herself at the creatures, but they shrugged her aside with flailing arms that felt like pillars of concrete. Implacable, they returned their attention to the older woman, their hands tightly pressed against her throat.

Joanna's skin was already overlaid with blue, her eyes bulging.

Before Ace could react, a third scarecrow lunged at her, knocking her to the ground.

The creature reached down, as if offering to help Ace to her feet. Then the musty hands covered her face, the harsh prickles of straw pressing against her eyelids and into her nose and mouth.

And Jack threatened to engulf her utterly.

The Midnight Hunter reached down to pat the broad neck of the horse, drawing the last drops of patience from the snorting creature. The Hunter's grey eyes were fixed on the village, as fascinating a prospect as any quarry he had pursued. Centuries-old hands gripped the reins tightly, feeling the pent-up power of the horse, and of nature itself. The force that invigorated the Hunter, that spurred on his followers, came up from the ground and out of the trees. The breath of life, as ancient as the creation of the world.

With the silence of a midsummer zephyr, the Wild Hunt began to gather behind their leader. First came the foxes, lithe darts of red, noses alive to the smell of the midday soil. Then came the Yell Hounds, their breath like fire, their eyes glowing like metal daggers in a forge. Their claws bit deep into the earth, but left no mark. Finally all the creatures of the forest came. Stoats and weasels, badgers and deer, harvest mice and bats. Hawks flew overhead, calling out in joyous celebration, eyes alive with inspiration and desire. An owl settled on the Midnight Hunter's arm. Its eyes imparted all the information the old warrior needed.

He straightened the old metal helmet as if for war, and took a deep breath.

With a great cry, the Hunter spurred his horse, and the creatures swept as one down into the village.

The Wild Hunt, after centuries of rest, was resurrected.

Rebecca let out a piercing wail that could have been death or childbirth. Trevor's blood was like ice flowing through a long-dead body. Only his eyes were alive, watching the scene, transfixed.

Trevor saw Hatch return to his car. Moments later the politician was driving away, the engine note dwindling as the country lanes swallowed him up.

Rebecca pulled herself from the ground where she had fallen. There were flecks of mud on her face and dress, her forehead damp with sweat.

Her eyes were terrifyingly alive, reaching out to Trevor. As he struggled he became aware of the straw hands holding him in place, of the seat at his back, and the strewn splinters of glass that lay in his lap.

Rebecca walked towards the car, her mouth hanging open. Saliva trailed down her chin. Her hands were outstretched, the blood-red nails sharpened, like claws.

With a shriek Rebecca pulled the scarecrows away, hurling them contemptuously to the ground. Her prize was Trevor.

She dragged him from the car by his hair, raking her fingers down his face. Cutting his eyebrows and lips. Smashing her small fist into his nose.

Her hands raked down again and again.

Steven Chen glanced over his shoulder. Three scarecrows were still in pursuit, scything through the cornfields like the shadow of sunset. Denman was struggling to keep up, his face red with exertion.

'Come on!' shouted Chen. 'They're right behind you.'

'I'll be OK,' said Denman, his breath coming in ragged bursts. 'You cut back and find that woman of yours. And Ace.'

Chen was about to protest when the policeman fell to his knees, his energy spent. Steven stared in horrified fascination as the first scarecrow reached Denman. The policeman's head snapped up and his eyes connected with Steven's, burrowing into his soul.

'*Run!*' screamed Denman, as arms of straw and corn fell upon him.

* * *

Suddenly the hands came away from her face, and Ace sucked in a whooping gasp of air.

The scarecrow staggered, batting feebly at the flames that tore at its chest and arms. Its cloth head smouldered, the brim of the floppy hat on fire. As it crashed into the ground a shower of sparks leapt into the air, glowing brightly in the sky.

Ace turned, wondering who had come to her rescue. She expected to see Steven Chen or Denman or one of the others. Instead, standing some fifty yards away, was an archer. A quiver of impossibly burning arrows was slung from his belt.

The man was only partly visible, the line of a hedge running straight through him like a razor. He wore ancient clothing, dominated by an enormous bearskin that hung on his back like a cloak.

Ace shook her head. 'I've flipped,' she said, under her breath.

She glanced down at the scarecrow corpse. The creature seemed dead, but there was not a trace of the fire she had seen earlier.

Joanna appeared at her side. 'What happened?' she demanded.

'Haven't the foggiest,' admitted Ace. She looked back towards the archer, but he was gone.

The courtroom dissolved around the Doctor, scenes from the outside world scudding across the sky above him. He saw the ethereal hunters sweeping over the village, attacking the scarecrows. He cried out in delight as Ace was saved by a man with a longbow. Just for a moment there was silence across the land, interrupted only by the distant call of a woodcock.

'It is the triumph of the human will,' the Doctor exclaimed. Before him, only the judge was left in the barren wasteland that had once been a courtroom. But no trace of Jeffreys remained. The eyes, flaming like the burning scarecrows above them, told the Doctor that he was again in the presence of Jack i' the Green.

The Doctor pointed to the sky, awash with primal colours.

'Instead of using the dark legends which you made more terrifying – the wicker men, the pagan gods of the corn harvest – the villagers have called up the Wild Hunt. An ambiguous enough legend, not good, not evil, but moral. Just the sort of thing to slip past you, unnoticed.' The Doctor paused triumphantly. 'Your ancient victims are turning against you, Jack. Human souls cannot bear your form of reality. They'll be at the palace gates soon. You're under siege!'

Still Jack said nothing. The landscape changed again to the village green in the seventeenth century, surrounded by oak-beamed Tudor buildings. The people of the village stood around the edges of the green, shouting, their fists raised.

'You've lost, Jack,' said the Doctor. 'Their strength is too great. They are using the power of the land, the ley lines, the stone circles. Legends of God and man and nature. They're taking back what you stole from them over three hundred years ago.'

'Battle is not yet won,' said the judge suddenly. The Doctor looked up to find the court room re-forming around him. Jack's eyes were glowing within a human face once more, a black cloth on his head. 'Thou hast been found guilty by this court. It is my duty to pass sentence. Dost thou have anything to say?'

'No,' said the Doctor, surprised. 'My mother always told me if I didn't have anything good to say about anyone, I shouldn't say anything at all.'

'The sentence of this court,' said the judge, 'is that thou shalt be taken to a place of execution, and there done to death. And may Jack have mercy upon thy soul. Take him.'

Guardsmen, with Jowett and Long John helping them, grabbed the Doctor and held him aloft, marching towards the green, at the centre of which a freshly dug pit glowed blood-red.

'Greetings.' The voice was as ancient as thunder, and caught Ace completely unawares. A huge armoured man on a horse had appeared a little way behind her. Owls and geese flew over his

262

head, and foxes danced around the motionless hooves of the steed. Like the archer, the man and his creatures were partly visible, as if only gently overlaid on reality.

'What the –' began Ace.

'I am the leader of the Wild Hunt. I have my freedom, and my instructions, which I chose to follow. Come with me.'

Ghost or not, Ace bristled at the man's patriarchal conceit. 'Why should I?'

The Hunter snorted, as if unused to dissent. His reply was to flick the reins of the horse – a big brute of a creature, more at home on a farm than a racecourse, thought Ace – and he swept down towards her.

The hooves pawed at ancient ground that was no longer there. Even so, the Hunter was swiftly at Ace's side. He reached down to pick her up, pulling her on to the saddle behind him.

Ace instinctively struggled against his grip, but there was little to kick against. His arm was broad and strong, but the moment she pushed against the hunter he became as substantial as a half-remembered breeze.

'Put me down!' she exclaimed, not used to being treated like this by anyone.

'Be not afeared,' pronounced the man, as the horse swept high into the air.

'I'm not,' said Ace, through gritted teeth. 'And why are you leaving Joanna behind?'

The Hunter laughed. 'Because,' he said, '*you* do not show fear. You have been chosen.'

'Chosen?'

'There is work to do.'

Ace smiled for the first time. 'Wicked,' she said.

The landscape blurred beneath the ghostly horse. The view was certainly extraordinary, the village a hive of activity as scarecrows and hunters wheeled in combat.

Ace reached down to pat the flank of the horse, but only the faintest tingling reached her hands where the creature's flesh should be. Pale against the dark greens of the fields, the horse's skin was slick with sweat, and the smell prickled at Ace's nostrils. If this was all an illusion, it was an extraordinarily convincing one.

Without thinking, she tried prodding the rider in the back, but her finger went right through the thick cloak and ancient armour.

'Oi,' she said loudly. 'Where are we going?'

'The centre of all things,' said the Hunter, as the horse began to plummet like an aeroplane hitting turbulence.

Ace groaned as her stomach lurched. 'Fine,' she said. 'Wherever.'

They were coming down towards the village green. Ace's eyes opened in alarm. The whole area, encircled by lanes and cottages, was open, like some great wound. The centre of the green, now a deep pit, seemed as dark as midnight. The tarlike soil was alive with the fluid, alien mass.

The horse plunged down, as if impatient to be consumed by the open mouth of the creature.

Just as they were about to reach the ground, the Hunter swivelled in his saddle, pushing at Ace with his broad hands.

Ace slipped from the horse, her hands scrabbling at thin air.

Then she fell into open space, and the pit at Jack's heart.

Rebecca seemed to have been walking for ever. She did not know why she had left the unconscious Trevor and walked half a mile down the road to A Taste of the Orient. Neither could she recall exactly what emotions ran through her mind as she saw the bodies of Mr and Mrs Chen, lying in pools of their own blood in the road outside.

She couldn't even remember what prompted her to pick up the carving knife, which lay abandoned beside the jade lions, caked with blood. She knew only that she held it in her hands, and it was good.

She stumbled back towards the Land Rover. Her feet ached and her head was full of voices.

Do it.

Do it.

As she neared the vehicle, she could see Trevor stretched out on the grass verge. He was just beginning to stir, his face bruised and lacerated from the earlier attack.

Finish him off.

The sensation of falling had been as awful as in a dream, but Ace neither woke up nor lapsed into unconsciousness as the ground hit her.

Somehow, she had landed on her feet, and was unharmed. She felt her legs and ankles gingerly. Not a bruise.

The pit extended fifty feet beneath the writhing surface of the green, and was the size of a house. The cavern walls – alive with the alien creature – were of natural rock, dominated by a large silver mirror.

Ace ran towards the mirror, but saw only her puzzled reflection staring back at her. 'What's this doing here?' she wondered aloud.

Suddenly something moved behind her, reflected in the mirror. She turned, and saw an impossibly tall man, dressed in white robes, held in place with a silver sash. His hair gleamed like gold.

'Right,' said Ace, 'I've had enough. Who the hell are you?'

The tall man stooped to look down at Ace, as though he hadn't noticed her before. His face creased into a frown, and he didn't answer, seemingly unused to such communication.

'I watched the battle at Mons,' he said, obviously considering this explanation enough. His eyes were wet with an extraordinary sadness.

'The bloke who brought me here,' explained Ace, 'said I had something to do. A mission.'

The tall man nodded, but said nothing more.

Ace sighed. 'Well?'

'Smash the mirror,' said the man, as if that was the most obvious thing in the world.

'Why?' asked Ace.

The man smiled, his face lighting up like early-morning clouds. 'Because you want to.'

'Why can't *you* do it?'

The man pushed his arm through the mirror, as if by way of demonstration. 'We can have no direct impact on Jack,' he said.

'Then the mirror is… Jack?'

The man shook his head. 'A mirror into his soul. It was an unwanted gift to Jeffreys, and was left in the pit when he sacrificed the villagers to Jack's greed.'

'Jeffreys?' asked Ace.

'Smash the mirror,' said the man, turning away from Ace. Moments later he was out of the pit, and striding across the countryside.

'I thought you guys had halos and little wings,' called Ace after him, but the tall man was long since gone.

Ace scrabbled in the writhing soil for a rock.

The Red Lion was an old-fashioned-looking public house on the edge of the village of Yarcombe, some twelve miles from Hexen Bridge. Matthew Hatch caught a glimpse of the swinging sign out of the corner of his eye, and slammed on the brakes. With barely a glance in his rear-view mirror, he engaged reverse gear, and the limousine accelerated into the car park, throwing up gravel and splashes of mud.

Hatch got out, whistling and tossing his keys from hand to hand. The barman was equally pleased to see him.

'What can I get you, sir?' he asked.

Hatch glanced around him. The place was surprisingly busy, a few tourists picking at their ploughman's lunches while a gaggle of students played pool in the far corner. Suited refugees from the nearby town huddled on lonely stools around the bar, studying the beer mats as intently as the news pages of the *Financial Times*.

Hatch returned his attention to the rotund barman, and grinned.

'Ask not what you can do for me,' he said. 'Ask what I can do for you.'

'Sorry, sir?'

Hatch reached out for the man, gripping his forearms in his hands. The barman shook, as if he had plugged himself into the National Grid. His mouth hung open, high-pitched whines escaping from prodigiously rounded cheeks.

Hatch let go, and strode towards the pool table. As he brushed against customers, arguments and fights broke out behind him. The sudden commotion disturbed the students, who looked up in alarm. Three boys and a girl. Perfect.

Hatch shook the hand of one of the uncomprehending young men, and turned for the door. There was a low thud as the girl was thrown to the floor, almost unnoticeable against the animal screams that filled the bar.

Behind him, the first window shattered just as Hatch opened the door of the limousine.

From the hillside Joanna watched in amazement as the ghostly hunters slaughtered the scarecrows. The stickmen were easy prey for the apparitions and their charging horses, falling beneath rushing hooves and exploding into pillars of flame. It was as though some celestial power was having its revenge on the scarecrows for having dared cheat death.

Joanna stared with horrified fascination as one barely defined figure, like campfire smoke glanced through trees, bore down and slew three stickmen, his iron sword slashing them to firewood. She thought she saw two enormous oriental lions lunging into the air, but when she shook her head they were gone.

Joanna heard the sound of approaching feet, and turned, ready to scream, until she saw Steven striding up the hill.

'Where's Ace?' asked Steven, before he reached the brow of the hill.

Joanna pointed. 'She was taken by one those . . . people.'

'I had to leave Denman,' said Steven. He surveyed the carnage, his eyes wide. 'It's about time those scarecrows got a dose of their own medicine,' he said.

'It's horrible,' said Joanna, turning away.

Rebecca raised the knife high above her head. Trevor lay at her feet.

Do it.

Trevor tried to sit up, his confusion visible even through the bruising that covered his face. One eye was swollen shut; the other blinked open.

Rebecca let out an animal scream of utter desolation, and clutched the knife tighter, her knuckles straining white. He was defenceless beneath her.

Do it.

Rebecca felt a blow at the base of her skull.

She dropped to her knees, the knife flying out of her hand and sticking upright in the soft earth. Trevor was backing away on his hands and knees. Rebecca turned her head, despite the pain, and saw what looked like an ancient soldier made of glass.

'What are you?' she screamed.

The Doctor was dropped at the grassy edge of the pit. He tried to stand, but Long John and Henry the idiot kicked his feet from beneath him, and he lay on the undulating earth, looking up at Jowett.

Jowett's eyes were as red as the pit beneath the Doctor.

'Listen to me,' said the Doctor. 'Jack's losing. Fight the power.'

'Richard,' said Jowett to the blond man at his side. 'Get him up.'

Long John and Richard dragged the Doctor to his feet.

'Thou art but a worthless sinner,' said Jowett. 'Thy maker awaits thee with open arms… To damn thee to hell.'

The two men pushed the Doctor towards the lip of the pit.

'Cast 'im down, cast 'im down,' chanted Henry, his eyes bulging in their sockets. 'Do 'im murder!'

'Execute him,' said Jowett, turning away.

'Aye,' said Richard, turning and pushing the Doctor with both hands over the edge and into the hellish pit.

As the Doctor fell he grabbed clods of earth with desperate hands, his fingers digging into the turf. He tried to push against the side of the pit with his feet, but they kept slipping, sending stones spiralling into the darkness.

The sound of an impact never came.

Richard looked down at the Doctor with a look of remorseless evil on his face. 'He still lives, Joseph,' he called over his shoulder.

'Then make it so he does not.'

The Doctor cried out as he felt the pressure of Richard's boot on his fingers.

Ace found a suitable rock, jutting from a patch of dark soil where the angular cavern walls had collapsed. She tugged at the stone, and it shifted, but then stopped, as if Jack knew what she had planned. Ace pulled harder, and the rock flew free in her hands.

Ace ran to the mirror. Just for a moment she thought she could see a small man struggling at the top of a pit that glowed like a furnace, but when she looked closer she could see only her own worried face shining back at her.

She raised the rock above her head, and brought it down on the quicksilver surface of the mirror.

With a crack like breaking ice, a transverse fracture appeared across the mirror.

There was a sudden moan of pain far above the Doctor's head. He tried to look up, but succeeded only in knocking himself off balance.

One hand, pushed away by Richard's boot, came free, flailing out into space.

His other hand gripped the top of the pit tightly, bearing his whole weight.

His fingers began to slip across the muddied grass.

* * *

Ace turned at the sound of galloping hooves. The ghost rider had reappeared. Rebecca was slung over the back of the horse. Some distance behind came another with Trevor clinging to his back.

With the same disdain as he had shown to Ace, the huntsman picked up the body of Rebecca, and hurled her through the air like a disobedient doll.

She hit the mirror with shocking force but, incredibly, the metal parted to let her through.

Then it closed around her.

Ace swung at the mirror with her boot – hoping at least to rescue her friend – and the surface fractured still further into a spider's web.

The police car approached the Red Lion suspiciously. The juke box was blaring like the PA at Castle Donington, and every window was broken.

'Blimey,' said one of the officers. 'When they said there'd been a disturbance –'

The Red Lion exploded in a mass of tentacles.

Ace lashed out at the mirror again.

It shattered, showering her with glass.

Chaos engulfed the Doctor.

He began to fall, but a stillness surrounded him, like the eye of a hurricane.

A shrill gale of psychic energy surged across the green. Fractured patches of reality broke through the illusion as the Doctor clung to the shattered ground by his fingertips.

'This isn't happening,' he said, his eyes tightly closed, as if the words were enough to change the world.

Then he looked up and saw the hand reaching down towards him.

* * *

Something like a train thundered into Ace, tossing her to the floor. Around her, the cavern began to crumble, the very earth collapsing with a deep moan.

Raging storms coalesced, faded, and re-formed overhead. It was like watching speeded-up photography, the clouds expanding and shrinking as if alive.

A moment later, the ice-cold wind forced her eyes shut, and the soil began to rain down upon her.

'Ah, good,' said the Doctor, grasping the hand with both of his own, and smiling as he came face to face with an angel. 'How do you do?' He stood uncertainly on the soil that surrounded the pit.

Around them the gale was ripping through the representation of Hexen Bridge, throwing villagers, and the surviving scarecrows from the real world, to the ground. Near the Doctor and the angel, a stickman exploded in a flurry of straw, which was plucked into infinity by the screaming wind. The sky, like a Turner watercolour, crackled with lightning.

'A bit windy,' observed the Doctor as the angel turned away from him. 'If I'd known, I'd have stayed indoors.' The Doctor saw Jowett, Richard and Long John being thrown about like corn dollies by the forces that had been unleashed. He was aware of something towering above him, and he looked up to find a face in the sky, as big as the world, shot through with the green of nature. Staring eyes and a mouth of needle-like teeth were framed by strands of what looked like dying ivy and the thorny, flowerless stems of roses.

'Jack?'

The was no reply except for the howling moan of something dying.

A more human cry made the Doctor look down, and he saw Rebecca lying in the middle of the green, moving as sluggishly as a child fighting the dream-monsters of the dark.

'You're not having her, Jack,' he shouted above the sound of the tempest. 'You have too much blood on your hands. Nobody else dies. You've robbed these people of their dignity for three hundred years. Fifteen generations. No hope, no peace, no future. It ends now!' The Doctor crawled across the scarred earth and reached Rebecca, cradling her in his arms.

'What are you?' came a booming voice like the clang of a plague bell.

But the question was never answered as the ground beneath the Doctor finally ripped open, and the world turned black.

The car shook as the earth beneath it trembled. The escalating voices in Hatch's mind were crying out, chanting a siren song of unity and purpose. His lips parted in a smile of simple satisfaction. Soon, the whole world would be consumed by the will of Jack i' the Green.

And then the voices stopped. Matthew Hatch screamed out in unaccustomed terror, his last truly human act.

The road in front split open, and Hatch's car plunged into the darkness. Stone and tarmac tumbled into the crevasse as Jack imploded, his limbs shrinking back and dying. With a claustrophobic rush of soil, the ground closed up over Hatch, throttling his screams into silence. And he died as he had lived: alone, except for Jack.

The heart of Hexen Bridge opened up as the black earth, the tendrils of Jack and every trace of the alien creature drew back upon itself. The public house, standing on the edge of the ruptured cavern, shivered, stood solid for a moment, and then slid into the soil as a thousand timber beams cracked. A cloud of stone and brick mushroomed in the air.

The Green Man was gone.

For a moment there was silence, and then the ground erupted again, spewing out a stream of multicoloured butterflies which soared high in the air over Hexen Bridge.

* * *

Ace remembered to breathe when the noise finally abated. Her hands, as she raised them towards her face, were shaking.

She pulled herself from the rubble of the pub. Overhead, the ragged frame of the hole in the green showed receding clouds.

'Wicked,' she said, her voice a funereal whisper in the face of the destruction that had consumed the centre of the village.

The hunters had gone. She was quite alone except for Trevor Winstone lying beside her. She checked his pulse. It was faint, but regular.

She crawled across the scree towards the remains of the mirror. She could just make out the glittering slivers of glass beneath the muddy bricks and planks of wood.

A sudden chill gripped her. 'Professor?' she asked, her head snapping from side to side. The monster was defeated, so the Doctor should return now, right? 'Doctor!' she cried in desperation.

A hand, pushing up through the debris, grasped her ankle. She stifled a cry, and was about to kick at it when she recognised that the hand was human.

Covered in dust and tiny scratches. Flexing and twisting, as if trying to communicate in some form of sign language.

Human? Well, something like that.

'Professor?' She began pulling at the stones and soil beneath her feet.

'Get me out of here, Ace!'

It was the Doctor. He only ever sounded this flustered when the *trivial* things in life went pear-shaped.

'You OK?' she said, pulling away a thick beam of wood.

'Of course I'm not,' came the irritated reply.

She could make out his coat, the arch of his slender back. Some distance away was a horribly begaitered shoe.

'All right,' she said, idly hurling a vast chunk of masonry into the air. 'What've you been up to?'

Finally the Doctor was revealed, curled up like a foetus. In front of him was Rebecca Baber. It looked as though the Doctor had tried to protect her the best he could when the world collapsed around them.

The Doctor sat up, brushing the dust from his sleeves. 'Oh, you know, Ace. This and that. Gangsters to overthrow, dark forces to combat.'

'The usual?'

The Doctor paused, a sombre look crossing his dirt-flecked face. 'Perhaps not this time, no.'

Denman massaged his temples, groaning. The ground around him was littered with corpses he did not recognise. People from the recent and ancient past, held together and manipulated by Jack, now released. Some were already beginning to crumble as held-off decay tore into them.

Denman remembered stumbling under the weight of creatures, a claustrophobic wave of darkness. Hands had pressed into his mouth while unceasing blows came down upon his back and legs. It was as if he was being disassembled in the most excruciating manner imaginable.

He was on the verge of unconsciousness when the stickmen had started to fall away. There was the faintest impression of people on horseback, and animals tearing into the evil creatures.

Moments later a storm, the like of which he had never experienced, had ripped over the land. It had raged like a battle in heaven, and finally died.

Denman held his head in his hands, waiting for the pain to go away. Then he remembered what had happened in Liverpool, and realised that it never would.

Steven Chen and Joanna Matson held each other tightly as the storm faded, like a nightmare blurring into welcome reality. The last finger of the wind caressed their faces just as the rain began to fall.

'Is it over?' asked Joanna.

Steven smiled and nodded, water droplets falling off his nose. 'Yeah.' He breathed deeply. 'Feel that? The air's fresh. Clean.'

'The thunderstorm?' queried Joanna.

'No,' said Steven. 'It's deeper than that. Something's changed.' He laughed, an earthy, throaty chuckle. 'I don't believe it. After all these years. It's all over.' His eyes roved over the chalk hills and fields, a green cloth with Hexen Bridge a jewel held delicately at its centre. Towards the horizon, a dim rainbow reached for the clouds.

He looked back at Joanna, and noticed, as if for the first time, that she was still in his arms. They parted, blushing.

Rebecca and Trevor looked like sleeping children as the Doctor and Ace laid them together at the side of the pit that had once been the village green.

'Will she be all right?' asked Ace, wiping the welcome rain from her face.

'She's free of the taint, if that's what you mean,' replied the Doctor, looking into the middle distance, at the smoke rising from some distant catastrophe.

'That *isn't* what I meant.'

The Doctor shrugged. 'They'll all have to rebuild their lives. It'll be hard, without Jack, but I have a feeling they'll survive. Humans usually do.' He paused, picking up a piece of glass from the mirror. The clouds parted, and it glinted in the light of the afternoon sun. 'Jack was attacked on many fronts, but he was ultimately defeated by humanity. I appealed to those feelings that Jack had spent hundreds of years repressing. Those people trapped inside Jack decided that true death was preferable to the hollow existence they had. Deep down, I believe every human being, no matter how evil, would have made the same choice.'

'Even me?' asked Ace.

'Especially you. With no energy, no substance, Jack – Jerak –

effectively ceased to exist.'

'Jerak?'

'That was Jack's real name. A creature manipulated by the Hakolians to become a war machine.'

'Hakolians?'

'I never did finish telling you about Little Hodcombe, did I?' The Doctor smiled. 'Oh, well, there's plenty of time for that. Perhaps I'll take you there. Jane still makes an excellent cup of tea.'

'What about those hunters?' asked Ace. 'Where did they come from?'

'Psychic extensions of the villagers' attempts to buy out of the system before they died, couched in the only mythic expression that seemed appropriate. Rebecca and I were spewed out because we didn't belong...'

'And the butterflies?'

'Yes,' said the Doctor, weighing the glass in his hand, and looking at the sky through it. 'They didn't belong there either.'

'Is that part of the mirror?'

'It is,' said the Doctor. 'Jack used the mirror as a direct access point to himself. Destroying it rendered him incapable of escape. That was a good idea of yours to smash it.'

'It wasn't mine,' said Ace.

'But you *wanted* to do it,' said the Doctor with a knowing smile. 'If anything of Jack i' the Green did survive,' he said at last, 'then he's trapped in here.'

The Doctor dropped the piece of glass, and ground it to dust beneath his foot.

FIRST EPILOGUE
ENGLISH SETTLEMENT

Several hours had passed and night was just beginning to blanket the land, free of fear. In the vicarage doorway, the Doctor stood watching the flashing lights of fire engines, ambulances and police cars as they clustered around the remains of the green and the pub. There had been much official scratching of heads, at least until the soldiers turned up. They wore the unmistakable winged-globe emblem of the United Nations, and had been summoned by a phone call from someone who claimed he had once assisted them.

'Only sixty-three people unaccounted for,' Ace told him after having spoken to one of the army men. 'And another thirty-three found dead. That still means most of the villagers survived. They found a lot of people hiding in their homes, delirious. Of course, they're not saying much.'

'What can they say?' asked the Doctor sadly. 'Who would believe them? Earthquakes aren't common in England, but then neither are aliens menaces destroying whole villages.'

'Just a minute ago you said this sort of thing happened –'

'Twice,' interrupted the Doctor. 'And both times the official explanation was a natural phenomenon. Lethbridge-Stewart's successors will have this one under wraps for a few weeks, and then it'll be as if nothing ever happened.'

'Isn't that a bit cynical?'

'Maybe. In a way, not much has changed. The people of Hexen Bridge have always been good at keeping secrets.' The Doctor paused, and then began walking away from the village towards the TARDIS. Ace hurried after him, slinging her backpack on to her shoulders as she did so.

'I'm glad the rain's stopped,' she said, remembering the thunder storm a few nights before, and her desperate attempt to find the Doctor's craft.

'Oh, a little rain never hurt anyone,' said the Doctor. 'It washes away the madness.' There was a dip in his voice as they passed A Taste of the Orient, and he removed his hat as a mark of respect. 'It seems so long ago,' he whispered.

'What, the meal?' said Ace. 'Yeah. Ages.'

'I meant when I first came here,' said the Doctor. 'It's been a shadow at the back of my mind for so long. I can't believe it's gone.' He sighed. 'Still, plenty more where that came from.'

'I've been thinking,' said Ace. 'How much of the violence was Jack's influence, and how much was what was normal for these people anyway?'

'I can't answer that,' said the Doctor. 'Only each individual can. They'll notice a change in each other. But they'll be just as imperfect as any other group of people. At least Jack won't be there, making them worse.' He pushed his hands into his pockets. 'I said I'd take Denman back to Liverpool – he's waiting for us at the TARDIS. Anyway, I want to see for myself what's happened up there.'

'You said Hatch released something into the water supply.'

'Yes. Jack was beginning to travel to Merseyside, you see. Like a bee to a psychic honeypot. Of course, he'd have overwhelmed the entire country in time. Maybe the world…'

'What'll happen to the people in Liverpool?'

'They'll recover,' said the Doctor. 'I managed to minimise the damage to the water supply. There'll be something of a crime epidemic – but then, that's not unusual in the summer. The sad thing is, I'm not sure anyone will notice.'

'Sad?'

'None of us need much encouragement to do evil,' said the Doctor. 'Even so, it was difficult to leave the city behind. I knew I had to confront Hatch in London, and Jack in Hexen Bridge. But I can't help but feel guilty at what's happened in my absence.'

'So that's why we're going up there?' asked Ace, but the Doctor did not answer.

'Say goodbye, Ace,' he said as they passed the little sign that said HEXEN BRIDGE: PLEASE DRIVE SLOWLY THROUGH OUR VILLAGE. 'I don't expect you'll ever come here again.'

'Oh, I dunno,' said Ace. 'Looks like the perfect place for a holiday. Not.' She helped the Doctor over a stile, and they set off across the fields, the grass glossy with rain. 'I would like to have said a proper goodbye to everyone, though. Especially Rebecca.'

'Grief and departures do not sit well together,' said the Doctor. He pointed to an indistinct hillside in the gloom. 'Look, nearly there.'

'You said *I* wouldn't come back,' said Ace. 'What about you?'

The Doctor came to a sudden halt. There were droplets of water on his face, but Ace guessed that it must have been splashes of rain falling from the trees that edged the field. 'I always have unfinished business, Ace,' he said.

Some hours later, Steven Chen and Rebecca Baber were sitting side by side on the wall overlooking the graveyard. In the circumstances it was a morbid place to be, but it seemed just about the only part of the village that wasn't swarming with policemen and soldiers.

Neither knew the other especially well, but their shared grief was beyond words and understanding. Weak with crying, they had lapsed into hushed silence, thinking only of their dead parents, and wondering if life could ever be the same again.

'I'm sorry we didn't tell you about your father in the restaurant,' said Steven suddenly, making Rebecca jump. 'It's just… Well, you know.'

'I understand,' said Rebecca, her voice a hoarse whisper. 'We had to survive. At that point in time, that's all that mattered.' She wiped a hand across her face. 'Look at me,' she said. 'Snot everywhere. Have you got a tissue?'

Steven passed her a handkerchief. 'I suppose we should be grateful we made it,' he said, his voice weak with doubt.

Rebecca blew her nose. 'My beliefs in a cause nearly killed me,' she said. 'But it's no consolation, is it?'

Steven shook his head. 'No.' He paused, trying to control his emotions.

'That's what you get for sleeping with the enemy, I suppose.'

'I can't believe they're dead,' Steven said at last, the tears prickling at his eyes again.

Rebecca shook her head. 'I lost my mum years ago, and I still miss her.' She sighed. 'You'll never get over that.'

'But life goes on? Is that what you're going to tell me?'

'Yes,' said Rebecca defiantly, despite the tears that coursed down her cheeks. 'My father always used to say that life is more important than death.'

The sun rose over Liverpool, forcing its heat through the thin covering of cloud. It was going to be another hot day in the city.

Denman turned to the Doctor. 'Thanks for the trip,' he said. 'It was certainly different.'

'My pleasure.' The Doctor stood framed in the TARDIS doorway. It had landed inside a subway, its battered shell not out of place against the graffiti. Perhaps he ought to move it before it, too, became daubed with spray paint. After all, it wouldn't be the first time.

'You think the village will be OK?' asked Denman.

'It'll be fine,' said the Doctor. 'More than enough survivors to keep a place like that ticking over. Still, it won't be easy, but at least they won't have Jack to worry about.'

Denman nodded. 'Oh, they're tough enough, I think.' He looked around him, at the familiar streets, still wrapped in the cotton-wool cocoon of early morning. 'For all our faults,' he continued, 'we know what's what. And *I* know when it's time to face the consequences of my actions.'

The Doctor nodded. 'Yes. We all must learn to do that.'

Joanna Matson spent the next few days at Trevor Winstone's parents' house, as her own home was rubble at the bottom of a pit. The Winstones had always organised the pub skittles team, and were keen to offer Joanna shelter. Of Trevor himself, however, there had been no sign. Tony Winstone had not been unduly worried, as his son had a habit of disappearing whenever the police or armed forces were nearby. 'I think it all goes back to when he was caught smoking dope in the school toilets,' Tony had said. 'He's always considered himself *persona non grata* where the constabulary are concerned.'

'Oh yes,' chimed in Christiana, with a false optimism that Joanna had found somewhat annoying. 'I expect we'll get a postcard from him soon. It's usually Kenya or Indonesia or somewhere exotic like that.'

A week passed, and still she had not heard from Bob. Joanna was becoming increasingly worried, but the police had so many missing people to investigate that they couldn't give any one case special priority. It was only when she had given up all hope of ever seeing him again that he finally turned up.

Joanna was in the Winstones' garden, weeding their rose bed, when she heard the scrunch of feet on the gravel path.

Bob was trudging towards her, looking like – well, there was no other way of describing it, a tramp. 'Someone told me I'd find you here,' he said with a grin.

'Bob!' Joanna ran towards her husband, embracing him warmly. 'Where the hell have you been?'

'Staying out of trouble,' said Bob.

Joanna took an instinctive step backward. 'Sorry, Bob, but… You stink!'

'I've been sleeping rough.' Bob sighed. 'Living with bloody gypsies. You won't believe what I've been through. I was…' He paused, searching for the right word. 'I was expelled, I suppose.'

'I said you'd get in trouble if you carried on like that.'

'I was lucky not to be killed. Jack deals harshly with those who draw attention to him.' Bob looked around him. The swifts were arcing overhead as if nothing had happened in the village. 'Is it safe to come back?'

'Oh yes,' said Joanna. 'Safer than ever.' She paused. 'But only if you have a wash.'

'I can't wait.'

'The Winstones have a corner bath set into the floor. You'll love it.'

Bob looked around him. 'They're…?'

'Away on holiday.' Joanna Matson extended her hand towards her husband. 'Come on. I'll even scrub your back for you.'

SECOND EPILOGUE
THE ANGELS KEEP TURNING THE WHEELS OF THE UNIVERSE

The small man was in the library again. This time there was no ghetto blaster with him, no musical accompaniment. And, as the boy walked in, the man seemed almost embarrassed.

No, embarrassment was too trivial a word to describe the anguish that crossed the dark-haired man's face. 'Are you OK?' blurted out the boy.

'I'm fine,' said the man, though he clearly wasn't. 'Not sleeping again, Kenny?' He paused. 'Do you mind if I call you that?'

The boy shrugged. 'It's me name,' he said. 'You doing some more research?'

'Oh, no,' said the man. 'The time for research is long past.'

'But you were here only last week and –'

'Was it really only last week? *Tempus fugit.*'

'Time flies,' said the boy.

'You always were very good at Latin,' said the man.

'Were?'

'Are, I mean. Tell me,' said the man, getting to his feet, and looking out of the window into the blank darkness. 'What did we talk about last week?'

The boy smiled. 'I said I was nothing special, and you said that I was. You said that I was "important", which is the most frightening thing in the world.'

'And did you understand what I meant?' asked the man.

'No,' said the boy. 'Well, not at first. But then I remembered *On the Waterfront*. Marlon Brando. "Charlee. I could have been someone, Charlee. I could have been a contender." 'The boy laughed. 'Maybe I don't want to end up like that, a nobody. When

283

I grow up, I wanna be somebody important.'

The Doctor turned. His face and eyes were pale, as if all the colour had been washed out of them.

'Kenny, I'm sorry,' he said.